t t r p
Time Travelers' Rally Point

By Justin Mitson

Red Team Ink
DBA of Zealot Solutions, Idaho LLC
5447 Kendall St.
Boise, ID 83706
Copyright© 2017 by Red Team Ink

For permission requests or information about discounts for special bulk purchases please contact: redteamink@gmail.com. Substantial discounts on bulk orders are available to corporations, professional associations, and small businesses.

Printed in The United States of America

ISBN: 978-0-9984881-7-2

Title: Time Travelers' Rally Point
Description: First Edition

Chapter One

Bassett Clark is aging. Not at a rate that is visible to the naked eye, nor at a pace that is quicker than anyone else's pace, but aging, nonetheless. Lately, he can feel it in his bones. He used to think that was an expression, but now he knows better. At 2 a.m., when he typically shuts down the bar, he moves slower than he used to, back when the whole place was shiny and new. Well, it was never shiny: Margarita Jones, the cleaning lady he hires, never works any harder than she needs to for her minimum wage paycheck from Bassett, which is usually late. He's also noticed silver hairs in his goatee, which he's been growing out lately to seem more hipster. He didn't used to have to work so hard to make his appearance mediocre. Hence, the goatee.

"Phat with a PH, man," his best friend, Stoop Mackenzie, had told him. "Phat in a good way. You know, like you're so hot you're cool? Right, man?"

Stoop said a lot of things Bassett didn't take the time to decipher. Stoop was a mixture of African-American, Cuban, and Scottish. This interesting gene pool had made him unusual and exotic to look upon. Stoop was over six feet tall, skinny, with mocha skin and a huge red afro that was a great source of delight. But his DNA had also given him some sort of a right to speak in odd and indistinguishable lingo. He called it Scottish Street Pride, or Cubano Gangster...or something like that. Bassett usually just poured him another Guinness and called a cab when Stoop got overly bizarre. They had been best friends since junior high when Bassett was a chubby outcast with an addiction to Dungeons & Dragons, and Stoop was a gangly outcast with acne.

Anyway, the goatee had been coming in quite nicely, and Bassett was pleased with his phat, hipster appearance, until the arrival of the silver hair (and seven of his clingy friends). Now, he was glumly considering shaving off the whole kit and caboodle, but then he ran the risk of the opposite effect: without any facial hair at all he looked like freshly born baby. He had the peaches and cream complexion of an infant's backside. He also had dimples. The five o'clock shadow around the goatee hid them, but not very effectively. He was thinking of trying out a Matlock type mustache. *Had Matlock been gone long enough for the look to be fresh and in style again?* he wondered. Maybe a killer mustache would distract from the dimples.

Bassett loaded the last of the shot glasses and wine goblets in the dishwasher as he reflected. His feet hurt, which was an absolute riot considering business had been so slow he'd barely even been on his feet. He pictured his aging self, with a sore back and a baby face, along with a Matlock mustache made of silver hairs, and orthopedic shoes. Life was not going well for Bassett tonight.

The bar was out of dishwasher detergent, which made him kick the door in frustration. There was no way Margarita was going to do these by hand in the morning. She'd just leave them there, with their lipstick stains and peanut dust. They'd be disgusting and Bassett's mild level of OCD kicked into overdrive. He didn't have to be surrounded by cleanliness all the time, he just preferred it to be that way, and he was a bit perturbed by odors and smears and germs. Fine, maybe he did need to be surrounded by cleanliness all the time. He blamed his mother: a dear woman who, while excellent at macramé and Jazzercise, would never have put Martha Stewart to shame. She had not passed on her bohemian way of life to her only son.

Well, there was nothing for it but to leave the dishes behind, as they were, dirty and full of the questionable germs of 12 strangers. That was the grand total of customers Bassett had seen that night, and two of them only drank ice water. Life was *seriously* not going well for Bassett.

He was also confident he'd never see those 12 strangers again either, which was awfully pathetic in his line of work. If he couldn't even bring in the usual suspects anymore, the regular crowd, the good old barflies, what kind of business man was he? It really should not be this difficult to get people to drink. What, was the whole city taking a vow of prohibition? He blamed Oprah, or maybe that new guy on television, Doctor Oz. He was likely behind this health kick that was taking over his city.

Bassett retrieved his phone from beneath the cash register and checked his messages. There was a voice mail from the water company, one from his mother, who had recently learned the art of texting, one from his on-again-off-again girlfriend, Emerson DuPree (you wouldn't call her Emmy unless you wanted a knuckle sandwich). He was late on his payment, his mother was going on a date with a 'fox' from the Retired Seniors Bingo Club she had joined, and Emerson Don't-Call-Her-Emmy was taking her weenie dog to the vet tomorrow and wouldn't be able to hang out.

Winnie the weenie was not Bassett's favorite accessory to Emerson's life. He preferred his girlfriend's long curls of golden red that always reminded him of strawberries and champagne, her toned legs (she used to be a competitive gymnast), and her smart mouth that could keep him guessing as to whether she was going to kiss him or annihilate someone with witty remarks and sarcasm. Both options gave him full body chills.

Winnie, on the other hand, was a pain in the neck. Bassett was certain she thought she was a Doberman and acted accordingly, with apologies to every Doberman alive today. She was yappy and yippy and had a 'delicate digestive system,' which was basically her excuse to pee or crap all over Bassett's shoes at a moment's notice. She was the world's worst dog, but Emerson loved her, and Bassett loved Emerson. So, Winnie was still alive and still taking a dump in his (not yet orthopedic) shoes at least once a month.

He scrolled down on his phone as it pinged. The other messages were hours old. Who in the world would be texting him this late? Bassett squinted at the words and the sender. It was a number he didn't recognize. The message read,

Don't shave the 'stache. ~ ME.

A text message from … ME. Who the hell was ME? Bassett ignored the butterfly feeling in his gut, putting it down to hunger, and swiped the screen to clear it. Obviously, a wrong number. He should play along like those witty, smart thinking people on YouTube and Instagram that kept messages going with unsuspecting strangers, sending them random photos of cats and such. Much hilarity could ensue. But Bassett was too tired and annoyed with life to be witty and he didn't have any photos of cats on his phone. Just Winnie. And he wouldn't wish her on any stranger.

The 'stache comment was weird though. Bassett stroked his goatee and wondered. Just a coincidence.

*   *   *

Emerson DuPree wound her mass of strawberry and champagne curls atop her head and fastened them with a #2 pencil inside the bar. Bassett was fascinated when she did that. She was always messing with her hair like a teenager and could anchor it with whatever she had handy: pencils, chopsticks, rubber bands, or those claw-shaped clip things that Bassett secretly found disturbing. They looked like giant, plastic tarantulas. Sometimes she would leave them on his couch or a barstool and they nearly gave Bassett a heart attack every time.

"It's definitely IBS," Emerson went on, oblivious to Bassett's daydreaming about her hair. "Irritable bowel syndrome. I knew it! She wouldn't be so cranky for no reason, poor baby."

Bassett nodded, but didn't reply. He had opinions on Winnie and her crankiness but he didn't think they'd go over well, and he didn't want to ruin the moment. After all, Emerson had come by the bar (before 3 p.m. it was merely a restaurant that specialized in cheap diner food), and wonder of wonders, she was going to have to leave the pooch at the vet overnight. Bassett was already graphing out a romantic night in his head, quick, while they had the chance, and while he had dry shoes.

"Anyway, I want to check on her again later and bring her some of those peanut butter treats she likes. Here's your detergent." She plonked a container of soap on the counter. It advertised lemony smelling satisfaction. "But you owe me. That was not cheap, and now I'll have to wash my own dishes by hand." She pouted.

Most girls pouted as a way of flirting, but Emerson didn't flirt. If she was pouting, she was honestly put out about the soap. She was probably nearly as broke as he was: Emerson was a Jill-of-all-trades and was out of work as often as she was in it. She'd been a dog trainer, a personal chef, a gymnastics instructor, a mural artist, a barista, and for a short time, Bassett's waitress. And that was all in the past six months. Some people found Emerson flighty, but Bassett only found her restlessness sexy. The only problem was the thought of making an honest woman out of her. They could barely support their own single lives. Bassett had grown up without a dad and had no idea what a husband and father was supposed to look like, but he was fairly certain they didn't look like him. They fixed their own lawn mowers, knew a lot about sports, could help with math homework, and they could have conversations about the meaning of life and important subjects like that. Those weren't strong suits for Bassett. He got clammy when religion or politics came up in conversation, and he didn't even own a lawn mower. He paid some teenager from around the block $20 a month to mow the grass around the bar. It was painful that the teenager was a girl, too. Even she would be a better dad and husband than he would. So, every time he got close to proposing, he panicked. This probably explained why Emerson tended to break up with him every few months.

"I'll pay you back right now," he promised, opening the cash register. "By the way, do you like my facial hair? Maybe just the 'stache?"

"I do love me some Tom Selleck," she answered. "Or better yet, Sam Elliott. Yummers." She tucked the ten he had handed her in the pocket of her jean shorts.

Sam Elliott? Yummers? Bassett's chest tightened near his heart. Still, he shouldn't have much to fear from a celebrity. He changed the subject. "Do you know anyone with the initials M.E.?" Bassett handed her his phone next with last night's weird message pulled up.

Emerson shrugged. "Mary Elizabeth? Monty Edwards? I don't know. Are you taking personal appearance advice from strangers?"

"Do we know a Monty Edwards? And no, it's just something I was thinking about anyway and then this showed up. Hey, I know a Mitch Ellery now that I think about it. Went to high school together ..."

"Look what the cat dragged in," Emerson interrupted. She stuck her tongue out at Stoop, who had just walked through the door. Stoop and Emerson had a rocky relationship. Emerson found him annoying, and Stoop found her terrifying. Bassett was all they had in common, and he also served as the buffer.

"Hullo, chicky. Morning, Bassett." Stoop helped himself to the coffee.

"Call me chicky again and I'll break your face," Emerson growled.

As a sign of both repentance and submissiveness, Stoop held up the coffee pot. Emerson shuddered. "I brought my own, thanks," she responded. Emerson was a coffee freak and never went anywhere without a spare French press in the car. Highly caffeinated, she was a strong woman who knew her worth. Decaffeinated, she was a she-beast from the bowels of the underworld. Bassett liked her just fine both ways, but he still kept a fresh container of half and half in the fridge just for her. The paying customers got powdered milk from a tiny package.

"Suit yourself." Stoop shrugged. He had no coffee palate. "Hey, I like what you're doing to the place."

"Huh?" Bassett looked up from where he had been admiring Emerson's legs in her shorts. "What'd I do to the place?"

"You know," Stoop gestured across the room with his coffee mug, splashing liquid sludge over the sides and onto the carpet. Margarita Jones was going to be livid. "The vintage look you have going. Sparse, but I get it. Minimalistic."

Bassett followed Stoop's stare and so did Emerson. There was a nautical helmet, the kind old-fashioned scuba divers would have worn back in the day, sitting on the corner booth table. The flickering light above it lit it up in an eerie fashion, giving the appearance of a decapitated head sitting in the bar. Bassett hadn't even noticed it until Stoop pointed it out. Emerson's hair had distracted him.

"I mean, one piece does not an antique vibe make, but I see where you're going with it," Stoop continued, draining the last of his coffee. "What's old is new again, yadda yadda, dude. At least you're trying to fix up this dump. Kudos to you, my man. I respect that kind of commitment to your craft."

"What the hell …?" Bassett walked over to the helmet with a cross between a scowl and a frown on his face. It made his goatee quiver and transform into a snarly mess. "Emerson?"

She was busy pouring hot filtered water over her newly ground Fair Trade Sumatra Roast and didn't reply at first. She swirled her brew with a spoon and capped the French press's plunger in place. Then she looked up.

"Tiger, if you want to redecorate you hired the wrong designer." She stifled a laugh. "What is that monstrosity anyway?" She moved out from behind the counter and came closer.

"Someone's idea of a joke, I guess." Bassett scowled for sure this time, and he poked at the helmet experimentally, as if it might explode or dislodge something distasteful from its depths. Next to the helmet was an antique looking photo album. That didn't look at all familiar either.

"And why is it wearing spectacles?" Emerson wiggled the eyewear. They were gold and looked like some old lady's reading glasses from the '60s. The cat-eye shape, like a stereotypical librarian would wear, complete with gold chain. They were definitely out of place on the scuba helmet, which was out of place in this bar.

Bassett thought back to last night's patrons. He may have been out of it what with his sore back and mustache worries and lack of income, but he certainly would have noticed someone wearing such an unusual thing, or even toting it under their arm. Wouldn't he?

"Someone must have left it here accidently," he offered, even though he was having a hard time believing that. There wasn't any other explanation he could come up with. He picked up the helmet. It was surprisingly heavy. Part of that was the mechanics of the thing; it was made of iron and shaped like a bulbous, exaggerated bobble-head, and it had definite weight. The other reason it felt so heavy dropped out on the table with a sickening clatter, and rolled to a stop.

A human skull.

Chapter Two

"Are you done screaming like a girl?" Emerson asked, dryly. She sipped her coffee and elevated her eyebrows over the rim of the cup as she did so. She hadn't been overly reactionary to the skull, but instead was flipping through the photo album.

Stoop obediently shut up. He swallowed so hard his Adam's apple bounced. "Dude, that's badass."

"Yeah." Bassett was at a loss. The skull looked up at them from its spot on the floor.

"At least it's not juicy," Emerson continued. "It's gotta be old. Real old. That's comforting … right?"

"Yeah." It seemed to be the only thing Bassett could come up with to say.

"These pictures are really weird. Look at this." She passed the album over to Bassett, who flipped half-heartedly through it. They were all vintage photographs, black and whites. They didn't seem to have any kind of theme or value, and Bassett closed the collection, uninterested.

"I'm going to have a drink." Stoop shuddered and returned to the bar, backing up as if afraid to take his eyes off the thing.

"Not a free one, you aren't." Bassett finally found his tongue, and with it, his sense of monetary survival. "Your tab's full. And besides, it's 10 a.m."

"Yeah, well, by my clock, it's skull-thirty and time for a beer."

"Maybe it's not even real." Emerson put down her beloved cup of coffee and bent down to retrieve the skull. A bit of dirt drifted down like some twisted and perverted snowfall. "Then again … maybe it is." Gingerly, she set it down next to the scuba helmet. "How do we even tell? And what do we do?"

"Yeah." Bassett replied. Then he shook his head to clear the cobwebs out. "I mean, right. What do we do? Um, call the cops, I guess?"

"It has our fingerprints all over it, man." Stoop hollered from the kitchen area. He was making himself a sandwich. Stress made Stoop hungry. "You do not want to do that." He punctuated each word with slap of cheese and ham. "I watch Dateline, man."

"Well, I watch *Antique Roadshow*," Emerson retorted. She put her hands on her hips and cocked her head as she stared at the helmet. "This thing has got to be worth a fortune. Even with that busted up part of its jaw."

"It's not mine," Basset answered, firmly.

"I'll put an ad on Craigslist for you. We'll find the owner." Emerson had recently begun writing ads for people for a small commission. She could sell anything. It didn't exactly pay the rent - she was hoping her newly found love of writing romance novels would pan out for that - but it helped with Winnie's vet bills. Bassett was secretly worried about the 'Personals' section of Craigslist though. What if she wrote up one for someone better than him? And answered her own client's ad? Pina coladas and getting caught in the rain and all that junk? He pushed the worry aside. They had bigger fish to fry. Like how to compose a query about a found human skull.

"Maybe we'll just put it in the back and the owner will come back to find it. We could get a finder's fee or something for our emotional trauma."

"Okay," Emerson sounded skeptical. "Unless they left it here on purpose and aren't coming back. In which case ..." she trailed off.

"What?" Bassett narrowed his eyes. Emerson had that look in her deep green peepers; it was that look that meant a crazy idea was forming. Last time she got that look, Bassett was dressed as Little Red Riding Hood and Winnie was dressed in a wolf costume. That look scared Bassett even more than the discovery of a skull in his bar did.

"Nothing really." Emerson shrugged and the look dissipated. "I was just thinking it does look cool. Not the head part, I mean, the scuba part. It's all old and vintage and really makes this corner pop."

Bassett wasn't sure where she was going with this and said so.

"I just mean it gives me some decorating mojo, that's all. This place has no atmosphere, you know that. Maybe this guy is here to give us a swift kick in the derriere, you know? We need to overhaul this dump. Change the name and everything!"

"Whoa, gorgeous, one thing at a time. And what's wrong with O'Malley's, anyway?"

"The banshee is right, dude," Stoop said. He came out of the kitchen with a huge sandwich. "O'Malley's is kinda dumb. The Pina Colada song and all that. We get it. But it's not funny or cute or what have you. It's just … dated."

"Well, that's hurtful." He'd spent a whole 24 hours thinking up that name back in the day. Maybe not a whole day, but at least an hour. Ten minutes, minimum. He'd thought it was hilarious and relevant and would bring customers in in droves.

Emerson went up on her toes and gave him a quick peck on the lips. She always had to tip-toe to do that. Bassett was not particularly tall, but Emerson only reached a full five feet when she stood up straight and teased her hair. "I mean, don't totally ignore him, because he's right, but ignore his phrasing. Let's go thrift shopping!" She rubbed her hands together with something that could only be described as glee.

Bassett felt a sinking in his gut: shopping. Ugh. He hated shopping more than he hated paying bills, or drinking light beer. Warm, light beer. On the other hand, the alternative was staying here with a sad lack of customers and only a human skull for company. What the hell were they going to do with that thing?

"Let's do it," he said, resigned to his fate.

* * *

Bassett wished that hanging a Closed sign on the restaurant would deter loads of customers, but he knew it was more likely that not a single soul would notice. His heart felt heavy as he flipped it over and locked the door behind him. O'Malley's did need an overhaul or he was going to lose this place. Maybe the strange appearance of the helmet was some sort of turning point.

A sick, twisted turning point, but whatever. Beggars couldn't be choosers, and Bassett certainly felt like a beggar these days.

Emerson knew her way around the Goodwill and the Salvation Army. Stoop even got into it, showing depths of decorating skills and especially color and pattern knowhow that Bassett didn't realize he even possessed. And wasn't sure he needed to know. After what felt like the millionth attempt at matching a plaid kilt to a set of candlesticks, Bassett wanted to light himself on fire in protest.

"I can't do this anymore," he said, through gritted teeth. "Can you guys finish up without me?"

He'd never seen his best friend and his girlfriend get along so well, he did have to admit that. So, he may have lost his soul and his man card with all this junking, but he did gain that. Maybe the whole afternoon hadn't been such a waste.

Emerson patted him on the back absently. "Okay, Tiger, we're almost done here. Buck up."

"Yeah, man, suck it up. Look at this beauty!" Stoop held up an old-timey camera.

Bassett stared at it blankly. "I think the odds of that working are nil."

"Dude." Stoop was losing patience and his voice was sounding annoyed. "It doesn't have to work, remember? Ambiance! Atmosphere!"

Bassett let his eyes roam their cart of atmosphere. Ambiance? More like scabies and salmonella. He shuddered. This stuff was going on his beloved bar's walls? On the plant shelves? Near him? He didn't see the treasure trove they saw. He also didn't see much of a pattern or theme.

"So, it'll be what … pirate?" He gingerly poked at a pair of weathered and cracked leather boots. "Or … wild west?" His eyes roamed back to a fringed vest and a pair of chaps. "I don't get it."

"Think of it as Americana," Emerson chirped up. She was positively glowing. Bassett hadn't seen her this cheerful in quite some time. She was in her element. "Each booth will have a kind of theme, but they'll all tie in together as a piece of history, a moment in time. Hey, that's good! A Moment in Time Bar and Grille?"

Bassett didn't want to crush her good mood, but he had to draw the line somewhere. "Uh, no. That's a negative. It sounds like some crummy made for TV romance."

"Well, we agreed we have to find another name, so get cracking." She tossed her hair, defiantly. "If I'm going to write up some ads for you, much less paint you a new sign, you need a name."

"Bassett's Bar and Grille?" he suggested, weakly.

"Dude, you're so lame. And wouldn't that be false advertising? You don't grill. Bassett's Bar and Crummy Microwaved Food would be more appropriate. At least, 'til I saved your butt." Stoop tossed a top hat and cane in the cart and gestured to Bassett. "If you can't be helpful, at least push."

"Who's going to pay for all this?" Bassett grumbled, though he knew the answer. He hoped the water company had other things on their minds besides collecting his payment this month.

*   *   *

Bassett halfheartedly reopened the restaurant as soon as the three got back with their loot. Or their booty, as he was wont to call it. What little customers he ever had were going to get a good laugh at the pirate corner. Inwardly, Bassett groaned. Outwardly, he tried to smile and gave a thumbs up as Emerson began unloading the goods. They spread out everything on the same booth as the scuba helmet, except the skull, which was in the back apartment where it couldn't look at them. Stoop said the eye sockets were following him around the room and he couldn't properly redesign anything under that kind of supernatural scrutiny.

What if it belonged to a murder victim? Some poor, long lost soul whose body had never been found? Come to think of it, where *was* the rest of the corpse? Bassett shuddered, a full body shudder. And there was that busted jawline. *Didn't that suggest some sort of violence? What if he held the link, the missing clue, to some cold case file?* Fingerprints or no fingerprints, he was going to have to call the authorities.

But first, a drink. Most definitely, a drink.

Bassett poured himself a scotch and soda and tried to look busy, or at the very least, enthused. Each time Emerson looked over at him, with that cute and optimistic look that made her Grecian nose wrinkle up, he gave a thumbs up and tried to widen his eyes in what he hoped was a delighted expression. And honestly, after a bit of reworking and shoving rubbish around, it wasn't looking too bad. Or maybe it was just the scotch talking.

"What the heck is an AED?" Stoop asked as he pried open the box that had just been delivered.

Bassett looked up. "What? I don't know. Who's it addressed to?"

"To you," Stoop said, pulling off molded foam blocks and popping the tightly sealed plastic.

"Then why did you open it?" Bassett said, walking over to get a look at this new surprise.

Stoop pulled out the oddly shaped device, clearly ignoring Bassett, and read from the instruction manual. "Automated external defibrillator."

"How about in English?" Bassett asked, gently moving Stoop out of the way. He picked up the case and surmised it was some sort of medical equipment.

"Says it's meant to be used in life-threatening cases of cardiac arrhythmia," Stoop continued.

"Again, English?" Bassett turned the case over and examined the device inside the clear case. It was made of a hard, yellow plastic, and almost reminded him of an oversized child's CD player or his old George Foreman grill. Except it had the look of medical equipment, with a digital screen and various cords. No one would be playing the Best of Barney or making turkey burgers on this thing.

"Like to stop a heart attack, man. You hang it up on the wall like a fire extinguisher. You know, in case of emergency."

Bassett rumpled his hair with his hand. "Huh." He didn't want to think about emergencies, so he used his scotch and soda break to look through the weird photo album again. Emerson was right: the pictures were odd. Not at first glance necessarily, but once you zeroed in on each one, there was something not quite right on every page. A photo obviously from the 1930s or 1940s, but with a modern looking hipster standing in the crowd. He was taller than all the others and dressed completely differently, from his haircut to his clothing to his sunglasses. He flipped the page: a disheveled looking man sitting at some sort of digging site or mountainside, looking completely out of place among the others. Someone had handwritten in pencil the date: 1917. The disheveled man didn't look like someone from 1917. The men sitting next to him were staring at the other in disbelief, as if he had popped out of the rock right as the shutter clicked. He carefully closed the album. He thought his family was weird. Whoever put together this awkward jumble of photos came from a strange line of lunatics.

Bassett stood and surveyed his castle. Slowly, he nodded. It really was coming together. It was … *eclectic*, if nothing else. Gave a bit of punch to the place. He still didn't get it – this whole Americana mishmash thing – but it had something. He just wasn't sure what it was.

"You're sure about the egg beater collection?" Bassett drained the last of his scotch. Most people had their go-to liquor. Bassett liked them all, which probably sorted the typical drinker from the barkeep.

"Totally. It's whimsical." Emerson brushed off her jean shorts. She was delightfully mussed and sweaty and giving Bassett ideas. "I'm going home to shower, then to the vet to see my baby girl. When I get back, I expect you to have come up with a snazzy name for this place, okay? I can't wait to see the customers rolling in! Congratulations, Tiger." She threw her arms around his waist and squeezed.

Bassett squeezed back and breathed in the apple scented shampoo that always lingered in her hair. He wasn't so optimistic, but what choice did he have? The bills were piling up, and even the regular bar-flies weren't so regular these days. He was pretty sure they were spending more time over at the new Buffalo Wild Wings. For God's sake, a chain bar? It was incredibly insulting. No, this had to work. O'Malley's was a thing of the past. The future was now. Tomorrow was the first day of the rest of his life! He couldn't help a wry smile as his thoughts became so pithy and upbeat. He sounded like a psychiatrist, or a faith healer. *By golly, Bassett, you're worth it!* His wry smile turned to a full-on grin as he kissed Emerson goodbye. *And gosh darn it, people like me! I'm beautiful and special!*

"Are you having a stroke, man?" Stoop looked at his friend, concerned. "You look weird."

"I think I'm happy," Bassett declared. "Yep. That's what this is. Happiness. I'm pretty sure."

"Well, it doesn't look good on you." Stoop went back to hanging a canvas of a mermaid posing like a pin-up girl. It was in the corner booth where the scuba helmet still sat, creating a nautical theme. "Go back to being our melancholy bartender, would you?"

"I don't think so. We're changing, right? The whole place? Well, maybe I'm changing with it. No more Mr. Curmudgeon."

"So, drinks on the house is what you're saying?"

"Not in a million years. What's that?" They both froze at a sound. It was a knocking sound and it was coming from the back room.

"Dude!" Stoop paused, mid-hammer. He looked panicked. "Dude, if that skull comes waltzing out right now …" He didn't finish the sentence. He didn't need to. Waltzing or rolling or bouncing or flying, neither man wanted to see the head enter the room in any way, shape, or form.

"Someone's at the door." Bassett let out a huge sigh of relief, and Stoop lowered the hammer where he had been suddenly brandishing it like a weapon. "Hell, we're jumpy! I'll see who it is. And uh, a little to the left. Yeah."

Normally, people came in through the front. No one entered or exited the back room unless it was Bassett himself, or sometimes a confused delivery man with a crate of liquor for the bar. Still, it wasn't overly bizarre and Bassett found himself humming as he worked his way to the door, side-stepping a box of juice glasses and a mop bucket filled with cleaning supplies. The skull was where he left it, thank goodness, and when Bassett swung open the door, he was surprised to see his mother.

"Baby!" Lila Clark wrapped her little boy in a patchouli-scented embrace. Bassett had forgotten his mother typically used this entrance, but it had been a while since she had visited him. Normally, they met for a lunch out, or he went to her house.

"Mom, hey, good to see you." He untangled himself from a strand of beads that had gotten stuck to his buttons during the hug. "You look good."

"I am good." Lila's voice was dreamy, not unusual but normally a sign of something flighty or ridiculous she was planning or scheming. Bassett's good mood waned a bit. His mother could be childlike. It was cute, but also tiring. "I came to say farewell, adios, bid thee goodbye, toot toot, cheerio! I'm off to Paris for the weekend, darling. Yes, my silver fox – I told you about him. Yes?" Bassett thought back to her text message. There had been mention of a suitor, but he had tried not to think too hard of what that might entail. He nodded. "Well, darling, he's simply the best! Lovely, lovely man. And rich too! We're going to France right now, right this very minute! Can you believe it? It's so romantic."

"Sounds ... great, Mom. Have a good time." He brushed the top of her white hair lovingly, with a little pat, and kissed her forehead. He knew sometimes he treated his mother like a cocker spaniel, but honestly, she was a bit flaky at times. She bounced around from adventure to adventure, never worrying too much about responsibility or being an adult. She was the most immature grownup Bassett had ever known, and as a child it was never clear who was the accountable mature parent in the house, but he loved her dearly. It would have been impossible not to. "And what is this fox's name?"

"No, no, no you don't, Bassy." She waggled her finger at him playfully. "No background checks this time. Your mama doesn't need to be babied. I know what I'm doing."

"Sure you do, Mom." Bassett stopped himself from rolling his eyes just in time. Laidback and a leftover hippie from the '60s she might be. (Bassett himself was evidently conceived at Woodstock, a fact he wished he hadn't been told at the very tender age of 12.). But even she wouldn't tolerate cheekiness from her only son. "Have fun. When you get back, you won't recognize this place. Emerson is doing a total overhaul of this dump."

"Good for her, it needs it. I'll bring in Jonathan on Monday so you two can meet. And don't worry, he's not trying to replace your father."

Bassett hardly thought anyone could replace the non-existent man he'd never met. Or maybe on the flipside, *anyone* could. But she always reassured him of this promise. It was par for the course in Lila's dating life. Kind of a ritual, a tradition. Lila had never been married, likely never would be, but her love life was anything but stale.

"But maybe get that thing out of here before Monday." She gestured to the skull with an expression of revulsion on her face. "Jonathan is a cop you know. I don't know what you're doing with that thing, or what you've done, Bassy, and I promise not to judge, but put that in a closet or something."

"Good Lord, Mom, I didn't do anything!" Bassett hurried to explain himself, but as usual, Lila hadn't stopped to listen and was still talking.

"I know, a cop! Can you imagine? Me? Being held down by the Man? Ha! Well, being held down by this man might not be so bad, let me tell you what! He is delicious." She burst out laughing and Bassett tried not to grimace but failed. His face scrunched up like a dried-out loofah. "Anyway, Bassy, I'll smuggle you back something in my suitcase from Paris. Would you like that? Now be a good boy while I'm gone." She squeezed him again and stepped lightly out the back door with nary a glance back.

Okay, his mother was dating a cop and Bassett had an unexplained human skull in his restaurant. Not ideal, but workable. If no one had returned to claim it over the weekend, he'd just turn it in to this Jonathan fellow. In the meantime, Bassett would devise a new name for the bar and they could get to advertising. It was a plan.

Chapter Three

In the morning, day two of the remodel experiment, Bassett stared at his bar with fresh eyes.

He still didn't get it.

He tried closing one brown eye and cocking his head. Doing that made him think of the head in his back room, so he straightened up hastily. Okay, he didn't *get it*, but he could admit it looked a bit better than it had before. Back when he thought a Glade air freshener plugin was haute couture. There was the nautical booth, which looked cool with the mermaid canvas and the scuba helmet, a lantern, and a shell collection. The pirate section was not nearly as kitschy or dumb as he had first worried it would be. There were some ships in bottles that they had found in Emerson's attic, a spyglass (likely a reproduction, but still interesting to look at), the leather boots that stood in the corner as if the owner had kicked them off, and a plumed hat sat jauntily on the plant shelf. The whimsical area, as Emerson had deemed it, was full of a mishmash of antique kitchen items and yard art. There was a booth with stacks of old books and globes and some pocket watches that dangled off the crummy, cheap chandelier. All in all, it was weird, but it worked. It looked like it didn't belong in any era. Or perhaps like it belonged in every era.

A Moment in Time Bar, no. But something with time and eras and the like mentioned. A place for weary travelers to put up their tired feet and get a stiff drink.

Time Travels Tavern? Time Travelers' Tavern? He was getting closer. Bassett stroked his goatee. A place for travelers to meet up. A rally point.

Time Travelers' Rally Point.

It was good. It had flair, a bit of whimsy and fancy. Bassett liked it.

Just then, his phone pinged in his pocket and made him jump. Having a skull in the vicinity was really make him edgy. He needed to figure out what to do with that thing, and soon.

It was a text message.

Winnie relapsed. Has a fever and needs to stay another night. How's Hemingway? ~E.

E was, of course, Emerson. Bassett said a silent prayer of thanks to the god of dogs who was sticking it to Winnie, and returned a message.

Hemingway?

He had no idea whom she meant. He didn't know a Hemingway. His phone pinged again.

Skull needed a name. He had a very classy appearance about him. His friends can call him Ernest.

Bassett laughed aloud. Trust it to Emerson to find a human head amusing and classy. He sent off one more text wishing Winnie well (he tried to keep a straight face) and asking Emerson to come over for lunch and more brainstorming. She promised to be there soon and Bassett got that butterfly feeling in his gut that he always got when Emerson was just moments away. Damn, he loved that girl.

Please let this overhaul of the bar work, he thought. *She deserves better than a loser. She deserves a successful man.*

* * *

"I love it!" Emerson had squealed when Bassett unveiled the bar's new name. Normally, Emerson would never squeal because she would consider it to be too girly a thing to do, so Bassett knew she was beside herself. "It's great! Totally unusual but not so weird that your patrons will forget what it's called. Perfect. Okay, I brought paint. Get your sign down and I'll get going on the new lettering."

"About that." Suddenly, Bassett felt shy. His head was coming up with more ideas and he didn't know what to do with them. Normally his head was full of thoughts of Emerson and her jean shorts and maybe the promise of a cold beer in the evening. Honestly, there wasn't much else in there, taking up real estate. Now, he was suddenly entrepreneurial and the shift was unnerving. "What if we don't?"

"Don't?" Emerson raised her red eyebrow. It was shaped like a Christmas candy cane now that Bassett looked at it. Even her eyebrows were adorable. He wanted to nibble on them.

"Have a sign."

"Confused girlfriend here. Do elaborate."

Bassett felt himself blush. Okay, the goatee was staying. It hid his girlish blushes. In fact, a full-on beard was needed. "So that it's more of a word of mouth, hole in the wall, secret society kind of thing. Not a club exactly, but you should know it's here. You know?" He trailed off a bit, staring at Emerson, hoping against hope she wouldn't find this moment to realize her boyfriend was a total nut job. After all, a secret business wasn't a lucrative thing to own. And yet, he'd loved the idea more and more ever since he'd had it, oh, 10 minutes before.

"So," Emerson pursed her lips as she contemplated. "No sign?"

"Maybe a plaque. You know, like on the door, a small, bronze sign. Like 221B Baker Street for Sherlock Holmes's house?"

"Can we get a door knocker for the entry?"

He chuckled. "Sure, I guess so. But they can also just come in, seeing as how this is a bar and all."

That being settled, Bassett went to fetch his ladder and removed the old O'Malley's sign. He decided to keep it. After all, with this theme in the new bar, the old bar had a place too. Maybe he'd hang it in the men's room. A little nod to the past, like the rest of the things in this place.

"Well, Tiger," Emerson chattered from the kitchen, where she had begun making coffee and assembling a collection of cheese and crackers for lunch, "if I'm not going to be painting today, what shall I do for you?"

Bassett could think of several nice options that would show off her skills in plenty of ways, but he knew that wasn't what she meant. "I still don't know what to do about the scuba helmet and Ernest. And, if we aren't advertising by having a large, neon sign, maybe you could use your ad writing expertise for those two problems? A grand reopening ad? Can you scribble one out?"

"Calling all time travelers?" she teased.

Bassett shrugged. "Kinda, I guess. You're the one with the skillful pen. I trust you. It'll be great. The customers will be showing up in droves."

"Let's hope so." She licked her fingers where some cracker crumbs had stuck to them. "I brought more stuff in my truck. My great aunt made me clean out her storage unit not too long ago and let me keep a bunch of great antiques, so you unload while I write. Let me know if you need my muscles: there's a trunk in there that weighs a ton. And a cello."

"A cello?"

"Yup." She grinned. "Music is timeless, Tiger. It'll look awesome next to the grand piano we will someday be able to afford."

"From your lips to God's ears," he replied. "Will you wear a slinky dress and sing torch songs all night?"

"Totally. I sound like a suffering frog when I sing, but no matter. Everyone will be drunk anyway, right?"

"Let's hope so. I know I plan to be."

*　*　*

Day three of the grand remodel came and went, with even more found and purchased junk. Bassett still didn't enjoy shopping, but he tried to keep his complaining down to a minimum. And the bar was looking amazing. Weird, but amazing.

The plaque was the biggest splurge. It literally took the last bit of the only not-maxed-out credit card he had, but he wanted it to look authentic and sophisticated. It was small and rubbed bronze and placed directly at eye level on the front door. Only the initals, **ttrp,** gave away the name of the bar. He thought the lowercase letters made it even more cryptic.

Meanwhile, Stoop was coming up with new menu items, easy to make but fancier than the typical crappy bar food Bassett used to serve. He was getting into it so much that Bassett wondered if he should hire him as a cook. Talk about hidden depths: Bassett had had no idea his friend could be so driven and creative.

The ad written by Emerson was finished and recently published.

time travelers' rally point. Nosh on pub food and have a great drink while you dream of the good old days, or the ones to come. Whatever your generation, your creed, your past, your future, or your methods, put up your feet at time travelers' rally point and change the world for the better. What do we want? Happy Hour and half-off appetizers! When do we want

them? It's irrelevant when you time travel!

Bassett thought it turned out witty and amusing, with just the right amount of secrecy. He hoped the readers would feel the same. He would probably need some business cards, too. Small ones, with very little wording. Maybe just the name and address, no explanation. Just the initials, **ttrp**, on a matte black card with gold wording.

He wondered if there was just a smidge more room on that credit card.

They spent the next couple hours sampling Stoop's menu. He was managing to make the cheap ingredients Bassett had into some interesting and tasty plates. And for now at least, he was working for Guinness.

"This is so exciting, Tiger," Emerson said, around a mouthful of grilled bleu cheese with thinly sliced pear and bacon. "It's going to be successful, I can feel it. People are going to love this place." She wiped the tip of her nose where the sandwich had bumped it. She had a longish, Grecian nose that most people would say was too large for her small frame, but it was just another part of her that Bassett found flawless.

Bassett glanced at his wristwatch. He was literally the only person he knew who still wore one, but he was always misplacing his phone. It was a knockoff of a Rolex, or at least he'd always assumed it was, and he'd had it since he was 12. That same year his mom had told him about his hippie father and gave him the watch. She had said it was his dad's but Bassett wasn't so sure. It would be like Lila to make up a story like that to make her little boy less sad. Still, he had worn it every day for 25 years now. Cheap knockoff it may be, but it kept time perfectly.

It was 4:48. They had changed their hours along with everything else about the old O'Malley's. Now they were opening at 5 p.m. every day.

Ten minutes to the grand reopening. What if not a single soul came?

What if they were all at Buffalo Wild Wings? Bassett felt like he was going to vomit. The anticipation was worse than his junior year of high school when he took three weeks to get up enough courage to ask Shelly Bennington to the prom.

When he finally gathered his nerve, she laughed in his face.

Bassett downed a shot of bourbon and poured another one. He could see Emerson eyeing him warily. Easy for her to stay sober; she was perfect. She'd probably been asked out to prom by every hot guy in high school. Twice. Bassett downed his second shot. Emerson frowned and took his glass, walking over to the sink and washing it by hand.

Five minutes to the grand reopening. He was going to be sick. Maybe he wasn't cut out to be a successful business owner, after all. The pressure was too much. He was better at failing. If it ain't broke, don't fix it, right? The old bar was okay. Bassett shook his foggy head to clear it. He must be tipsy if he was getting nostalgic over his old place.

Two minutes to the grand reopening. Stoop was hollering for someone to go out and get more bread and butter pickles. The fate of a pulled pork sammie was evidently at stake. Emerson found another jar in the pantry and talked him down from his ledge.

Bassett stared down at his not-a-Rolex. It was time. He walked to the front door and his legs felt like iron. He felt like he was in a slow-motion dream. He was sweating, and he wiped his forehead with the back of his hand before he reached out and twisted the knob of the sliding lock on the door. There could be no one on the other side. Or there could be a mob. He didn't feel emotionally prepared for either option.

The door swung out and the sunlight blinded him. The bar was dark, partially for atmosphere and partially due to poor lighting in general, and Bassett squinted. There were people. *Holy heart failure, Batman, there were people!*

Chapter Four

It was nearly two weeks after the opening of **time travelers' rally point**. Any skepticism or cynicism Bassett may have had was gone. The bar was a success.

Well, if not a booming success, at least a growing and promising success. And they already had regulars, which as Bassett knew, were the bread and butter of a bar owner. It was only a matter of time before they were thriving.

There was a group of young men and one girl: they all looked like teenagers but had the ID to prove otherwise. Bassett assumed they were from the local community college. The boys had patchy facial hair and acne, and the girl was one black lip liner away from full-on Goth. They always brought their laptops and what looked like textbooks and they spent their time arguing and debating over subjects Bassett didn't listen to. The young men drank light beer and the girl – Bassett had overheard her name was Tess – drank fuzzy navels. They had been here every night since the opening. They tipped in crumpled one dollar bills and random handfuls of change, and they never ordered food, which irked Stoop.

Another group of regulars were three business men. They dressed in trench coats and suits and carried briefcases. They were well-groomed and serious. Bassett assumed they were lawyers. They spoke in hushed tones with papers spread out on the table in front of them, highlighting things and circling sentences. They always sat in the vintage book section, farthest away from the other tables.

There were a few loners, too, like you always got at bars. There was a grizzly bear of a man with a navy shield-front shirt and tan wool trousers held up by leather braces. Bassett sometimes wondered if he was about to rob a stagecoach, or ride off to join the cavalry. But he was quiet, so Bassett left him alone. The man solemnly drank gin and tonic until exactly 10 o'clock, then he would glance up at the clock, place a tip on the table, and leave. There was a middle-aged woman with sad eyes and premature wrinkles who sipped on coffee with Irish cream in the kitschy corner. Tucked into her long paisley skirt was a high-neck blouse, topped with a flounce of delicate Irish lace. The blouse had a soldier-like row of buttons, which was echoed atop the scuffed, black granny boots beneath her full skirt. Her wavy red hair was often escaping the tight bun into which it had been neatly pinned, presumably hours earlier.

Well, one thing's for sure. My customers are doing their part to keep the thrift shops in business, Bassett pondered.

There was an old man who wandered through the bar with his whiskey, looking at the décor and the patrons and writing things down in a small notebook that fit in his shirt pocket. At first, Bassett was worried he would annoy the other customers but no one seemed to pay him any mind.

An old married couple always sat at the bar, perched on the stools. The woman was named MJ (Bassett found that delightfully young sounding for a blue-hair), and her husband was Bruce. They were old-fashioned in their manners and great tippers. Bassett heard them request watercress sandwiches once, as well as clotted cream and lemon curd. Bassett didn't know what either of those things were, but they sounded disgusting and made him feel queasy. Nevertheless, Bruce always ordered the daily special, which Bassett never knew the description of until he probed Stoop. But Stoop loved MJ and Bruce and started building his specials around their preferences.

There were a few people that only came once, like the rockabilly greaser boys in their dungarees and leather jackets, and the couple in the spats and flapper dress who couldn't keep their mitts to themselves.

Apparently, this is the place to pre-game for costume parties, Bassett figured.

But he wasn't worried. They'd only been open a couple of weeks; just because they hadn't been back yet didn't mean they wouldn't ever come around again. Most people only went out on the weekends anyway. He was excited for the weekend crowd. All in all, he was enjoying getting to know the regulars and adding to the list. It was like an eccentric cast of characters.

Emerson was over the moon about the success, and Winnie was back.

Well, you can't have everything.

Winnie's lifespan wasn't going to put a crimp in his happiness, hard as she was trying (four ruined pair of Nikes later). It wasn't that he hated Winnie, or wished her dead. Not exactly. But he was more of a cat person. He'd grown up with cats, and they were a low-maintenance sort of pet, in the grand scheme of things. They weren't so needy and they didn't hog his girlfriend the way Winnie the weenie did. He liked dogs, but he wasn't convinced Winnie really was a dog. He was thinking maybe a Dachshund got overly frisky with a rat one drunken night.

No one had returned to claim the scuba helmet, the photograph album, or the skull. The more Bassett examined the skull though, the more he was inclined to believe it was only a manmade replica. Probably used for medical instruction or something. He thought about putting an eyepatch over one socket and sticking it in the pirate booth, but it seemed a bit too macabre, just in case it was, after all, human remains. Emerson had written up an ad in the 'Lost and Found' section:

Found: vintage nautical item with questionable contents inside. Also, one pair of granny glasses. Please call to identify. No questions asked.

Bassett had gotten a few calls about it, but no one could identify the helmet, so here it sat. It looked at home in the bar.

Bassett pulled up a barstool and shook the hand of the man next to him. He had told Bassett he had question for him.

"Shoot," Bassett offered. "I'm listening."

The man introduced himself as Lizard Buttons. He pointed to the stage at **time travelers' rally point** and asked if Bassett would consider it as a venue for his band, The No Talent Hacks.

"So, it's, like, ironic?" Bassett took a drink of his scotch. He had ordered in a new label: not bad, smooth and fiery. A higher caliber than the swill he typically ordered.

"Nope." Lizard grinned. He was a youngish man, maybe 30 years, with a long beard and one of those man buns that were cool one or two years ago. He wore a flannel shirt and a kilt. He was eccentric for sure. He also looked just right in the bar, a bit like the helmet did. Fit right in with their respective oddness. "We're just really, really bad, and we feel people shouldn't get their hopes up."

Bassett stared blankly.

Lizard hurried to explain. "You don't have to pay us, we'll play for tips. Mostly, we need a place to practice. So we don't, you know, suck so hard."

"What kind of stuff do you play?" Bassett asked.

Lizard's face brightened. "All sorts! But we specialize in 1950s style punk rock."

"That's a thing?"

"Not yet. But we're optimistic."

"Ah ha. How many in your, um, ensemble?"

"There are four of us. Marcus plays the flute, I'm the drummer, Angel plays electric guitar and keyboard, and Cat sings."

"And you really are awful?"

"Oh my God, we're terrible. Angel has the most talent because he took some lessons at some point, but the rest of us, well, we have heart and that's about it. What do you say?"

Bassett wasn't sure what to say. He liked Lizard Buttons. Couldn't help himself. To do what you loved even if you were bad at it … well, he could relate to that some. "Okay, you can play tonight for tips, but if you drive away my paying customers we'll have to call it a day. Fair enough?"

"Absolutely!" Lizard beamed behind his whiskers. "You won't regret it. The audience will love us. Also, they'll be at least somewhat drunk, right?" There was some anxiety in his voice.

Bassett raised his glass in a toast. "Let's hope so."

If Bassett thought that conversation was weird, he had to re-evaluate his barometer. His next dialogue ended up being with the lawyer group. One of them got his attention by motioning with his empty glass. Bassett obediently brought over the rest of the bottle of cognac they had been drinking and topped off their glasses.

"How's it going, friends?" he asked. "Gonna have some live music here soon. Hope you can stay for it."

One of the lawyers nodded. "We wanted to ask you something, sir. We are in need of a room. A private room. Do you rent out anything like that?"

Bassett was surprised. No one had ever asked him that before. He did have a back room, but it currently held cleaning supplies and a skull that may or may not be human. He cleared his throat. "Like for a private party? Or a meeting room? Something along those lines?"

"Yes, sir." Another man spoke this time. The three of them were similar in appearance, especially in their clothing. Bassett hoped he didn't have need to tell them apart: they were all tall, slim, and had middle of the road type features. Clean cut, non-descript, medium brown hair, no distinguishing marks or abnormalities. Yep, lawyers. Or CIA spooks.

"But we'd like to rent it for a long period. Say, a month?" It was the first man speaking again. "Money is no option. We just need a quiet room that is easy to find when we need it. When we're in town."

Out-of-towners then. Bassett tried to school his face to appear nonchalant. Money may be no object for them, but he was rather fond of it himself. He could clean that room in next to no time. "When would you need it by? I might have a space that will fit the bill."

"We aren't concerned with a time table," the man replied, and smiled. "We find those things tend to work themselves out perfectly."

"All right then." Bassett named a sum that seemed fitting for renting out a whole room for an entire month. He was shooting from the hip, but they seemed nonplussed, and the original lawyer and he shook hands on it. "But you won't have access unless it's normal business hours."

"No worries. But if you would, please keep it under wraps. It's a closed group. We aren't opening membership opportunities at this time."

"Um, sure. Just you three allowed, got it."

"It's just that," the man leaned in and lowered his voice, as if telling a secret, "our calibrations and calculations are at a critical point. The last thing we need is amateurs looking over our shoulders and planting recording devices. You know what I'm talking about?"

"Sure, sure." Bassett waved his hand as if he had a clue. He had no bloody idea what they were going on about. "Total privacy, you got it."

"We'll also need a launch point, and we were hoping to pick your brain about that as well." The second lawyer looked at Bassett with expectation in his unremarkable brown eyes. He seemed to be waiting for something. "Any suggestions?"

"For a, a," Bassett stumbled over the wording, "A *launch* point?"

"Certainly. You're the expert. This is our first time jumping off."

"Jumping off?" *What, was this some sort of suicide squad?*

"Going back."

"Going *back*?"

"Or forward."

Bassett was tired of parroting every word, so this time he remained silent as he regarded the three lawyers. They were still looking at him with expectation, though now it was mixed with some confusion. Hell, they were confused? Bassett was baffled.

"Well, if you let me know what it is you're uh, launching, that would give me some frame of reference. Then I might be able to suggest a location."

"Ah!" The first man smiled. "Good point. Nothing too large."

"Smaller than a bread box?" Bassett answered, dryly.

The other men chuckled. "Maybe the first time. Then, it's the big one."

"The big one?" There he went, parroting again.

"Us. Well, maybe not James here. He's just here for the scientific aspect."

"Got nothing to go back for," the man Bassett assumed was James spoke. "I'm good."

It was beginning to dawn on Bassett what they were intimating. He eyed the bottle of cognac. They hadn't drunk *that* much. No, they weren't snockered. Just crazy. They thought **time travelers' rally point** was a real rally point for time travelers. Awesome. And he'd just promised these whack jobs a whole room to themselves. They'd probably burn down the whole bar with their experiments.

Still. Their money was just as good as anyone else's. What was it to him what they did in that room?

"Work on your calibrations," Bassett said. "And I'll find you the perfect … *launching point*."

Chapter Five

"Yeah, I don't think they're the only ones, man," Stoop said. The bar was closed and they were cleaning up. He wiped some water spots off a pitcher. "I overheard the Goth saying something about what kind of weapons to take. She said a knife because it was best for any era, wouldn't be out of place. Then her boyfriend said she wouldn't be thinking that if they ended up anywhere – or excuse me, I think he said, any time not anywhere – where someone was pointing a gun at her."

Emerson chimed in. "I think we've got ourselves a certified secret society here, Tiger. Just like you wanted. Except a bit loonier."

"Wait a minute," Bassett called out, while digging through a stack of video tapes in the back room. "Do you think they're really loons? I mean, I know it sounds crazy, but maybe there's something to this time travel deal. And maybe these people are coming here to, I don't know, *prepare*? Does that even make sense? At any rate, maybe they're coming here, to this bar, to get themselves ready and test it out time travel."

"Whoa," Stoop said, his head drifting back.

"So this is like a dress rehearsal," Emerson mused.

"Exactly," Bassett said. He loved that he could always count on his girl to make sense of things.

"That explains all the odd getups," Stoop said, running his fingers through his red curls.

"Oh yeah," Emerson said, "like that stagecoach guy, and the greaser gang. Goth Girl."

Stoop shot her a glance. "Let's not jump to conclusions about perfect goddesses just yet."

Emerson rolled her eyes and Stoop broke into a grin. For a minute, Bassett thought they might actually be getting along.

"Well," Emerson said, "in order to reach conclusions, we clearly need to look into this."

"Exactly," Bassett said as he fiddled with the kitchen's TV, an older set, with a built-in VHS player. He'd found the movie he had been looking for in the back room. The back room that was soon to belong to a group of nuts.

"So, your answer is to watch *Back to the Future*?" Stoop asked, skeptically. "The 1980s Sci-Fi flick with Michael J. Fox?"

"It's research."

"It's ridiculous."

"Well, it's all I got. You got any better ideas? They think because I own this place that I'm some sort of time travel wizard." The word wizard reminded him of Lizard. The No Talent Hacks were exactly what had been promised. And yet, they were sort of addicting. Like stale pretzels. Not good, but if they were in a bowl in front of you, you'd eat them.

"There's a copy of Jules Verne in the book section," Emerson offered. She yawned. "Didn't he write time travel stuff? Am I getting my high school lit mixed up? Where's Ernest? I think we should put him in the décor after all."

Bassett was still nervous about that. "I don't know. It's kind of ghoulish."

"Goth Girl will love it."

"I love Goth Girl," Stoop added, waggling his eyebrows. They were like oversized, plump, red caterpillars above his eyes. "She scares me. I like it."

"You'd be a bizarre couple. She'd eat you alive."

"Yum. What a way to go."

"She's too young for you," Emerson effectively ended the bunny trail. "And she's crazy."

"All your patrons are crazy, but their checks clear." Stoop removed a pick from his red afro and began absentmindedly detangling one side. It grew right before Bassett's eyes into a giant puff. "I got to hand it to you, dude. You're making this place run."

"Well, you're helping." It was the nicest thing Emerson had ever said to him. They were getting along surprisingly well these past weeks. "Your food is pretty decent." Her eyes widened as she realized how kind she was being. "I mean, for a high school dropout." That dig wasn't as mean-spirited as it would have sounded to an audience that didn't know Stoop. He, in fact, did not graduate high school, but that hadn't hurt him. Somehow, he had made a fortune designing and building aquaponics: self-sustaining fish ponds and gardens. Bassett didn't understand Stoop's profession any more than he understood most of his lingo and slang.

"My Baja fish tacos were a big hit," Stoop bragged. "Even frozen fish sticks taste good covered in my pico de gallo. My brotha from another motha, I need a raise."

Bassett built him a Guinness. "Here's your raise. And thanks. Both of you. Maybe our clients are nuttier than a chocolate bar, but for the first time ever, my bar is a success."

"Don't talk about time," Emerson quipped. "Apparently, it's more of a serious business than we used to think."

Bassett shushed them both. The movie had started. He pulled out a pad of paper he normally used to take drink orders. He had a feeling he needed to take notes.

* * *

The next two weeks were spent with Bassett channeling Dr. Emmet Brown, the nutty doctor character from the movie. Stoop was Marty McFly, and Emerson rounded out their cast as Claudia (though Bassett found Emerson much, much sexier). Bassett wasn't sure if it was a testimony to how great the film was, or how unsophisticated the group of lawyers were, but the bluffing seemed to be working.

Until today.

The day was just weird from the get-go. Winnie had snuggled up to Bassett that morning over his bowl of cereal, which was suspicious, and then he had gotten another text message from the ever-mysterious ME person.

UPS delivery happens today. This is where you have to start paying attention. ~ME.

This time he answered it with a short 'you have the wrong number' reply, but it returned to him as 'undeliverable.' *One more and I'll just block the number,* he decided. Why he was creeped out by it he didn't know. For goodness sake, he slept with a skull nearby. He shouldn't be so sensitive over a wrong number.

It didn't help when UPS delivered a package right after lunch. Margarita Jones had come by for her paycheck (which, in an out-of-the-ordinary gesture, Bassett had ready and waiting for once) and brought it in with her.

"This was on the porch," the cleaning lady said, plonking the box on the counter. It landed with a thud. Bassett felt his heart race a bit. He got nearly all his deliveries from the liquor guy. He couldn't even remember the last time UPS had called. Christmas, maybe? Hadn't his sister, Peggy, sent him something? A set of dishes, perhaps? But it was nowhere near Christmas, nor Bassett's birthday.

He felt ominous as he reached for the box. *Bigger than a bread box …* hadn't he said that to his lawyer group? He didn't even know if they were lawyers. And he was certain this was no bread box.

Margarita studied him with her dark eyes, the lids as thin as crepe paper. She was a grouchy old thing, prone to cussing and drinking, two things that probably kept her coming back to **time travelers' rally point** even back when it was just O'Malley's. "You going to open it or what?" she barked. She had the husky, scratchy voice of a smoker, which ironically, she wasn't.

"Yeah." Bassett paused for a moment, his hands on the wide band of packaging adhesive that crisscrossed over the box like a cop's caution tape. He bent forward and put his ear on the box, listening. There was his name, written in wide-point purple permanent marker. In fact, it wasn't just addressed to Basset Clark, but Bassett Z. Clark. He could count on one hand the number of people who knew his middle name was Zechariah. It was for his wayward, hippie father, the man he'd never known, so he didn't exactly advertise it.

"Animals?" Margarita interjected.

"Huh?" Bassett raised his head. He'd forgotten she was still there.

"What are you listening for? Animals?" she rasped.

A bomb was more like it, but Bassett just grinned. "Yeah, um, chickens. Baby chicks. I think Stoop ordered some. You know, for his sustainable, uh, fish coop."

"A fish coop?" Margarita folded up her paycheck and tucked it firmly in her shirt pocket. She wasn't the type to carry a purse. "Good lawd, what will they think of next?"

"Right?" Bassett smiled weakly. He hadn't meant to say fish coop, but she didn't seem too phased by the lame explanation. She had to be at least 70 years old and probably thought anyone under 45 were simple-minded whippersnappers. "Well, see you later, Ms. Jones."

Once she left, Bassett still sat staring at the box. Finally, he grabbed a steak knife and split open the tape, pulling the tabs aside and muttering under his breath the whole while. It actually looked a bit like a breadbox once he brushed aside the packing peanuts and pulled out the contents.

Only instead of cheap plastic with the stenciled word of Bread done up in swirly lettering, it was a red, metal box with a handle. Dented in several places - whether through a careless UPS worker or simply by age Bassett couldn't determine - it had a rusty silver flip-type hinge. It also had a sticker on one corner, a colorful horse that looked like it belonged in a little girl's sticker album. Bassett recognized it as one of those My Little Ponies Peggy had collected as a kid. Cotton Candy Surprise, or Rainbow Jubilee, or Peachy Cloud Princess, or some such thing. Bassett had once cut off the tails of Peggy's favorites after she had taped over his recording of Star Trek. She had wailed for hours.

Butterscotch. That was the one.

The sticker looked out of place on the toolbox, which was definitely what the red box was. He grasped the handle and pulled it out of the box, packing peanuts drifting off and floating slowly to the ground like giant puffs of snow.

Bassett Z. Clark opened his gift.

It was money. Stacks and stacks of money, bundled together with rubber bands in neat little rectangular mounds. He'd never seen so much cash before, and suddenly he was afraid to touch it. It might as well be snakes for all the warmth and goodwill he felt oozing from the box.

But that was silly. Bassett shook his head like a spaniel bounding out of the lake after a swim. He closed his eyes for a moment and when he opened them again, the money stared back up at him. There had to be … hundreds if not thousands and thousands of dollars in there. There was also a note, written on yellow, lined, notebook paper. Bassett pulled it out gingerly.

Backing and start-up monies for **time travelers' rally point**. *Investment made in good faith that one Bassett Z. Clark will wisely instruct, counsel, and provide discretion in all matters of time travel, including but not limited to, points of location/eras/positioning, client confidentiality, rules and regulations, and high quality drinks and refreshments for said travelers. Sum: $2,000,000. Non-transferrable.*

Have fun and be safe out there.

*   *   *

Three hours and four white Russians later, Bassett still sat where his shaky legs had deposited him: in his upstairs apartment sprawled across his old La-Z-Boy recliner. The toolbox of money was on his lap. He was still dressed in his bathrobe, a worn-out but comfortable plaid number. The plaid was beginning to dance and blur as Bassett's eyes bore holes in his lap. He wasn't sure if it was all the white Russians on an empty stomach or if shock was setting in. Maybe he was slipping into a coma.

He had to open the bar soon, which meant he had to figure out what to do. What did all this mean anyway? First the scuba helmet, skull, and photo album, then the strange text messages, and now a fortune left to him by a mysterious benefactor who seemed to believe Bassett had actual, bone fide, time traveling capabilities.

Would it be unsavory and unethical to take the money?

On the other hand, he couldn't return it. The box had no return address, and the note was unsigned.

He stared morosely into the bottom of his glass. His life had gone from rather boring to preposterously thrilling. Well, if not thrilling exactly, at the very least, *interesting*. Which was new to Bassett.

His phone pinged a notification and Bassett jumped as though he had been shot. The last of the white Russian seeped into his bathrobe and the toolbox slid to the floor with a thud. Some of the money spilled out on his apartment's raspberry red carpet. He left it where it lay and fumbled for his phone in his robe pocket.

Hands shaking and with a sense of foreboding, Bassett squinted at the small screen. If it was another premonition from ME, he was going to shout or throw things or move to Minnesota. But it was only Stoop informing him he was out on the street waiting to be let into the bar. With trembling fingers, Bassett hurriedly texted a typo-riddled reply that he would be down in just a few. Walking like someone who had just seen a ghost, Bassett went into his bedroom and changed out of his liquor-soaked robe and into a green button-down and jeans. He felt like some sort of yuppie when he wore flip-flops with jeans, but he had no energy to pull on socks and shoes.

When he turned the lock on the front door and saw Stoop – his normal, cheerful, completely sane friend in a world that had gone topsy-turvy on him – he wanted to weep and embrace him. He settled for grabbing him by the collar and yanking him inside, slamming the door and locking it again as soon possible.

"Thank God you're here." Bassett shoved his friend towards the stairwell. During business hours, he kept the door locked to keep inebriated customers out of his personal space, but when the bar was closed the door stayed open.

"I got watercress I need to put in an ice bath, man! What gives?" Stoop tried to backtrack, but Bassett was determined. He blocked the bottom stair. "Whoa, you got crazy eyes. What happened? Did the shrew dump you?"

Watercress? What's next, curdled cream and lemon clots, or whatever that stuff was?

"Huh? No, no, just keep going. I need to show you something. Go, move it, *move faster!*"

Stoop put his hands above his head in surrender, watercress and all, and together they entered the apartment. The tool box was still on its side, spilling obscene amounts of money onto the shag carpeting. The scent of white Russian lingered in the stale air.

Stoop stared blankly at the floor for a good two minutes. "Okay, dude, this is what we do," he finally said. He set the watercress down gently in the La-Z-Boy. "We don't tell Emerson about the gambling. We get you to one of those rehab places – the good ones, like the ones celebrities go to. I can get you in. I helped put in one of Charlie Sheen's ex's nanny's aquaponics. Then we tell your customers you are closed due to toxic mold. Then we—"

"No, no, I don't have a gambling problem, Stoop." Bassett bent down to start piling the money back into the toolbox. He handled it tentatively, as if it would self-destruct at any time. It was crisp under his hands. Every bill looked new.

"No? Okay, man. This is bad. I don't really have a lot of wriggle room with the mafia." Stoop looked very concerned. His mocha colored skin had gone a bit pale. He pinched the bridge of his nose as if he had a headache. "I get like one favor with them, man, and it's gotta be worth it."

"What are you going on about? What mafia?" Bassett flipped the latch to close the toolbox.

"Come on, man, you gotta tell me. No gambling, no mafia? Ah man, it's drugs, isn't it?" Stoop went boneless all of a sudden and sat on his watercress as his long legs gave out. He buried his head in his hands. "Duuuuuuuuude," he drawled out in a muffled tone. "Whhhhhyyyyyy?"

Bassett rolled his eyes. "I'm not a drug lord, Stoo. Come on, you know me better than that."

"I thought I did." Stoop said, his hands still over his face.

"Look, you need to focus. This arrived in a box for me this morning. This note was with it." Bassett thrust it into his friend's hands.

Stoop read it and his lips pursed in thought. His forehead creased and his left foot started twitching. These reactions were exactly why Stoop did not play poker for money. "Whoa."

They sat in silence for a bit.

"Whoa," Stoop said again.

"Yeah."

"This is weird."

"Yeah. And that's not all. Right before the package arrived I got a text message telling me it would."

"So? Probably a service UPS offers nowadays. Like a confirmation that delivery is on its way. Yadda yadda. Tracking."

"Nuh uh. It wasn't from UPS. It was from ME."

"Me?"

"No, *ME*." Bassett frowned. "Wait. I thought it was initials. M.E. Like Mitch Ellery."

"The little guy with one leg from high school?" Stoop was lost. "He works for UPS?"

"No! Geez, Stoop, I need your clear head on this. It wasn't initials. I think it was me. I sent that text message. To myself."

Stoop's foot went from twitching to positively river dancing. "Duuuuuuude."

"I sent it myself. From the future."

Chapter Six

"Nope. I'm just not going there yet." Stoop was trying to salvage the watercress and was washing it in the bar sink. They had left the toolbox upstairs, came back down to the business area, and locked the apartment door. Now Stoop was refusing to look at facts and was instead mapping out his watercress flatbread pizza with a ferocious one-track mind.

"Well, you're going to have to if you're going to keep working here."

"You don't even pay me, so I don't work here." Stoop brandished a zucchini at him. "Which means I can leave anytime things get too weird. And things are getting weird."

"I know! Don't you think I know that? That's why I need you. Keep me sane. Help me figure this out." He raked his hands through his brown hair so that it stuck up in clumpy spikes.

"You don't really think it's possible, do you? Come on, Bro. Time travel? What, like with the Doctor and the Tardis and all that?"

"I think that's more like space travel, but yeah. Come on, how much do we know about the universe, about time and space continuum, about the theory of relativity? Didn't Einstein believe in this stuff? And he was what? Like a rocket scientist or something."

"Not exactly." Stoop began kneading his pizza dough that he had prepared the night before. He pounded it more than was strictly necessary.

"Well, my point is, smarter guys than us have believed in this. Maybe there's something to it." Bassett sounded defensive, and he wasn't even sure what he was defending. He didn't believe in all this either, did he? He didn't know anymore. All he knew was the coincidences were piling up faster than the explanations. And he didn't like it. Minnesota was sounding better and better. "And whomever sent us the money believes in it. And idiots aren't typically millionaires, so that's something."

"Wealth does not care about your brain capacity, Bro," Stoop replied. He threw the dough up in the air and caught it. "Rich guys can be morons, too. Cash doesn't discriminate."

"Stop hitting me with logic. This is not a logical problem we're having here. We need to think outside the box. Haha, outside the toolbox!"

"You know what I think? I think that photo album went to your head."

Bassett had been flipping through it lately. It had gone upstairs to his nightstand and was interesting to look at if he couldn't sleep. He'd stared at all the strange photos several times over. Not all were photographs though: there were also newspaper clippings, internet printings, images torn from books. They all concerned time travel. "You're probably right. It's going to my head. Especially since it's the last thing I see before I fall asleep."

They were silent as Stoop built his pizzas. He spread garlic, olive oil, and red pepper flakes over the dough, then added goat cheese and mozzarella. The watercress would be tossed with lemon and salt and pepper and added on top after baking. Bassett thought it sounded kind of feminine for bar food but Stoop had assured him it would be a big hit. Besides, he now had bigger things to worry about than happy hour snack foods.

"So, what'd the instructions say again? I mean, what was the gist of it? You're supposed to use the money to fund this place. Only this place is supposed to function as a genuine, in-your-face **time travelers' rally point**? A meeting place for honest-to-goodness time travelers?" Stoop forgot about his pizzas and leaned up against the counter. He was covered in flour, but his left foot had quit its frantic twitching.

"I guess." Bassett scowled. "I can't believe a trip to the Goodwill got us into this mess.”

“What mess?” Emerson entered the kitchen area. She put her keys to the bar on the counter as she leaned in to kiss Bassett. For once, her boyfriend’s peck was absentminded and less than passionate. She sat down as the two men began to explain the situation to her, including the part about the text message that may or may not be from Bassett himself. Her face went from skeptical to leery to baffled to excited in the space of a few minutes.

“Don’t you see?” Bassett ended his story. “I’m at a loss.”

“About what, Tiger?” She bounced to her feet. “This is amazing! Two million dollars! Do you know what we can do with that kind of cash?”

“Simmer down, Imelda Marcos,” Stoop answered. “It’s for the bar.”

“Duh, I wasn’t suggesting otherwise. Go burn something.” Emerson sniffed. “Or plant a fish.” Evidently, Emerson wasn’t sure what aquaponics were either.

“It’s a lot of money for décor. Hell, we could move locations if we wanted to. I mean, if you wanted to. Buy a whole new building!” She clapped her hands like a little kid.

“I like this place.” Bassett felt panicky. This was moving way too fast. Suddenly he realized something: he missed his old life. Boring and stale it may have been, but this was too much too fast.

His girlfriend picked up on his panic. “Okay, we don’t have to move. How about a franchise?”

Stoop snorted. “He can’t handle the one, you want to add to it? Our melancholy bartender wasn’t meant to be this busy.”

"Well, what do you suggest, genius? Wait for another cryptic text message from the future to tell us what to do?"

Bassett was getting a headache. He was also feeling annoyed at their lack of faith in his entrepreneurial proficiency. He could buy another building if he wanted to. He just didn't want to at this particular time.

Time.

It was getting to be funny stuff.

*   *   *

Despite not having touched the money in the toolbox or told of its existence to anyone else in the bar, some of the now regulars were treating Bassett like he really was some sort of time lord. He wasn't sure whether to laugh or cry. A few weeks ago, when he had realized the lawyer group (or whatever they were) took time traveling seriously and he was channeling his inner Dr. Emmet Brown, he didn't mind so much. Now, with two million on the line and sitting upstairs, it felt more dangerous and daunting to pretend. Like the fate of the world was resting on his small shoulders.

Now it was the young group, the one with Goth Girl, who were treating him like the boss. Word seemed to be getting out, despite himself. He sighed inwardly as they picked his brain (such as it was) over a pitcher of hard cider. That was a splurge for them; it was twice the price of light beer.

"It's just the ripples, the paradox, the morality of the thing, you know what I mean?" This particular guy was named Adam and he functioned as the leader of the crew.

"We talked about this!" Goth Girl – Tess – was irritated. She had two bright spots of hot pink color in her cheeks, which were normally a ghostly white. "We were all in, remember? You don't want to mess with the big stuff, fine. We never said we'd change the world, just *our* world."

"And the difference is ...?" Bassett trailed off. He found this was an excellent way to avoid getting super involved in the conversation. He felt like a psychiatrist. *And how do you feel about that?* was becoming his mantra. Left to their own discoveries and thought processes, they usually came to their own conclusions and he was off the hook once more.

"It's just a ripple, not a splash."

"Every ripple has a consequence, that's all I'm saying." Adam held up his hands. "It's a risk."

"You're right." Bassett nodded. "It is. Is the outcome worth the risk? After all, you're not doing anything immoral or wrong, correct? Just changing a few things?" He was genuinely curious about what they were all attempting to go back for.

"But if your plan works," Adam turned his attention back to the girl, "and you stop your parents from divorcing, your mom will never remarry and have another little girl. The girl who will one day," he lowered his voice to a dramatic whisper, "discover the cure for cancer."

"What little girl?" she exploded. "My mother hasn't even remarried!"

"Not yet." Adam waved his hands and fingers in the air as if blurring the lines of reality and fantasy. Bassett was beginning to think those lines were indeed blurry. He sighed.

Tess was starting to look murderous. "Fine, I'll join someone else's group if you don't want me around. Good luck without me." She started to stalk off, but Adam pulled her back.

"Okay, okay, fine. I'm just messing with you. You're right. I'm thinking too hard about this. The mission is back on. I'm done, I swear." He looked like an over-eager puppy with big, blue eyes. "I'll behave."

"Fine," she groused. The pink spots in her cheeks faded and she sat back down.

Disaster averted, Bassett wondered if he was free to go. He started to edge away from the group, dishtowel in hand, but was soon apprehended by one of the lawyers. He couldn't remember which one; they all looked so similar.

"Mr. Clark, sir?" the lawyer asked.

"Yeah?" He paused mid-step, dishtowel poised for action of the wiping tables variety.

"I was, er, wondering about security? I mean, I know you're the expert, I don't mean to insult you or anything like that. It's just, well, we're getting close to our rendezvous and well, you understand. This technology … the competition. Etc, etc! So dull. I know. You're a busy man and of course I comprehend that your brain works at a level mine does not, so again, I apologize for even bringing such mundane things up. But I just wanted to check." He seemed embarrassed. Bassett was embarrassed too. He didn't deserve their admiration in the way they all thought he did. He felt like a fraud.

"Er, yes. Security. Well, I don't like my patrons to have to worry about those types of annoyances so I make sure that, er, I make sure that my security is chameleon-like, I guess you could say. After all, if it's noticeable, what kind of security is it, am I right?" Bassett chuckled nervously. "The best kind of security is the type you don't even see." He realized, belatedly, that was what people said about background music, not security, but oh well. It seemed to placate the lawyer. "If you notice it, I'm not doing my job."

He smiled in relief. "I thought so! The others, well, they were a bit anxious about the lack, but I told them, I said, 'Don't worry, Mr. Clark has it under control!'"

"Yes, I certainly do." Bassett tried to smile back, but it came out a little sideways, like he was seasick. "No need to worry. We take our clients confidentiality and safety very seriously here. Lots of, um, experience. Definitely."

The lawyer shook his hand, dishtowel and all, full of energy and pep that hadn't been there a moment before. "I'll tell them! Thank you again, Mr. Clark. Really, you are simply wonderful. We recommend you all the time to our comrades."

"Great," Bassett answered. He kept his seasick smile in place all the way back to the kitchen.

"Okay, this is getting ludicrous," he announced to Stoop, who was piping filling into deviled eggs. "Now they're wanting extra security."

"Who?"

"The clients. The customers. The lawyers."

"We have lawyers?" Stoop frowned as an egg rolled away.

"The back room renters."

"Oh, those guys? I don't think they're lawyers, man."

Bassett growled a deep, guttural noise. "Whatever they are! They are, what did he call it? *Getting ready to launch*, I guess. Which probably means they're going to blow us all to kingdom come. And they want to make sure no one steals their secrets."

"Well," Stoop stuck his tongue between his teeth as he filled an egg with an extravagant swirl and topped it with paprika, "that's not too unreasonable. After all, they're paying a small fortune. Give 'em what they want."

"What, like a bouncer? Some big lug to stand by the back door with a rope around the line of unsavory time travelers trying to get in?"

Stoop shrugged. He capped the paprika. "As a street kid, I can say the best security system is just a group of people who notice things. Out of the ordinary things."

"A street kid? Are you kidding me? We grew up on the same street. It was suburbia."

"You never saw the darkness in the 'hood like I did, man."

"You're an idiot."

"You want my ideas or not?"

"Fine. What's your idea?" Bassett popped an egg in his mouth whole and spoke around it.

"I'll take care of your security breach. No worries, man. Now, keep these refrigerated until Happy Hour, all right?"

"Where are you going?"

"To my actual job. You know, the one that pays me?" Stoop looked pointedly at him. Bassett felt guilty, especially since he had a toolbox full of cash money upstairs, but he just wasn't ready to use any of it yet. It seemed like a point of no return somehow. "And, to get reinforcements. We'll be back in the morning."

"We?"

"Yup. We."

Bassett wasn't sure whether to be cheered or apprehensive. He didn't have time to be either because just then the bar exploded.

Chapter Seven

"I can't believe you blew up my bar." Bassett wiped dirt off his face with a grimy hand. All he succeeded in doing was to smear it all the way into his hairline.

"I'm really sorry. I didn't mean to. I apologize," one of the lawyers gasped.

Again with the apologies.

"I knew this was going to happen." He regarded the lawyer group. He now knew – since explosions tend to bring people closer – that they weren't lawyers, they were accountants, and their names were James, Robbie, and Casey respectively. It was Casey who had caused the explosion that was thankfully much louder and impressive sounding than the damage turned out to be. He had been experimenting with a Bunsen burner and some sort of blue goo. Evidently the goo was highly flammable – who knew? The hole in Bassett's back room was now the world's largest sideways skylight with a view into the alley, large enough to be considered a security breach in anyone's opinion. Bassett had spent a whole 10 minutes staring at it, hands on his hips, in silence, while the accountants stood by in mortification and shame. Whenever someone tried to speak to him, Bassett would hold up one finger and they would immediately stop talking. It was finally Emerson who broke his stupor by literally using all 4'11" of her height to shove him out of the room and upstairs, where he collapsed on his La-Z-Boy. He spent the next hour conferring with Ernest, a fact that had Emerson drinking red wine nonstop.

"Well, at least you have the money to fix it," she pointed out, topping off her glass again. She motioned to the toolbox.

Bassett muttered something incomprehensible and gathered Ernest onto his lap, where he stroked the top of its head. It calmed him.

"Should I call your mom?" Emerson bit her lip. Normally when she bit her lip, Bassett got those butterflies in his stomach, but now all he felt was dread. "I think you're taking this pretty hard."

"No mom necessary. I'm fine. I'm good. I am A-Okay." His right eye began twitching, as it did when he was feeling stressed out. For example, when he failed algebra the second time, when he wrecked his first car, the first time he laid eyes on Emerson and her radiance, and that time when his beloved bar blew up.

"Okay. Good. That's good. Because there's a hole in your bar."

"Yes. I saw it."

"But the guys feel super bad and they're cleaning up the mess right now."

"That's wonderful."

"We could, um, put up a tarp for tonight. Or I could, um, park my car in the hole. You know, to discourage looters?"

"Wouldn't want anyone stealing our Goodwill treasures, would we, Ernest?" Bassett tickled him behind his nonexistent ears. "That would be a travesty."

"Okay, mister, enough. It's time to put you to bed. You're obviously in shock. Things will look better in the morning." Emerson swallowed the last of her wine and got shakily to her feet. She looped her arm through her boyfriend's and pulled him up.

"Can my friend here sleepover?" He cradled Ernest to his chest protectively.

"Yeah, sure. Bring your friend. Nothing kinky though, all right?"

"Your wish is my command, Madame DuPree!" Bassett saluted her like a soldier. "Wake me when this over!"

"You got it, Tiger."

* * *

"You did the right thing by calling me." The 12-year-old girl speaking was Stoop's sister, Joey. She had shown up the next morning after the explosion, walking in like she owned the place, with her frizzy red braids and Converse high tops.

Bassett hadn't said anything yet – not since Emerson had tucked him in - and wasn't sure he would. Confusion showed in his features as obvious as a sinner in church. He knew Joey of course, but the site of seeing a preteen in a bar was disconcerting, not to mention he had the sinking feeling that this was Stoop's solution to his security problem. He tried to school his face into something less than horrified and/or insulting. He was beginning to feel his face was made of Play-Doh.

Joey slung her backpack on the nearest table – the one with the broken pocket watches dangling from the old chandelier – and crossed her arms over her skinny chest. "I have school in, like, 10 minutes though, so spill."

"Um, Stoo?" Bassett finally broke his silence and turned to his friend for help.

Stoop looked amused. "I said I'd take care of the security issue, didn't I?"

"By hiring a rugrat?"

"Hey!" Joey glared at her Uncle B, as she called him. "I don't have to work under these conditions, you know."

"Sorry, kid." Bassett arranged his Play-Doh face into what he hoped was a smile. Hadn't her brother said the same thing recently? "It's just ... you gotta admit, you aren't exactly much of a deterrent to a bunch of thugs or drunks. And, you can't be in here, legally speaking."

Joey rolled her eyes. "It's not *just* me. I have friends, you know."

"Oh, that's comforting."

"Are you going to listen or not?" Joey turned up her glare a notch to full-blown nuclear level. Her freckles stood out like angry polka dots.

"Yes, ma'am." Bassett nodded. "Present your security expertise, if you please."

"I just so happen to be the leader of the local neighborhood watch group." Joey announced it as though she were the CEO of a major company. Her voice got lower and more secretive as she went on. "We're a specialized group, I guess you could say. We are very experienced in undercover work, and I'm proud to say our crime level has gone down substantially in the past 14 months since I took over."

"Is that so?"

"It is, Uncle B. Like, no car vandalism or nothing. We're good at it. So, I think you should hire us. We'll report back to you anything we find suspicious. What do you say?"

There was plenty Bassett wanted to say, but he didn't want to hurt Joey's feelings. He also didn't want his bar crawling with toddlers either, so he was going to have to tread carefully. "Well, you'll have to be discreet …"

"Discreet is my middle name!"

"Your middle name is Dorothy. I was there when you were born." Joey was a surprise baby; born to Stoop's mom, Betty, when she had assumed she was past the age of childbearing. Betty still seemed a little shell-shocked and it had been 12 years.

"Pfft. Whatevs. Believe me, you won't even know we're here. We'll be like ghosts. Plus," she grinned, "we work for cream soda." She twirled the end of one red braid and gazed expectantly at him.

"Working for beverages seem to run in the family." Bassett glanced at Stoop, who raised his glass to him. "Okay, you're hired."

* * *

"Seriously. A hole in my wall the size of a small aircraft, a fortune that appears out of nowhere, text messages from the future, people think I'm some sort of time travel guru, and now I have a band of pint-sized security experts on my hands. I don't even have enough liquor to get me through the weekend, E, and I own a freakin' bar." Bassett groaned, his head in his hands.

Emerson reached down and pulled off his flip-flops. She kneaded his toes in a sympathetic fashion. "Okay, Tiger. Look on the bright side. You've got me! But I will need my car back ASAP. Sorry to remind you in your time of need."

Bassett groaned again. Emerson's Ford Fiesta was blocking the entrance at the hole in his back room; otherwise, who knew who could just come in and help themselves to whatever they liked, including the accountants' *secret calibrations*. Bassett was, of course, more worried about the safety of his inventory, especially since he planned on drinking a large portion of it himself. "I'll get it fixed, I promise. The accountants said they'll pay for it so I don't have to worry about insurance covering it. I wasn't sure how I was going to explain it anyway. Nature of claim: exploding time machine."

"Well, money isn't a worry for you these days anyway." Emerson popped his big toe and he gave a sigh of relief. "You've got stacks of dough just waiting for you to spend it on something."

"Don't remind me. I still don't know what to do with that."

"Well, you could start paying Stoop for starters. And pay off that credit card we maxed out with our shopping habit. And take me to Cancun." She tickled his sole teasingly.

"It's just if I start spending, there's no going back, you know what I mean?"

"Yeah. But it can't just sit in your apartment next to Ernest forever." They sat in silence for a bit. Bassett regarded the love of his life as he reflected on the state of his reality. Life had gotten so weird so fast. He was glad he had Emerson around to keep him centered and sane. Her sparkly peach nail polish on her pretty hands were at war with his ugly feet and knobby toes.

"Okay, my coffee break's up." He sat up and stretched. "Evidently, I have to meet Joey's neighborhood watch team." He stifled a chuckle. "Pray I can keep a straight face. Oh, and also please rack your brain to come up with an actual security idea, would you? We do, after all, have some serious whackadoos to protect, not to mention a box full of money."

She saluted smartly and kissed him full on the mouth. "Aye aye, O captain, my captain! I'm on it."

Bassett wasn't particularly comfortable with the proposed plan of meeting the watch team on the bar's grounds, even if they weren't open for business for another hour, so he had arranged to meet Joey on the playground a block away. He had to chuckle at the irony of meeting his bouncers at a park. Why was he even wasting his time with this? Because Joey was like a little sister to him, he figured. Sure, he had Peggy, but she had been adopted at the age of 5 by Lila when Bassett was 10; not the best age to suddenly become an older brother. They had bonded eventually, but Joey held a special place in his heart somehow. He peeked at his watch as he walked down the street. He'd patronize Joey and her pals for 15 minutes; then he really had to get down to business about the goings-on at **ttrp**. He needed to decide about the money, and hire a team to fix the hole. Not to mention, dedicate some time to viewing *Back to the Future II*.

When he got to the park, it appeared empty at first glance. Then, as he swiveled his head side to side, he spotted Joey at the top of one of the playground structures: a swirly turret that capped a slide. Her long legs dangled over the sides and she was slumped over, hugging it with her full body. Then he looked again and saw a mom with an infant lying in the shade beneath the same slide. Her baby was in one of those sling type things. Then he noticed a teenage boy straddling the top of the swing set, and another person – looked like maybe a grandmother – up a tree. That last one made him gape, a bit astonished. He'd never seen a treed grandmother before. She caught his eye and jumped lithely to the ground near him.

"Son of a biscuit!" she announced, thrusting her hand to Bassett. "You saw me! I gotta work on my camouflage. Sorry about that. Was hoping to make a better impression. Name's Barbara. You can call me Babs. Just like Streisand. Ha!" She shook her hand impatiently as Bassett had not yet taken it. He had only gawked. "This is my group, such as they are. Everybody! Front and center!"

Bassett found himself taking the strange woman's hand and as he did so, he was swarmed. Joey was there, and so was the woman with the infant, the teenager, two others he hadn't seen before: a middle-aged man with a poodle, and another mom-type. They must have been better with their camouflage. He swallowed a hysterical laugh that had bubbled up in his throat and schooled himself to stay serious.

"We understand you're looking for a neighborhood watch," Babs continued. "We want to say, look no further. We know this 'hood like the back of our hands, and we are a specialized group that can meet all your home security needs."

"It's a bar, actually." Bassett sounded apologetic, but didn't know why. He cleared his throat and tried again. "A very successful bar." Words he'd never uttered before. They sounded peculiar but rather nice in his mouth.

"Well, here's our flier. You won't find any other group that will do a more satisfactory job than us; I think you'll find us a perfect fit. We have stealth and skill, plus the advantage of blending into the crowd."

Bassett found that debatable, especially with Babs herself. She wore heavy-duty coveralls over a white t-shirt that was rolled up at the shoulders, revealing some tattoos. Her combat boots were as old as she was, and her hair was salt and pepper gray and cut in a flat-top. He didn't think she'd blend in anywhere, except maybe a biker convention.

He took the flier he was offered and read it.

He flipped it over. It read: **We are watching you.**

"Very, uh, thorough."

"We think so. Crime has gone down 50 percent since we joined up. Amy here is excellent for stake-outs," Babs nodded towards the mom, "since she always has an excuse to be out walking with the kid. Plus, little Junior keeps her up all night anyway, so she likes to have things to do."

Amy smiled at Bassett. She was the definitive picture of a tired new mother, but she seemed up to the task.

"Same with Pam here." Babs gestured to the other mom. "She doesn't have babies, but she has teenage twin daughters, so she doesn't sleep either. Joey, of course, is our go-to girl with the plan. This here is Walter and his partner, Nugget." Bassett could only assume the man was Walter and the poodle, Nugget. "And this is Quinn. He's mostly used for muscle." The teenager flexed in response. He was an oversized young man, looked to be of Inuit descent, and he was more French fries than actual muscle. He wore a poncho to cover his pudge and had a cheerful grin. He held up his phone and Bassett heard that distinctive clicking sound that meant he had taken a photo. "And you met me," Babs concluded. "What do you say?"

Bassett didn't know what to say, so he said the only thing he figured he could say. "You're hired."

Babs spit on her hand and offered it again, as she beamed at him. "You won't regret it."

He already did but didn't want to admit it, so he smiled. The handshake was moist and he tried not to shudder. He was going to have wash in Purel. "Remember, the best security is the one we don't notice, so, uh, feel free to stay in the background. Like, way back."

"Not a problem. You won't even know we're there. Just put out some cream soda in the back alley once a night or so and you got yourself a Neighborhood Watch."

Awesome.

Chapter Eight

And so, it came to be that Bassett Clark set out two six-packs of high quality cream soda in the alley each night for a week. It was becoming less surreal each time.

As far as strange things went, this was merely a number on a sliding scale.

The hole in the wall of the back room had been patched up so nicely, you never would have known an explosion had ripped through it with the force of a hurricane (or a Bunsen burner manned by a lunatic). The accountants had ponied up the cash readily enough, though their first suggestion was to go back in time and prevent the explosion from happening in the first place. Bassett had politely but firmly declined the offer and took the money.

On this night, Joey had met him out back and confiscated her soda in person. They sat on the back stoop, Joey swinging her Converse clad feet off the edge, and Bassett sipping on a vodka cranberry.

"So," she asked, burping, "excuse me. How goes the bar ownership? Any disturbances?"

"Not a one." Bassett toasted her by clinking his glass against her bottle. "I'm quite satisfied with your work, young grasshopper."

"I knew you would be." Her voice was confident. "We've been keeping a close eye on all the regulars, especially the suspicious ones." She made a snapping motion with her fingers, in a Z-shaped formation. "Guess what I call that? A ginger-snap! Get it? 'Cuz I'm a ginger?"

Bassett nodded and chuckled appropriately, but had no idea what she meant. Also, he wondered which ones were the suspicious ones, but was afraid to ask. In his book, all his regulars were freaks. They all thought they could time travel. He *liked* them – in fact, more and more each night, but he wouldn't deem any of them normal or sane, and he would trust them about as far as he could throw them. As far as Bassett himself beginning to believe in the possibility of time travel, he had since amended his declaration. Text messages from himself from the future? He now disregarded that thought and wish he'd never mentioned it to anyone. There was something about your bar blowing up that restored your fragile sanity, he figured.

"Oh, and you really need to pay your water bill," Joey continued.

"Huh?"

"Your water bill. The water company dude is like, staking this place out, looking for his payment." Joey polished off her soda and twisted off the cap of a new one. "He usually just hangs out in his car out front."

"What water dude?" Bassett frowned. He did owe the water company … he'd forgotten. But sending someone to collect payment was weird. Wouldn't they just mail a notice or give him a call? Or if worse came to worse, shut off his water? "What's he look like?"

"Nothing."

He cocked an eyebrow at his companion. "Nothing?"

"He looks like nothing! Like, seriously, Uncle B. I couldn't describe him if you stuck a gun to my head. Sorry. I'm usually good at that kind of stuff, but I guess I need more practice. He looks like … everybody." She shrugged.

Like the accountants then, Bassett figured. Well, he'd look for him tomorrow. Look for a guy who looked like everybody. Shouldn't be too hard.

*   *   *

And it wasn't too hard. The street the bar sat on was hardly busy – it was in one of the most neglected and hard-up areas of town and wasn't exactly a thoroughfare. The car the water company man sat in was a black sedan. That was a little bizarre, Bassett thought, but maybe the company van was in the shop? Somehow, he didn't think so. He wasn't as paranoid as his patrons, but this situation was becoming fishy.

"What can I help you with?" Bassett leaned down conversationally, resting his arm on the top of the sedan. The man inside reluctantly pushed the button to roll down his driver's side window.

"Hello, there. Fine establishment you have here." Joey was right: the man was as blank as a sheet of paper. If Bassett had thought the accountants had a non-descript way about their appearance, they were full-on memorable and distinct compared to this guy. He had a face like a white dinner plate: empty and void and with not one blemish or mole or stray whisker to redeem it from utter vacancy. He had a color of hair that was neither brown nor blond, but some sort of dull hybrid of the two. He was of an average weight and of an average height (Bassett could tell even when he was sitting down), and wore an average black suit. His eyes were a light brown, no green or flecks of gold, not dark enough to be exotic and not pale enough to be striking. There was nothing remarkable or significant about him at all, other than perhaps he was a bit paler than the average person.

"It's even better on the inside," Bassett replied politely. "Why don't you come in and have a drink?" Silence. "Unless you're here for something else?"

The man scrutinized Bassett before replying. His eyes were unblinking and rather vacant, but Bassett got the feeling that could be an act. He might be taking in and seeing more than he liked to let on.

Hell, now he was getting as paranoid as the accountants.

"I'd rather meet elsewhere if you have time, Mr. Clark," he answered. His voice had a mid-level tone, pleasant enough but not friendly, with no discernable accent or lisp. His teeth were white but not too white, and his lips were neither thin nor full. "Say, IHOP on 53rd? Seven a.m.?"

Bassett sighed inwardly: people always forgot that bartenders did not keep normal hours. Seven a.m. was torture for someone who regularly stayed up past 3 a.m. and slept till noon, but on the other hand, he was curious. "Do you always meet at cheap pancake houses to collect payment for the water company?" He intentionally kept his voice dry and sarcastic.

The pale man smiled, and it was a creepy kind of smile. Bassett felt a chill. "Come now, Mr. Clark. I think we both know I'm not from the water company."

The chill moved up Bassett's spine and settled in his neck. "Yeah, I didn't think so. Can I at least get your name?" He rubbed his neck, smoothing out the gooseflesh.

"So you can find out as much as you can about me before we share a plate of sunny-side up eggs and waffles?" That smile again, if you could even call it that. It was more like the imitation of a smile, done by someone who hadn't had much practice with the real thing.

Bassett shrugged as if he didn't care one way or the other. "I'm a strawberry crepe guy myself."

"Linus Fields." The man didn't extend his hand for a shake, for which Bassett was thankful. He had a feeling his hands would feel clammy or corpse-like. "Feel free to do your research, but it won't help."

"No?"

"I don't exist, Mr. Clark. Not now. Not ever." The pale man's smile began to fade until it was gone and all that was left was his dinner-plate face:

empty and white and blank. Bassett had the impossible thought that the rest of Linus Fields was going to disappear the same way, right in front of him, like the Cheshire Cat.

Of course, that didn't happen. But he did drive away, the man who was not from the water company, leaving Bassett alone in the street, staring at the black sedan until it turned a corner, vanishing out of his sight.

* * *

ttrp was busy. If Bassett didn't know better, he'd say it was nearly at maximum capacity, per fire department laws and regulations. At least, it felt that way. He'd never had so many customers at once. Lizard Buttons and The No Talent Hacks Band were hurting everyone's ears with their punked out version of Blueberry Hill, and Stoop was making huge plates of onion rings with a homemade garlic aioli. Emerson had writer's block and was currently sitting toward the back, near the pirate area, glaring at her laptop and occasionally punching on the keyboard. Winnie was curled up beneath the table, growling at anyone who passed by, and Emerson sipped a merlot and snacked on a bowl of pistachios while she painstakingly came up with plotlines for her newest romance novel, *The Highlander's Mail Order Bride.* This was book two in a series. The first installment, *The Werewolf's Concubine,* hadn't exactly made her a household name, but she did have a few fans out there and she didn't want to let them down.

MJ and Bruce were up at the bar on their usual stools, and the community college group was bent over an oversized book. Tess's sheet of dark hair hid her face, but judging from her hand movements and the way she kept rubbing at her forehead, she was getting a headache. Bassett hoped they weren't doing some sort of complicated time travel equation involving advanced math, and if they were, he hoped they didn't come to him, the maharishi of time travel, for help. He'd barely squeaked by high school algebra and didn't relish that becoming common knowledge. Why? Maybe he kind of liked being the all-powerful boss and leading expert on time travel, even if he was just the man behind the curtain. Winnie would likely pull a Toto on him and expose him somehow, Bassett reckoned. He could see it now.

Lizard Buttons' band moved onto a strangely haunting cover of Mack the Knife. It wasn't half bad. Bassett eyed his drink. Maybe he'd had enough if he was picking out actual notes of music in The No Talent Hack's repertoire. He set his glass down and went to check on Stoop. Too many customers made Stoop nervous about getting behind on the tickets.

"How's it going?" Bassett picked up an onion ring and munched on it. It was perfect: hot and just the right amount of greasy. Personally, Bassett preferred regular ketchup over the fancy aioli sauce, but he wasn't about to bring that up.

Stoop wiped his brow with a dishtowel. He was sweating. The number of customers was stressing him out. Bassett gulped. He needed to start paying Stoop. Tonight. Next week at the latest.

"Rings are a hit, man." Stoop took a deep breath. "I think maybe I'm too good at this. I'm gonna need a sous chef."

Bassett snorted. "Let me guess, you have the perfect small child in mind? Jeez, you're like the Pied Piper or something. I'm going to get in trouble with Child Protective Services if you keep hiring me thigh-high employees."

"Nah, I'm outta sisters anyway. But seriously, Bro, if this keeps up ... this, uh, what do you call it?"

"Success?"

"Yeah, that. If you keep on being successful, you're gonna have to hire more help. Maybe even expand. Or franchise."

Bassett rubbed his neck, contemplating. The two million upstairs was starting to burn a hole in his proverbial pocket. Was he going to just sit on it for the rest of his life, on some sort of newfound morals? Was that realistic? Besides, whomever gifted it clearly wanted Bassett to have it for the bar. Honestly, it'd be morally wrong not to use it as it was intended if he thought long and hard about it.

"You're in luck, Stoo, my man," he said, finally. "Today's payday."

Stoop finished plating his last onion ring. They towered like an edible Pisa, listing to one side. He raised one eyebrow at his boss. "You been drinking the inventory again?"

"I'm serious. Payday and in cash, coming right up."

"Nah, brother mine. I'm good." Stoop waved a ring at him. He was flushed, like he was embarrassed, or maybe insulted. "Really, I don't do this for the money. I like doing it. I like hanging out here. Being a part of all this."

"I want you to take it. It's important to me." As he said it, he realized it was true. He was successful now, a real entrepreneur. He wanted paid employees under him. Not kids paid in cream soda, but real life, adult, paid in actual wages, employees.

"I don't need it, man. Just let me be a part of this. And when the time machine is built, I want on. In." Stoop frowned, thinking. "Whichever. I want to go."

Bassett had to assume he was only kidding, but he played along. "I can't guarantee that. I don't think the accountants are offering rides, like at an amusement park."

"Not the accountants, my main man. The college kids. My money's on them. They're gonna win this time travel race. Here, take these to table four before they get cold.”

Bassett obligingly took the offered platter. “We have a table four?”

“The pocket watches?”

“Ah. Right.”

“And better bring the rest of the bottle of Cab to the she-wolf, too. I don’t think her muse is musing tonight.”

He meant Emerson. Bassett took the suggestion to heart. If Emerson was having trouble writing her romance scenes he wanted to be the one to kick start her groove back on. In. Whichever.

Chapter Nine

"I love you, but go away." Emerson glared at him, her green eyes blazing over the top of her wine glass. "Thank you for the vino. Still, go away." From beneath the table, Bassett heard a growl and a snapping sound as Winnie found his shoelaces. He shook the Dachshund off with a kick, but a subtle one. It wouldn't do to upset his girlfriend more than she already was. He got a fierce bite on his big toe as retaliation. Bassett bit back a yelp. He pulled his long legs onto the bench, which was something of a feat. Emerson was as flexible as a stick of string cheese, but Bassett was about as pliable as a butter knife.

"Can I help?" He reached out and stroked her arm. She had a line of freckles there that was so darn cute he couldn't think straight when he focused on them. It was like a trail of stars going up her fine wrist to her adorable elbow to her delicious shoulder to –

"No, you can't help! Go away. I'm being taunted by this stupid plotline and I've written myself into a corner." Emerson practically wailed, a sound she didn't usually stoop to. She dropped her head on her arms, her hair spilling around her as the pencil holding it all up abruptly quit its job and broke. She made a sound like a smothered scream.

"How about the vampire turns from a bat back into a man but it happens during mid-flight and so he drops to his death, but you know, he's already undead, so PLOT TWIST. Yeah?" He didn't think it sounded so bad. He'd seen best sellers at the bookstore with less character development.

Emerson raised her head and leveled him with a stare. "It's a highlander, not a vampire. Pay attention. Did you even read the first one? The one that also did not have a vampire?"

"Um, yes, yes, I didn't."

"Yes, you didn't? That doesn't even make sense."

He was getting into trouble here. *Abort mission, Bassy*, he muttered to himself. "Let me get you something to munch on." He beat a safe retreat.

"You can't just feed me every time I get cranky!" Emerson hollered after him. Winnie yapped in agreement.

"Can too!" He hollered back. He would brew a whole pot of French press coffee. Yes, this would do the trick. And some of Stoop's BLT sliders from yesterday would hit the spot. No one could be sad or angry when eating bacon. It was scientifically impossible.

Speaking of scientists, one of the college kids nearly mowed him down on his way back to the kitchen.

"Mr. Clark!" He was breathless. Bassett thought it was Adam, but honestly, he had met so many new people in the past few weeks, he was having trouble keeping them all straight. He'd never had so many friends before, if that was what you could call them. Could you? He was unsure. Could customers be friends? When money was involved, maybe not. Wouldn't that be illicit or something?

"Having a good evening, Adam? Can I get you a refill on that beer?"

"Huh?" Adam looked down at his hand. He seemed surprised to find it clasping an empty glass. "Oh, no, that's okay. I need to keep my head clear tonight, if you know what I mean."

Bassett did not, but he was getting used to this kind of duplicitous talk. He was becoming an expert at finagling his way around it. "Ah. Well, you know best."

"I just," Adam looked over his shoulder. The sad-eyed lady smoothed her hair and sipped her Irish cream, then rubbed her thumb over a locket tucked inside her blouse. Adam continued, "I did want to mention ... Well ... that is ..." He scratched a bit of acne on his neck. He'd be a good-looking man someday, once he grew out of the pimple phase.

Bassett swallowed back a groan and an eye roll. *Spit it out, kid,* he thought. He had a bacon emergency here that was not going to solve itself.

"It's just that I saw you last night at the hardware store and couldn't help but notice that you were buying some things that could be used for, well, **you know what**," he dropped his voice dramatically. "And I thought to myself, I mean, it's none of my business, but I am just hoping that if you are working with the lawyers, you might reconsider throwing your lot in with us."

"They're accountants."

"Oh."

"And I'm not throwing my lot in with anyone, rest assured. My life is this bar. Gotta keep it up and running for you adventurers, am I right?" Bassett smiled, and clasped his hand on the young man's shoulder.

"Totally, totally!" Adam waved his hand so enthusiastically that his glass came narrowly close to clocking Bassett in the head. "Forget I said anything. I'm an idiot!"

"Also," Bassett went on, "I wasn't at the hardware store last night. You must have mistaken someone else for me."

Adam went from smiling to frowning. "I could have sworn it was you."

Bassett shook his head and took the empty glass from his patron. "Nope. Let me get that for you. On the house, okay? Just a half. You'll be clearheaded, I promise." *Not that you're that sharp to begin with, no offense. Good thing you're pretty.*

"Huh." Adam was clearly confused. "Sure looked like you. Although I did wonder at your Hawaiian shirt."

"I don't even own a Hawaiian shirt. Emerson would break up with me if I did." Sam Elliott wouldn't be caught dead in a Hawaiian shirt, would he? "I'll be back with your beer in a jiffy."

Bassett escaped, thinking all the while of how weird people got when they drank. Much less when they thought they could time travel. Maybe combining the two wasn't such a smart idea after all. They were starting to give him a headache. Maybe he should have started a coffee shop for people who thought they might be zombies. Or a gyro shop for descendants of royalty. A pretzel bakery for out-of-work spaceship pilots? Anything but a bar for time travelers.

And now they were seeing him in Hawaiian shirts, buying tools? This was getting to be too much. Then again, the alternative was being skewered by his girlfriend's laser beam eyes. He imagined the star freckles going all the way up her arm.

There were worse ways to go. He grinned all the way to the kitchen to brew his beloved a hot pot of Ethiopian Blend. He made her a BLT slider with extra bacon and cut it into the shape of a heart, adding a sprig of parsley on the side, forcing Stoop to make gagging noises at this gratuitous display of romance.

*   *   *

The next morning dawned fresh and bright and new. At least to some people. Bassett was not one of those people. It was 6:30 a.m. and his alarm clock had gone off three times. If he was going to meet up with the oh-so mysterious Linus Fields, he needed to get out of bed. But it was so early, and still dark, and he had only gotten three hours of sleep. He lay there, his grizzled goatee needing a trim and a shape-up, his breath smelling like last night's onion rings and the large Moose Drool he had used to wash them down with, and his not-a-Rolex watch sticking out of the covers on his wrist backwards. He groaned again, to no one in particular, unless it was Ernest (who thankfully didn't reply), and managed to slide out of bed on his knees. He smacked the alarm clock as it once again began to ring its ear-piercing screech, and knocked his head against the bed repeatedly. Finally pulling himself to standing, he yawned and scratched his butt contemplatively.

This guy had better have one hell of an interesting story to tell. He didn't get up this early for anyone. Bassett stumbled into the bathroom and left his upstairs apartment eight minutes later, mostly dressed, teeth sort of clean, and goatee still bristled and unruly. He yawned all the way to the IHOP and practically yanked the coffee pot out of the waitress's hand when he arrived.

Linus Fields did not have an interesting story to tell. He did not threaten Bassett, nor did he make accusations. He did not claim to know the secrets or the recipe to time travel, and he did not ambush Bassett during the strawberry crepes.

He didn't do those things because Linus Fields never showed up to the IHOP.

Linus Fields didn't show up to the IHOP because he was dead and lying in the back room of **ttrp.**

But Bassett didn't know that yet.

Chapter Ten

He found out soon enough when he got back to the bar – disgruntled and extremely cranky but full of crepes and coffee – where Margarita Jones was shrieking at the top of her considerably strong lungs.

He fumbled for the key as he listened to the earsplitting screams coming from within and willed himself not to have a heart attack. The woman's hollers were painful and Bassett was sure she was being murdered in lots of unsavory ways inside if he could only get this stupid key to cooperate and find out.

Finally, he won the battle and burst through the door. "Margarita!" he shouted over the screaming. "Margarita, where are you?"

It was a silly question since he could just follow the sound, but in truth it was echoing off the walls and it seemed the appropriate thing to shout anyway. Sort of like when people wake up after fainting and ask, *Where am I?* even though it's a dumb thing to ask.

"Margarita!" he kept shouting her name as he ran through the bar to the back room. He erupted through that door, stumbling over his shaky legs, and was privately proud of his bravery. But his sense and practicality were yelling at him to stop short and enter cautiously, if at all.

The scene before him was not what he had been expecting. No one was murdering his cleaning lady in unsavory ways after all. Margarita Jones stood in the middle of the room (still screeching, though her voice was getting softer as her throat got more and more sore) and she was looking down at the body at her feet.

Bassett's first thought was that she – Margarita – had murdered someone else in an unsavory way. Had someone snuck up on her, intent on robbery, and she had bashed them in the head with her mop? Thrown toilet cleaner in their eyes? Choked them with her scrubbing rags? But the possibility was too ridiculous to be true. Besides, if she had done in the poor soul with such malicious intent, she wouldn't be screaming about it so hysterically.

Bassett moved to the woman and put his arms around her protectively. It seemed the right thing to do, and she abruptly quit shrieking and moved onto babbling incoherently. Honestly, he was surprised at her lack of control in this situation. She had seemed a more practical person than this dramatic display. She'd likely be irritated at herself when she was more composed.

Bassett held onto his cleaning lady, patting her back in what he hoped was a gentle but reassuring fashion, but only seemed to initiate the hiccups for poor Margarita. He gazed down at the body. He'd recognize him anywhere, though he never could have described him to anyone. It was Linus Fields for sure. The strawberry crepes turned to a pit of writhing snakes in Bassett's stomach. Linus's body was stained with blood, mostly on the back of his head and on the floor beneath, where it had billowed out. Bassett was no detective, but Linus had obviously been attacked from behind, hit over the head with something, and had fallen forward. His head was twisted to one side in what would've been an awkward position to wake up in, had he been alive. Bassett didn't think he'd be waking up though. He looked very deceased, expired.

Still though, just in case ... he should probably check. He could merely be unconscious. Then he'd have to, what? Give him mouth-to-mouth? Bassett shuddered a full body shudder, not because of the idea of saving a man's life, but because Linus had been a creepy sort of fellow in life and he didn't relish the picture of him coming to and finding Bassett pursing his lips above his. Also, he was covered in blood. Bassett had never been very good with blood.

Bassett let go of Margarita – who promptly started screaming once again – and bent down. He felt for a pulse in Linus's neck, trying not to throw up as he did so, and felt none. He was dead all right.

Now what?

*   *   *

"Dude," Stoop looked awed. He had looked this way all morning, ever since Bassett had called him into the bar several hours earlier than usual, along with Emerson. There, Bassett relayed the story of his morning. "Your life is getting so friggin' weird. You know that, right?"

Bassett pulled his attention and gaze away from Emerson, whose messy hair and pajamas had been a very good distraction from the murder in his bar. He stared at his best friend and pulled a face. "Yeah, I've noticed that."

"This is getting yucky, Tiger." Emerson snuggled in closer. She was sitting on his lap, a location that Bassett was pleased to provide for all of eternity should he need to. "I don't like this. I'm worried about your safety."

The cops, including one named Jonathan Phelps whom Bassett had the sneaking suspicion must be his mother's 'silver fox,' had arrived and, so far, had not left. The statements had taken quite a while, especially with Margarita who was still not back to normal, and would probably need to be taken again at the precinct later.

"I'm sure the murderer is long gone," he reassured Emerson, nuzzling her hair with his chin.

"Not that. I'm worried that the police will think the murderer is you."

Bassett paused, a strand of red blonde hair between his lips. "I hadn't thought of that."

"Yeah, Bro. It is your bar. And it was locked. And you didn't like him." Stoop agreed.

"Well, nobody knows that … and I never said I didn't like him."

"You said he was a weasel."

"Yeah, well, I like weasels fine."

"Dude. Get serious."

Bassett waved away the suggestion. "I have an alibi. The waitress at IHOP will remember me."

"I don't think it happened this morning, Tiger." Emerson turned her worried face up to his. "I heard one of the EMTs saying he'd been dead for hours."

Bassett grimaced. "That can't be right. We were all here last night. I mean, like a full bar and everything. I'm pretty sure the accountants would have noticed a dead body in their room when they were doing their experiments or calculations or whatever it is they do back there when they're not blowing it to smithereens."

"Maybe *they* killed him." Stoop helped himself to Emerson's pot of coffee. He was either feeling brave or was distracted by the murder.

Emerson was distracted too, and didn't object. "That's the only explanation. They don't seem like killers, but … that's what they say about all killers, isn't it? It's always the accountants you least expect?"

"I don't think anyone has ever said that. Maybe he was killed elsewhere and the body didn't arrive until this morning." Bassett wasn't going to jump to the conclusion that the friendly accountants were cold-blooded murderers. It seemed too farfetched. They were so … boring.

"How does a body arrive?" Stoop snorted. "UPS? Like your toolbox?"

"Your toolbox!" Emerson gasped, and jumped off her perch on Bassett's knees. "If it was a burglary, the money could be gone! I mean, R.I.P. Mr. Fields and all that, but shouldn't we check?"

"Mr. Clark?" It was a policeman. The silver fox himself. He poked his head into the kitchen, where the three friends sat. Emerson nearly ran into him in her haste. "We're taking the body to the morgue now. We're going to need you and Ms. Jones, and those renters you were speaking of, to come into the station this afternoon. Really, any of your regular customers who were here last night and into the morning would be helpful for us to talk to."

"Yes, sir." Bassett wasn't sure he'd ever referred to anyone as 'sir,' (his hippie mother found it distasteful and didn't encourage such hierarchy in his growing up years), but there was something about a cop in his kitchen that suddenly brought out the respectful little kid in him.

"And I'm sure I don't need to say, Mr. Clark," Jonathan lowered his voice, "but don't leave town."

Only Babs' favorite cursing expression came to mind. "Son of a biscuit," Bassett muttered, but he nodded his acquiescence.

Emerson looked horrified as the police detective left the kitchen. "Tiger! What are we going to do?"

"Don't panic. We'll be fine. They'll get this sorted out fast. It's their job."

"Yeah, 'cuz no innocent person ever gets sent up the river." Stoop grunted and rolled his eyes. "And all of the popo are on the up and up."

"The *popo*? That's how you talk in the *'hood*?" It was Bassett's turn to roll his eyes. "And by the way, I'm firing your sister."

"Come on, man! This ain't her fault!" Stoop was appalled at his friend's seeming lack of trust in the neighborhood watch group, even if they had failed to stop a violent crime.

"I didn't say it was her fault. I just want her safe, that's all. I don't want her anywhere near this place until we get this solved. Come on, E, let's go check on the toolbox while they tote Fields out of here."

"I'm not staying in here by myself," Stoop came out from behind the counter. "I don't want to get bashed in the head."

"My hero." Emerson snorted a very unladylike snort. "So brave."

"I never claimed to be brave," Stoop replied. "I'm smart. I got no burning desire to die young, no matter how good looking a corpse I would leave behind. I still haven't met the girl of my dreams. Or maybe I have?" he continued to muse as they approached the stairs to Bassett's apartment. They all ignored the men in uniform who were wheeling a cart with a body bag attached right by the stairs and towards the front door. Bassett wished they'd use the back alley exit. This would not be good for business. And right when he was getting successful, too. This stunk. He felt a small pang of guilt for blaming poor Linus Field for his own murder, but really. Couldn't he have died elsewhere? It was beyond rude.

"You've met your dream girl?" Emerson asked Stoop.

"That Tess is a hotty totty with a naughty body, that's all I'm sayin'. There's something about her ..."

"Ew! She's too young for you, you nasty old man!"

"I got no problem being a sugar daddy, that's all I'm saying." They had reached the top of the stairs and Bassett turned the knob to his rooms. He hadn't been in there since early that morning, before IHOP. He felt a nervous knot in his stomach that clenched like a vise. What would he find in there? A missing toolbox? Another body? The murder weapon, planted in his rooms to frame him?

He focused on Emerson's pajama pants for a moment, to steady his suddenly racing heartbeat. His eyes fixated on the pattern made in the soft flannel. They were decorated with a sushi and chopsticks print. Emerson loved sushi. He loved Emerson. Those thoughts centered him.

He opened the door.

Chapter Eleven

There had been nothing amiss in his rooms. The toolbox was safe beneath the bed where Bassett had left it, untouched. The money was intact inside of it, still in messy bundles, still with the cryptic note on top. The scent of sour white Russian still lingered, no matter how hard he scrubbed the stain on the carpet. The photo album lay on his nightstand, open to what he had been looking at last: a photo taken off an educational film showing the score of a Rangers and Giants game, years before it had ever happened.

Bassett, Stoop, and Emerson had collapsed on the bed together in relief, and they were still there an hour later. Ernest Hemingway looked at them from his spot on the nightstand with what seemed to be a patronizing sort of stare. Bassett scooped him onto the bed in case he felt left out, and scratched him behind the ears affectionately. He was part of their gang after all, like a mascot. It wasn't his fault he was a little creepy.

"All right, Tiger," Emerson said, playing footsy with Bassett, "this just goes to show you should not keep millions of dollars in your house. Spend it, or give it away, or put it in the bank, okay?"

She was right, of course. She was Emerson. Bassett nodded. "So ... which one?"

She was silent and so was Stoop. Finally, it was the latter who answered. "It's your dough, dude. Do with it what you will."

"I just wish I knew who sent it. It's driving me nuts! I never wanted to be a hardboiled detective. This was not the plan."

"You're the only person I know who could complain about being gifted a fortune."

"I'm not complaining, I'm just – hey. What's that noise? Did anyone lock up the bar before we came up?" Bassett sat up straight on the bed. He could hear the distinct sound of someone walking around downstairs: not just walking around, but opening and closing doors, and being altogether not quiet. "Ah hell." He moved off the bed, his toes reluctantly leaving Emerson's, and moved towards the door, Ernest tucked in the crook of his armpit.

"Hang on!" Emerson got up too, and grabbed the bat from beside Bassett's bed. This was what it had been put there for years ago: as weaponry. It had been there so long there was a small dent in the carpet where it had stood, and the bat itself had a thin layer of dust on it. Bassett suddenly had the inane thought that his and Emerson's future kids would never use the bat to play baseball if they were about to murdered in the bar. This was a bad time to be considering a proposal but these morbid, end-of-life type thoughts always came to him in times of crisis. He eyed his beloved, decked out in her sushi pajamas and brandishing a Louisville Slugger like she meant business, a wild look in her deep green eyes. He wanted to drop to his knees right then and there and pull a (non-existent) engagement ring out of his chest pocket. He stifled the insanity and opened the door. Together, the three raced down to the bar.

It seemed to be in order, and no one bashed them in the back of the head like they had Linus. Bassett looked around blankly, finally spying someone sitting in one of the booths.

A shapely woman nodded at him as he caught her dramatically lined eyes. The trio slowly approached her booth.

"Can I help you," Bassett asked, trying not to stare at her escaping cleavage. She was tall, with a sleek blonde bob, full red lips, and dark eyes framed by long, fluttery lashes. Aware that Emerson was standing right next to him, Bassett averted his eyes from her curves, which seemed to be held prisoner in her clingy black dress. "We, uh," his voice cracked as he fixed his eyes upward, "don't open for hours."

"I'm here about the murder." The woman smiled, which seemed an odd thing to smile about, but maybe she was just being polite. "I'm from the police department. Special Agent Fitzgerald. Call me Katie."

Emerson stared pointedly at her bosom. Bassett wondered briefly why she got to look but he couldn't. He would have liked to ask, but valued his life. "Oh, we'll be calling you Special Agent Fitzgerald, thanks." Emerson's voice was frosty.

"I'm going to need to bring you in, Mr. Clark," Fitzgerald said in a slight southern drawl. We have some more questions we'd like you to answer. On record and paper all that. Tiresome, I know, but I'll have you back as soon as possible."

"Oh. Uh, sure." Bassett figured it wasn't a request. He felt the strawberry crepes creep back up in his mouth. He'd never eat those again. He swallowed hard. *Was he about to be arrested?* At the very least, he was under suspicion, he knew that much. *Would Emerson love a convicted felon? Would she marry a prisoner? Would there be conjugal visits where he was going?*

"I'm coming, too." Emerson spoke up. "No question."

"Well, munchkin, you aren't invited, but if you insist," Special Agent Fitzgerald replied. Bassett worried for her safety. Emerson didn't tolerate short jokes or being patronized, even if she was wearing sushi pjs. Also, she hadn't put down the Louisville Slugger. "And I'm going to need the addresses of your regular customers. The ones who were in the bar last night."

"I don't have any addresses," Bassett stammered. "I don't even have full names."

The detective turned her condescending look to him. "Of course you do, Mr. Clark. Check your credit card receipts. Or just hand them over to me and my team will do the footwork.”

Bassett nodded. Of course. Credit card and debit cards records. Most businesses wouldn’t have their customer’s addresses and information on their receipts. But Bassett still used a flatbed credit card imprinter, the kind with carbon copies. Weird that she knew that. Maybe he’d served her before. No, he’d remember the cleavage. “Do we have to pull them into this? I hate to bother them.” *Not to mention losing my only customers*, he thought. Talk about short-lived success.

“Bother them?” Special Agent Fitzgerald raised her flawlessly groomed eyebrows. “Mr. Clark, one of them just may be a killer.”

“Oh. Right. Let me get you those receipts.” He swallowed hard and moved to the cash register located behind the counter.

“Interesting what you’ve done here, as far as decorating goes.” The woman stood, looking around her. She laid her hand on the top of the scuba helmet, and tapped her long, blood red nails against it. “Quaint.”

“It’s not quaint.” Emerson tightened her grip on the bat and glared at her. “It’s meaningful. And timeless. You wouldn’t understand.”

Katie Fitzgerald ignored her. Stoop had said nothing up to this point. He seemed to be somewhat intoxicated by the detective’s arrival – or maybe it was her dress.

“Close your mouth. You look like a wide-mouthed bass,” Emerson hissed to him, as Special Agent Fitzgerald walked around the bar. Stoop obediently snapped his jaws shut with a clack.

Bassett stuffed the pockets of his cargo pants with the receipts from last night’s purchases. He looked up to find the detective watching him. She nodded. “Shall we?” She gestured toward the door.

Emerson, Bassett, and Special Agent Fitzgerald exited the bar, leaving a star-struck Stoop behind. An unmarked police car was parked in front, and the detective opened the back door for them. Bassett was extremely grateful she didn't place her hand on his head as he got in the car. He felt criminal enough.

He climbed in, Emerson directly behind him. He noticed she was still glowering as she settled into the seat next to him. He heard the door slam and then he noticed a strange smell filling his nostrils. The next thing he perceived was a thick smoke filling the car. He also noted the front door opening and Special Agent Fitzgerald climbing in, suddenly wearing a gas mask. That seemed suspect.

Those were the last things he noticed that morning. The smoke clogged his lungs and Bassett Clark fell deeply asleep, his head resting on his girlfriend's patterned lounge pants. She toppled over next to him.

*   *   *

They woke at the exact same moment, groggy and disoriented. Well, Bassett was groggy and disoriented; Emerson was fighting mad.

"What the hell?" she hollered, struggling against her bonds. They were each tied to a straight-back wooden chair that reminded Bassett of his grandmother's dining table at Christmas Eve dinner where he was berated annually for not sitting up tall enough. Their captor – they could only assume the fake policewoman – had secured their hands and ankles: Bassett with zip ties, and Emerson with rope. Bassett wondered halfheartedly why the discrepancy, but realized they had likely only planned to kidnap one. Emerson had insisted on coming. Bassett struggled weakly against the bonds. He felt seasick from the after effects of whatever had been used to knock them unconscious. Emerson, on the other hand, was struggling and thrashing about mightily, in between shouts of what she planned on doing to Katie Fitzgerald.

"Oh, stop. You're making me blush." Katie was sitting across from them. The gas mask was gone. She looked as un-mussed and perfect as ever. Even her impressive bosom didn't heave with exertion. Bassett wondered how long he and Emerson had been out. Katie seemed very well rested for a kidnapper. You'd think that kind of lifestyle would take it out of you, but perhaps she had practice.

"I'm going to kill you so hard!" Emerson hissed. The sound gave Bassett chills, but had no effect on Katie.

"Promises, promises," she replied, dryly. "Everyone says that, but no one follows through. Now, let's have a little talk, shall we?"

"We shall not!" Emerson spat toward her, but most of the glob landed soggily on her own chin. Bassett would have laughed but he was sure that wouldn't go over well. He settled for leveling his sternest glare at Katie.

"Be quiet, Oompa Loompa," drawled Katie, "I only let you come because I didn't feel like killing you."

Stoop! Bassett suddenly had to swallow his fear for his best friend. What if Katie had killed him while Bassett and Emerson were napping in the car? "What did you do to Stoop?"

"Who?" Katie frowned. "Oh. You mean Gregory Mackenzie? He's fine. Don't blubber."

"Gregory?" Emerson stopped thrashing for a moment. "Stoop's name is Gregory?"

"Yeah." Bassett didn't take his eyes off his jailor. She crossed her long legs, shiny black stilettos dangling in the air for a split second. "No one has called him that since elementary school, though. How do you know so much about us?"

"That's my job, Mr. Clark. I'd love to say you've been on our radar for years, but you've been a boring little fellow up until recently, haven't you? Nothing to make us suspect your activity until a few weeks ago, when you popped up from virtually nowhere. You're either incredibly good at covering your tracks, or you're brand new to this game."

"This game? What game?" Bassett was wary. He didn't like where this was going.

"Come now." Katie – if that was even her name. She didn't really look like a Katie. Who named a hired thug, a criminal, a kidnapper, Katie? Of course, her parents probably didn't know their baby girl would grow up to be on the wrong side of the law, but still. Katie leaned forward to stare intensely at the two in front of her. "The time travel game. Seems like you're an awfully important person to some extremely dangerous people, aren't you, Mr. Clark? They sure do look up to you. Poor Linus Fields was only trying to protect you from them. Tsk tsk. Blood on your hands. That can't be comfortable."

Bassett grimaced. "Protect me? I thought he was a bad guy." Whoops, that sounded incredibly amateur. "I mean, I thought he was the enemy." There. That was better.

"I don't think you know who your enemies are." She spoke slowly and clearly, as if she were a schoolteacher talking down to a dimwitted student in detention.

"Yeah, well, I think we can count the nut job that drugged us and kidnapped us as one," Emerson bit off.

"Excellent detective work, Nancy Drew," Katie chuckled. "A for Effort."

"So, who killed Fields?" Bassett didn't know much, but he recalled from some thriller he had read that you're supposed to keep the enemy talking. They usually gave up interesting facts and got distracted. Wasn't that how it went?

But Katie didn't look interested or distracted. She looked bored. She examined her long, red fingernails as if they were much more fascinating than her two victims. "I have no idea. One of us maybe. Who knows? The man had enemies, that's for sure. From just about every era."

Bassett let that sink in. Either Fields had been a time traveler, or Katie was insane. Possibly both. He missed the days when late water company bills and crummy microwaved bar food were his biggest concerns. He wriggled with renewed vigor against the zip ties and heard something fall out of his lap with a clatter. He looked down at his feet: it was Ernest. Weird. He must have had him tucked under his arm when he had gotten into Katie's car. It was rather kind of her to have let him keep the skull. Maybe, as a criminally insane person, she appreciated the morbidity of Ernest.

"Well," Katie stood and stretched. "I'm going to call it a day. Someone will be in to have a little chat with you momentarily. Tell the Butcher I said hello. I'd say see you later, but I think we both know I won't." She walked across the dimly lit room and left through a heavy door that rolled up when she yanked on it. They could hear a padlock being fiddled with from the other side.

"You won't?" Bassett whispered after Katie.

"The Butcher?" Emerson whispered back.

Chapter Twelve

"Good grief, you're sexy." It was the third time in as many minutes that Bassett had uttered those words, but he still meant them. The object of his adoration was managing to squirm out of her ropes, little by little.

"Well," she gasped, pulling her arms with a pop of the shoulders that made Bassett wince in sympathy, "all that gymnastics training was bound to pay off. My dad will be thrilled. He always complained about wasting the money." Her wrists had been tied behind her back, but she somehow rolled them over her head. Next, she began to nibble at the ropes, working them back and forth like a terrier.

Bassett watched, feeling helpless in his zip ties. There was no way he could do the shoulder trick. He'd had no gymnastics training. Also, he was confident he couldn't chew his way through the plastic anyway. If Emerson could get free, maybe she could find a knife or scissors lying around.

For the first time, Bassett looked around the room. It was a large room, practically warehouse size, empty for the most part, and windowless. A dim light came from a bulb dangling overhead. The door that Katie had rolled up and left through was the only entrance and exit. It seemed to be some sort of storage facility if Bassett wasn't mistaken, though he'd never been held captive in one before. Even if they could get free from their bonds, how were they going to get out of here?

Emerson read his mind. "Okay, Tiger," she said, around the ropes in her mouth, "here's the plan. Once I get you free, you pretend to still be tied, all right? When the Butcher comes in for our little chat, I'll be hiding in the corner with my chair. I'll bash him over the head and then we run. Got it?"

"Why do you get to do the bashing? Someone named the Butcher is bound to be tall. Are you going to bash him in the kneecaps?"

Emerson narrowed her eyes at him. "This is no time for short jokes," she said, as she snaked her way out of the ropes. She crowed triumphantly. "Fine. You can do the bashing of the Butcher." She hurriedly began untying the ropes that bound her ankles to the chair legs. "Unless it's not him. If Special Agent Fitzgerald comes back in, I'm doing the bashing. All the bashing will be mine."

"Yes, dear."

"The bashing will be fierce."

"Yes, dear."

"And the bashing will be merciless."

"Yes, dear."

"I'm gonna break her stupid face."

"Okay, okay, we've got to get some coffee in you before you turn into a homicidal maniac, E." Bassett was getting alarmed.

"And then her stupid legs. Definitely going to bash those. She called me an Oompa Loompa. I *hate* her." Emerson stood up, completely free from the ropes now.

"Let's focus less on making mincemeat out of Katie, and more on finding something to bust me out of these zip ties, okay, sweetheart?" He tried widening his eyes like Bambi.

"You look constipated," she replied fondly. "Okay, if I were a big ol' knife where would I be?"

They both looked to their lefts and to their rights. Up and down. In the empty corners and on the blank walls. There was literally nothing in the room but them and Ernest.

"Maybe under the chairs?" Bassett suggested. "Like Oprah. 'Look under your chairs! You get a knife! He gets a knife! Everybody gets a knife!'"

"Hardyharhar." Emerson collapsed at his feet. She laid her head on his lap. He longed to brush her frizzy hair, or at least give her a comforting pat, but … zip ties. "Hey." She sat back up and stared at the floor.

"What?" Bassett followed her gaze, focused on Ernest.

Emerson lifted Ernest off the floor and regarded him intently. The spunky gymnast and the expressionless skull were engaged in a staring contest and Bassett wasn't sure who was winning. But it was making him uncomfortable. "What?" he asked again. Then he got it. "You wouldn't!"

"Sorry, Ernest Hemingway," Emerson answered. She bit her lower lip. "But I gotta do it."

"No!" Bassett would have reached out to stop Emerson from flinging Ernest to the floor with a sickening crash, but … zip ties.

Ernest hit the floor with such force that he split open. Bassett closed his eyes in sympathy and revulsion.

"Okay, Ernie," Emerson said, as she started going through the pieces of bone, "let's find your sharpest fragment. Ah ha! This should do the trick." She held up a jagged piece of wicked looking bone.

Bassett was still mourning the loss of his mascot and didn't reply. He was silent as the grave as Emerson used the bone fragment to saw through the thin plastic of the zip tie on his ankles.

"This will be good as a weapon, too," she said, her tongue between her teeth as she worked. "I can shank Special Agent Fitzgerald with it. Good times." She worked in silence for a few minutes. Finally, she straightened up. "This isn't working." She frowned at the remains of poor Ernest. "It's not sharp enough."

"You killed him for nothing," Bassett said, morosely.

"Tiger, he was already dead."

"Can you use the tip to like, push the button thing?"

"What button thing?"

"You know, the square shaped button thing. Then slide it off the way it came."

"Hmm. Okay." She worked quickly for another few minutes, at one point slipping with her fingers and stabbing Bassett in the ankle with the bone. He blinked back tears. It seriously smarted. "Yeah, that's not working either. New plan."

"The new plan is, you get out of here and leave me behind. I'm not kidding, E. You have to get out of here."

Emerson stood and placed her hands on her hips. Bassett got a sudden view of what she would have looked like as a feisty five-year-old who wasn't getting her way. "I don't think so. Besides, nothing's changed, except that I'm going to have to be the one who does the bashing. That's the only new part of this plan. You'll just have to sit here and look pretty until I can get something to bust you out. Either that, or you just take the chair with you?" She raised her candy cane shaped eyebrows to punctuate her question.

Bassett gave it a try. To move at all, he had to hunch over and then jump like a kid playing hopscotch. *Escape by hopping. Great. He was going to look so cool in front of Emerson and his kidnappers. They'd probably die laughing.* "Yeah, I don't think that's going to work unless we've got a whole week to get out of this building. Moving at the speed of snail here." He stopped, breathing heavily at the exertion. He'd only moved a couple of feet. He sat back down, hard.

Emerson cocked her head as she regarded him. She leaned forward and grabbed at the front of his cargo pants. Bassett's eyes widened and he yelped.

"Honey, it's not that I'm not willing, but this is neither the time nor the—"

"The receipts," Emerson dug her hands in his pockets. She pulled them out, empty. "They're gone. Our customers are in danger, Tiger."

A sound came from outside the storage unit. They glanced at one another. "Go!" Bassett whispered. "Don't forget the chair!"

Emerson scampered to the corner, next to the roll-up door. She placed the chair in front of her, her elbows in an L-shape. The chair dwarfed her. She really was a munchkin – Bassett couldn't help but smile.

The door rolled open.

*   *   *

Emerson looked down at the crumpled body at her feet. She put the chair aside. "Well, I was hoping for Special Agent Fitzgerald or whatever her real name is, but that was oddly satisfying, too."

The body was a huge beast of a man. How little Emerson had managed to drop him was a mystery Bassett would have to solve later. It must have been the element of surprise. She couldn't even have reached his head. Maybe she broke his back and the pain knocked him unconscious? Well, they'd find out later.

"Okay, I'm going in." Emerson cracked her knuckles.

"Going in?" Bassett felt panic rise in him.

"A man named the Butcher is bound to have all sorts of knives on him. Or cleavers. Or one of those poky hammer things that they use to tenderize meat. Not that that would help, but here goes." She bent down by the body.

Bassett held his breath. How long did a person remain knocked out? Or had she somehow killed him? "I think you should just go, E. Just go!" He could see the outside of the storage unit, and Emerson had a chance to escape. She should take it.

"Shut up. You know I hate it when you tell me what to do." She used all 105 pounds of herself to roll the Butcher over, panting as she did so. She patted him down like an airport security officer. "Ah ha!" She crowed victoriously as she brandished a pocketknife.

Bassett breathed again. They were going to make it. They were almost free. Emerson ran over to him and began to saw on the zip ties at his ankles again. They snapped free almost immediately, and she went to work on the ones on his wrists.

Bassett used his newfound mobility to do what he did best: he grabbed Emerson's face between his palms and planted a deep, satisfying, romantic, passionate kiss on her mouth. If they got out of here, he was determined to make an honest woman out of this girl. Some of that toolbox fortune was going toward a shiny engagement ring, no doubt.

Without saying anything and still tingling from the kiss (it was, by far, the best of their whole relationship), they circled hand in hand around the body of the Butcher, threw a sad look backwards at the remains of Ernest Hemingway, and exited the storage unit at a run.

Chapter Thirteen

"When I dreamt of our future together, it did not include this!" Bassett's heart was pumping painfully hard and his lungs were fit to burst. He was not a runner and they'd been running at their fastest pace for what felt like hours.

"It's only been 10 minutes, Tiger," Emerson threw him an encouraging smile over her shoulder as she slowed to a jog, "but we can probably slow down now. I don't see anyone following us. You always promised to run away with me someday, remember?"

They stopped, Emerson with her hands on her hips, barely out of breath, and Bassett panting like the hound breed he was named for. They were in an unfamiliar neighborhood, if you could even call it a neighborhood. It was more like a storage unit out in the middle of nowhere, off the side of a highway, in the desert.

They didn't live in the desert.

"How long were we out for?" Bassett gasped for breath. He doubled over, his hands on his knees. He was sure he was allergic to running. He felt like passing out. "I mean, in the car?"

"Longer than we thought I guess. I suppose Special Agent Skanky didn't leave you your phone?"

He patted his pockets, but the cell phone had gone the way of the bar receipts. "Nope. Now what?"

"We've got to warn the customers somehow. She's got their information, or at least she's halfway to knowing it by now." Emerson bit her fingernails as she thought. Her hair was a halo of red gold frizz, and her pajamas were rumpled and dirty. "And we need to check on Stoop. Poor Winnie. I left her at the doggy daycare and she's going to be so frantic to be picked up.”

“This is a real sucky place to be,” Bassett answered. He was nervous. He didn’t want to talk about Winnie. “We’re like sitting ducks out here. If Katie or one of her minions come by, we’re toast.”

“I know. Hey, do you picture Katie’s minions driving an old flatbed pickup truck?”

“No, I picture them driving unmarked black SUVs. Maybe Hummers. Or helicopters.”

“Me too. Good.” Emerson suddenly stuck out her hand, thumb up. Bassett followed her gaze.

An old flatbed pickup slowed and pulled up next to the pair. In the back, precariously tied down with bungee cords, were the contents of someone’s house: a ratty couch; some mismatched dining chairs; several boxes; and a patio umbrella.

“Howdy.” The voice belonged to a grizzled man. He had bushy gray brows over piercing blue eyes which scrutinized the couple. There was also a large German shepherd in the cab next to him. “Goin’ to town?”

“Yep!” Emerson hopped in the passenger seat with nary a qualm. “Hey, wittle baby,” she cooed and scratched the shepherd on the head. He reciprocated by licking her face. She laughed.

Bassett started to crawl in next to Emerson. It was going to be one tight fit – the bushy man was not exactly small and the shepherd was enormous. Suddenly, it began barking ferociously, baring its teeth and lunging forward, over Emerson’s lap. Bassett stumbled backwards, out the door, and onto the highway pavement again.

“Best you sit in the back.” The old man nodded behind them.

Bassett waited for Emerson to join him. She continued scratching the dog and shrugged at Bassett. "Sorry, Tiger. See you in town."

"Really? I don't think this is the safest option when hitchhiking with strangers."

The old man guffawed. "Ah, ain't nothing gonna happen to your little woman here."

"I was talking about *your* safety with the little woman," Bassett muttered, but he circled around to the back of the pickup and heaved himself up and into the flatbed. He pushed his way past a stool and several suitcases, and settled himself on the floral couch. It smelled like old people and fried chicken. He arranged the patio umbrella so that it offered him some shade, and settled down for the ride. Might as well get some shut-eye. Who knew how long the promised 'town' was away from here … much less what town it was.

The ride was bumpy and long. By the time they got to their destination – some small city called Riverside that had no visible river in sight – Bassett was sure he had bugs in his teeth. His back hurt and he was sunburned (the umbrella had fallen over at some point). He was in a mood, and not a pleasant one. He wanted a shower and a tall scotch on the rocks. The truck pulled into a parking spot at a restaurant and the old man turned off the noisy engine. Bassett got out, legs cramping, mouth dry. He circled around the truck and met up with Emerson. She looked refreshed and cheerful. She'd twisted her hair up with a purple marker and was laughing with the man like they were old friends. Bassett crossed his arms over his chest and glared at her. He couldn't help it. His sunburned skin crackled and stung, and he felt dehydrated and angry at the world.

She leaned forward and kissed him thoroughly. "You look hot. Like Sam Elliott," she whispered in his ear.

He was instantly cheered and he led the way into the restaurant, smiling ear to pink-tipped ear.

*   *   *

Bassett washed his face and hands in the bathroom sink and then went to use the pay phone out front. *A pay phone.* He didn't know these things still existed, but thank goodness they did because old Cap (that was the man with the truck) didn't have a mobile.

"That's how the gov'ment tracks ya," he had said wisely, when asked. He'd tapped his head as if to prove a point, then taken off his cowboy hat and showed Bassett the lining. Aluminum foil.

Bassett had to bum some quarters off the waitress, who looked seriously annoyed. *Wait until you find out I have no money to pay for the bacon cheeseburger and fries I just ordered.* He dialed Stoop's cell. It rang and rang. Just when Bassett was about to compose a voice mail message in his mind, Stoop picked up.

"Hello?" His voice was suspicious. The caller ID would show an unknown number: he didn't know it was his kidnapped friend.

"Stoop!"

"Bass? What the hell, man? Where are you? What happened? What's going on?"

"Slow down!" Bassett laughed. It felt good to laugh. "I'm all right, and E's all right. We escaped. Wait, let me go back. You know that detective, Special Agent Fitzgerald?"

"Yeah, yeah, man, I know. She is no agent — at least not with our police. Dude! I watched her put that gas mask on and I was all, duuuuuuuuuuude!"

"Right? It was serious SyFy channel stuff. You have no idea. We were totally knocked out by this gas stuff she let off in the car, and the next thing you know, we wake up in this storage unit, tied up and everything."

"Duuuuuuuuude." It seemed to be Stoop's only response.

"Exactly. So then Emerson went all Mary Lou Retton on this mammoth body builder, and wham, we get a ride out of the desert with some ax murderer hick, and now we're eating cheeseburgers. Any idea where Riverside is?"

"Uh, yeah, I get some of my supplies from the quarry out there. You're like hours away from home, buddy."

"I figured. Hey, Stoop?"

"Yeah, my man?"

"You need to stay clear of the bar."

"Dude, I know. I cleared outta that place like my pants were on fire. I called the police too, but they seemed more annoyed about you leaving town after they told you not to. I don't think they believed my hot policewoman impersonator kidnapping you story."

"Damn."

"Yeah."

"Okay, well, I'll deal with that later. Another thing: you've got to warn the customers. The accountants, MJ and Bruce, the creepy old guy, the Neighborhood Watch Team, and the college kids."

"How do you expect me to do that? I don't even know these people's last names. Hell, I don't even know their first names."

"Well, think of something. It's a matter of life and death."

"Duuuuuuude."

"I got to go." He'd just spied the waitress through the window, fielding a platter of cheeseburgers. "With any luck, I'll see you soon."

Emerson was deep in conversation with Cap when he got back to their booth. The restaurant was a cheap, no-class, no-ambiance kind of diner that had hit its prime about 20 years ago, but beggars couldn't be choosers. The menus were made of cracked, stained plastic, and the tables were covered in hard, thick vinyl tablecloths. The whole place smelled of grease. Still, Bassett's stomach was about to crawl out through his ribcage in search of sustenance.

"So, you're saying you're in deep shit?" Cap asked, in a conspirator's whisper. Emerson widened her green eyes and nodded, very slowly. Cap bent his grizzled head low, his eyes shifting from side to side as he continued, "And you're saying, if I help, I would be risking my own life?"

Emerson shook her head, just as slowly as Bassett slid into the booth next to her. "Oh no," she whispered, "it's not a risk. It's a certainty."

"I ain't getting outta this alive?" Carefully, Cap removed his hat and set it next to his large Pepsi.

"It's highly unlikely."

The old man stared at Emerson, speechless for a moment, as was Bassett. Then, he chortled loudly enough to raise the heads of everyone around. "You got yourself a deal, Missy!"

Bassett sighed, but they weren't listening. The waitress brought his burger and the sight, not to mention the aroma, brought tears of happiness to his eyes. He reached for the ketchup and let Emerson and

Cap continue plotting to save the world.

Chapter Fourteen

"What we need is a bunker." Cap and Emerson had been hashing and rehashing plans all the way from Riverside. Now they were five minutes away from **ttrp**, and Bassett's only way of communicating with the pair was through the very small window in the back of the pickup. And if he stuck his head through too far to talk, Maggie, the German shepherd, tried to eat his face.

So, all in all, Bassett had had better days.

"Right? A bunker would be way cool." Emerson's voice was dreamy. She was really getting into this vigilante stuff. As far as Bassett could tell, they hadn't come up with a plan, but mostly talked a lot of smack about Special Agent Fitzgerald. "And a Batmobile."

Bassett groaned and pulled his head all the way out of the window and settled back down on the geriatric, fried chicken-scented couch. The town, his hometown, flew by. There was the old laundromat that Lila used to send him to as a kid, with a pocket full of quarters, pulling a red wagon of dirty clothes behind him. There was his favorite Mexican place, with the $1 tacos he craved when hungover. There was the movie theater where he liked to see midnight movies with Emerson, whenever he remembered to plan a date night. (Why was that always so hard? He needed to try harder). There was the construction on 15th street that had been there for practically forever. There was the smoke shop, the insurance office, the community college campus.

Those college kids. Bassett's gut clenched. If Katie and her minions had gotten to his customers before Stoop could, he'd never forgive himself.

Emerson stuck her head out the window. "We're headed to Lila's," she reported. "I don't think it's safe to go back to the bar yet, and they probably know where I live, too. We need to get to a phone and track down Gregory. And I need to pick up Winnie. At this point, I'm going to own stock in Poochikin's Pet Palace."

"Stoop's gonna kill you for calling him Gregory, but yeah."

Emerson snorted. "I'd like to remind him that crazier and bigger people have tried and failed." She was obviously proud of herself. Bassett could see her now, changing her career path from romance writer to freelance crime fighter.

Cap drove them to Lila Clark's house. This was the house where Bassett had grown up: a practical ranch house, with a sensible three bedrooms and two baths. There, the practicality and sensibility ended. Lila had decorated it in a smattering of macramé, tie-dye, pottery, beads, tapestries, and local art. There were plastic pink flamingoes in the garden, along with crystals, dreamcatchers, and large ceramic globes. She drove a purple Volkswagen Bug and it was parked haphazardly in the front yard, probably due to there being a gigantic teepee in her front yard. Bassett recalled dimly her mentioning that she was housing someone she met at an art colony in New Mexico. This was normal for Lila, who would give anyone the shirt off her back, providing she was wearing one. There had been a few months where she had dipped her toes into the water of nude living. Bassett had blocked out those months from his memory with help from a well-qualified and expensive therapist.

They skirted by a flamingo in a compromising position with a gnome, Bassett leading the way, and knocked on the front door. There was a fat Buddha on the front porch, along with a light-up plastic rendition of Mary and the Christ child that was probably meant to be a Christmas decoration but sat there all year around, and a Hindu symbol of an Aum on the door. Lila refused to be tethered by a single religion so she liked to combine as many as possible, like a spiritual cocktail. She covered all the bases.

Lila opened the door and Bassett breathed an inward sigh of relief that she was fully clothed. "My sweet boy!" she exclaimed, and threw her arms around her son. "Emerson! Darling!" She nearly threw aside Bassett in her hurry to embrace his girlfriend. Bassett knew his mother was worried he was going to lose Emerson if he didn't marry her quick. And since Lila wasn't a big advocate of marriage the irony was not lost on Bassett. She had no faith in him being able to keep Emerson without a ring and a minister.

"Hi, mama L!" Emerson squeezed her back. "This is Cap. We're here to borrow your phone if we may, and to protect you."

"Is this going to be a long story? Should I get some refreshments?" Lila pursed her lips thoughtfully.

Cap nodded as a response, and they all went into the house, where Emerson and Cap sat down in the living room, Lila went to the kitchen, and Bassett followed his mother.

"So, what's all this protecting me mumbo jumbo about?" Lila poured glasses of orange juice from a pitcher and arranged some cookies on a plate. "Unless you'd rather have brownies?"

Bassett grimaced. "No, Mom, none of your brownies. We need to think, not space out. But thanks. Here, let me." He took the tray of juices from her hands. "And I do need to use your phone."

"Well, you know where it is. I'm going to go have some girl talk with your lovely girlfriend and the transient you brought over."

Bassett rolled his eyes. "His name is Cap, and evidently he's ready to die for us, so mind your manners. Besides, you're one to talk; you have someone living in your driveway."

Lila tittered. "Well, the apple doesn't fall far from the tree, does it?"

Bassett kissed her affectionately before they went back to the living room.

He dispensed with the juices and helped himself to some cookies before going back to the bedroom to call Stoop.

"Dude. So glad you're in the land of the living. Great news: I have found and am currently with one whole, intact, and not murdered customer!" Stoop's voice sounded proud.

"One is better than nothing." Bassett tried to mask the disappointment. He wished, not for the first time, that he'd never turned over those receipts. "Who? Wait, let me guess, Goth Girl? Vampira?"

Stoop answered with a chuckle. "You know it, brother of mine! I've told her I will not leave her side until the danger is over. She doesn't look all that impressed, but I think she's faking."

"Yeah. Probably. Okay, well, stay with her, I guess. If you come up with a plan that's better than me heading over to the police station, let me know."

"Duuuuuuude, you do not want to do that. They're pissed at you. Plus, they're never going to buy your story, especially when your character witnesses all believe in time travel. It's not looking good for you, my man."

"Thanks for the vote of confidence. But I can't just sit around waiting to be kidnapped some more. Plus, the customers. Agent Skanky, as E calls her, is out for blood. Actually, I'm still not entirely sure what she's after …"

"Right?" Stoop mused for a moment. Bassett could hear something in the background. It sounded like kids. He must have the television on. "The secrets of the universe? Time and space continuum and all that? Wormholes?"

"Or she's after someone in particular. It was the customers she was interested in mostly. Who do you think is the least nutty in our little group?"

"Umm, I'd go with Tess. Totally."

"Are you saying that because she's sitting right next to you?"

"Yes. Yes, I am." Stoop laughed his deep, joyful laugh which signaled that he was in a good mood.

"Come on, buddy. You know you're too old for a college girl." Bassett put on his best stern, fatherly voice. They were in their mid-forties, he and Stoop; what did they have in common with a fresh out of high school kid? It was kind of … grody. To the max.

Stoop turned his laugh into a chuckle. "I think you'll be surprised, my brothah from another mothah. Come on over. And bring us some of your mama's most excellent cookies, would you?"

* * *

Bassett trooped out to the driveway with Emerson right behind him. Cap had wanted to stay behind in Lila's living room - he had discovered the brownies — but they needed his truck.

The flap to the teepee swung open, and a head poked through. The group waved politely as they traipsed past. The head slowly swung to one side, watching them, then went back inside, the flap shutting with a decisive smacking sound. The head belonged to the most Norwegian-looking Native American Bassett had ever seen.

Bassett crawled back into the pickup bed. He had barely gotten comfortable on the couch when Cap's truck came to a stop. Bassett hopped out and opened the door for Emerson. "M'lady," he said as he offered her his hand. Cap smiled and put the truck in park.

The address Stoop had given Bassett wasn't far; evidently, it was Tess's parents' home. Similar to the teepee man, Tess lived in the driveway, only in a decent sized RV. The door opened and out stepped Stoop.

"Dude! Dudette! I'm so relieved you two aren't pushing up daisies! I was so worried. You have no idea. I was like a mother hen, looking for her lost chickies." Stoop's eyes looked misty.

"What did I tell you about calling me Chicky?" Emerson retorted.

Another head popped up behind Stoop. It was a woman with a mop of curly dark hair, and a hot pink jumpsuit. Between the hair style and the outfit, she looked like she had stepped out of the 1980s. She also looked oddly familiar. Bassett stared, trying to place her.

"Tess?" It was Emerson who finally found her voice, and with it, her knowledge of how they knew this woman. They started up the driveway toward the RV.

"Where?" Bassett frowned, looking around.

"Right there."

The woman smiled. That didn't jog Bassett's memory. He'd never seen Vampira smile before.

"But where's the goth getup? And I thought you were, like, practically a teenager?"

She grinned bigger. "I guess my disguise worked then."

"Disguise? What are you hiding from?" He was suspicious. The last thing he needed was some teenager-impersonating, escaped career criminal seducing his best friend.

Tess shrugged. "I wanted to get in with those guys once I found out what they were trying to do. And it just makes it easier to focus on school when I've got a tough outcast thing going on. At my age, I need all the help I can get. I guess it's silly, but it's kind of fun. I never got to rebel when I was actually a teenager so I'm living it up now."

"So, you're not dating Adam?"

"Ew. What gave you that idea? Gross. I'm practically old enough to be his mother." She was appalled. "He's just super smart is all. Together I think we really have something."

Yeah, like a huge problem. Bassett refrained from speaking his thoughts out loud. "You mean, the time traveling stuff?"

"You are a believer, right?" Tess narrowed her blue eyes as she stared at Bassett. Then she turned to face Stoop. "You told me he's the real deal."

"Did I say that?" Stoop put on his best innocent face, but it made him look ill.

"Look, we have more important fish to fry." Bassett was not going to get into a debate over the possibility of time travel here in a stranger's driveway. "We've got big trouble, and we need to sift out the enemies from the friends, okay? We need to head back to the bar. I also need a new phone. And a shower. I also should probably head over to the police station at some point before I get myself arrested. I've got a headache now."

"My poor Tiger." Emerson took his arm. "We're in this together. Me, and Tess, and you, and Gregory here."

"Hey!" Stoop tossed a cookie in her direction, but she ducked.

"Knock it off, kids." Yep, Tess was definitely a mom. She had a clear and firm voice that meant business. "What we need to do is a stake-out. And my little RV here is perfect for such a thing."

"You want to stake out the bar in this thing?" Bassett wasn't sold.

"This *thing*? This thing has a name. It's Rhonda. And it'll be perfect, you have to admit."

"I love the idea." Stoop raised his hand as if casting a vote.

"Kiss up," Bassett muttered.

"It really is a good idea," Emerson agreed. "Bathroom, food, good camouflage, shower. We can swing by a phone store on our way. And go to my place for a change of clothes."

Bassett was so used to seeing her in her sushi print pjs he hadn't even thought about how she'd likely want to get dressed at some point. He missed the pajamas already. He conceded with a sigh. "And we should get that money in a bank. Even I agree this is getting ridiculous to keep it in the bar."

"And then after we deposit it, we take it out and spend it?" Emerson suggested innocuously. "Cancun, here we come?"

"What money?" Tess whispered to Stoop. He bent down and whispered back in her ear.

"Let's hope she isn't the enemy," Bassett muttered under his breath. "Tell her all our secrets, why don't you?"

Stoop was too preoccupied with sniffing Tess's hair to reply. "Mm, Aqua Net." He nodded in approval. She winked at him.

"Good Lord, they've been dating five minutes and they're already grossing me out," Emerson muttered back to Bassett. Then, louder, "Come on, squad. It's a plan. Let's go."

"What do we do with Cap?" Bassett glanced over at the truck, with Maggie hanging out the window, panting.

"Oh, yeah. Forgot about him. I feel kinda bad. I was only using him for his mode of transport, and I promised him a hero's death."

"Well, maybe he'll get lucky, go back for more brownies, trip over a gnome, and get impaled by a flamingo. Think positive. But seriously, I don't think we should bring him. I'm getting an ulcer keeping track of all the people I've put in danger. In fact, I think we should just take you to your dad's, E."

She leveled him with a green-eyed stare. "You cannot be serious."

"I am."

In reply, she kicked him in the shins. "Don't even think about it."

Bassett rubbed his leg. "Geez, thanks a lot. I was just trying to save you and keep you safe."

"Don't ever do it again."

"Fine. I won't."

"I'll let you know when I need rescuing."

"I said fine!

"IF I need rescuing."

"I SAID FINE!"

With that, Bassett walked down the driveway to talk to Cap, still waiting in the truck. "Hey, we'll take it from here, buddy. Thanks!"

Cap was a little spaced out, so it only took a little convincing for him to go on his merry way, doing whatever it was he had been doing before he picked up the hitchhikers at the storage unit. Bassett figured it had something to do with all the furniture in his pickup truck, but didn't ask. They assured him they would call immediately should certain death situations arise so he didn't miss out.

Cap nodded and started up his truck. "Good luck!" he called as he drove off.

"Do we have his number?" Bassett murmured under his breath to Emerson..

"Nope," she whispered back, waving sunnily, "but he doesn't seem to realize that."

One innocent bystander out of the way, a dozen more to go, Bassett thought. He had to get to his customers.

 "Are you two coming or not?" Stoop was amused. He held open the door to the RV and gestured inside.

"I'd hold the door for you but I don't want to get clobbered," Bassett said to his love as he climbed the step and went inside.

Chapter Fifteen

Bassett now had a sore shin and knew better than to have the audacity to protect Emerson from danger, but he still wasn't comfortable with her going back to her place. So, he reluctantly suggested they go back to Lila's. Tess cheerfully suggested they take turns showering in the RV, and Emerson emerged with freshly washed hair and skin, wearing Tess's clothes. They were way too long on Emerson's petite frame. But at least they were regular clothes, consisting of a flannel shirt and leggings, not the black getup Tess typically wore to the bar. Bassett was a little disappointed; E would have looked like a sexy ninja all in black. He rubbed his shin. A sexy, lethal ninja.

Bassett decided to use his mother's shower. He had a change of clothes there anyway, but not exactly a recent one. Evidently, he hadn't showered at his mother's house since 1984, judging by the concert tee that featured A Flock of Seagulls.

The quartet loaded up in Tess's RV. "Speaking of phone numbers," Bassett continued, "let's hit the cell phone store first. If we get split up at any point, I want to be able to contact you guys."

"I'm going to call The Butcher and The Skank on your old number and give them a piece of my mind," Emerson retorted.

"Let's not."

"Don't tell me what to do."

"Good grief, don't make me feed you." The only response he ever had to Emerson's anger was to provide it with sustenance.

"Kids, knock it off. Mama needs quiet to drive Rhonda." Tess's voice was no nonsense. She turned over the engine and The Cure began blaring out of the speakers. "Ahem." She cleared her throat and turned the volume down slightly, then pressed the accelerator.

Tess had reached out to her college friends to warn them while the kidnapping victims had been showering. Unfortunately, she hadn't bonded well enough with anyone else at the bar to exchange phone numbers. Still though, it was two fewer people to find. Adam and Gus had been impressed with her story, even though she kept the explanations to a minimum. Impressed, but not shocked. Bassett was realizing the expectations for conspiracy theories and the like were high with time travelers. Nothing phased them; they expected it all already.

"How long have you lived in this?" Stoop asked. He had automatically jumped in the passenger seat, while Bassett and Emerson had climbed back to the captain's chairs that swiveled to face the pull-out dining table. "It'd make an excellent food truck should you ever decide to sell. You can move in with me."

Emerson snorted. "Move a little faster, why don't you, Gregory?"

"Hey, I don't mess around." Stoop was nonplused.

So was Tess, who laughed as she merged onto the road. "You haven't met my kids, Casanova. They scare off all my prospective boyfriends, if my makeup doesn't do it first."

"Nah, not worried." Stoop laced his big fingers behind his head and settled his afro against the seat. "I can take kids."

"Teenagers?"

"Overgrown toddlers."

"That's pretty accurate actually." Tess smiled.

"Hey, speaking of your kids, aren't they going to worry if they come home, and *home* is, uh, isn't parked in the driveway?" Emerson interjected.

"Well, Sadie is at a robotics camp all week, and I already texted Sawyer. My parents are gone on a cruise, but I thought he could go over and cut Lila's grass, stay there until we're finished up here. He's always looking for spending money."

"Thanks for helping us," Bassett replied. "We really appreciate it."

"Well, I knew what I was getting into when I started this time traveling thing." She, too, was casual about the adventure.

"Really? I didn't." He was glum. He needed a rum and Coke and a cuddle session with Emerson, maybe while they watched John Wayne movies. He'd give anything to escape this new normal.

They stopped at a Sprint store and Bassett bought a new phone. Well, Stoop bought Bassett a new phone. He had no wallet. He hoped The Butcher used his loose change and debit card to buy a better personality. Thank goodness, he hadn't put any of his toolbox money in there. The bad guys wouldn't get far on the $37.70 Bassett had in his checking account.

Tess continued to drive – and Stoop continued to flirt – as Bassett programmed his new device. He groaned when Stoop texted him from the front seat.

Dude, I am loving this woman.

It wasn't the text itself that made him groan. He'd just figured out his new phone number. Bassett had never been good at memorizing anything other than drink orders, but this number he flat-out recognized: it was the number belonging to ME.

"Damn," he muttered under his breath.

"What?" Emerson looked over at him, frowning.

"Nothing." He pocketed the phone. So, it *had* been himself texting himself. He just didn't … remember? Or he hadn't done it yet? Time traveling was confusing. He wasn't up for this part. He erased the worry from his mind. He had enough things to fret about, like bad guys and protecting his customers and retrieving his toolbox. Oh, and that pesky warrant out for his arrest that was probably a certainty at this point.

Speaking of which, how was he even going to get into his own bar? The cops would have a lookout for him, wouldn't they? If they really thought he was a suspect in Linus Fields' death than they'd be waiting for him to come back to the scene of the crime. How could anyone think he was capable of murder? He'd been the only boy on the block who didn't burn ants under a microscope or pull the wings off beetles. Lila Clark had raised a pacifist and a lover, not a fighter.

He voiced his concerns to the others. Stoop and Emerson had no suggestions, other than to let them do all the dirty work, while Basset waited it out from the comfort of Rhonda's swiveling captain's chair. Bassett vetoed that insulting idea. But, Tess had a plan.

*   *   *

An hour later, while pulled over in a McDonald's parking lot, the three stared at Bassett, trying to control their laughter. Tess had done Bassett's face in full-on goth makeup.

"You look like a pissed-off mime," Stoop chortled.

The cherry on top was that Bassett was wearing a black turtleneck belonging to Tess. It was a woman's sweater and too tight. He looked ridiculous.

But on the plus side, he didn't look in the slightest like Bassett Clark, bartender and time-traveling (pseudo) guru. Defying the electronic warning, and at the risk of grave personal trauma, he'd shaved off his 'stache. It was an act he immediately regretted. Not only was the makeup causing his skin to dry out, but his face felt weird without the odd comfort of his whiskery lip.

"Doesn't it give you a feeling of power and self-discovery?" Tess was the only one not dissolved in laughter. She was proud of her achievement. "I think it's really you."

Bassett didn't favor her question with a reply. He was too depressed wearing all that black, not to mention the makeup was uncomfortable and itchy. He scrunched up his face. The pancake foundation felt like it was cracking and drying out.

"Let's get it over with," he managed to croak. If he survived this, he would never live it down.

"So, you are just going to walk right through the front door?" Emerson looked worried, now that she was done laughing. She snuggled up to Bassett. "Maybe we should rethink this." Bassett nuzzled the top of her head. "Hey, don't get eyeliner on me."

Bassett sighed. "I'll go through the alley. If they do have police watching and they stop me, I'll pretend to be a waiter who has a key." His own key had been in the pocket of his pants, along with his cell phone and wallet, but there was a spare under the potted plants.

"You don't have any waiters."

"Yeah, but they don't know that. I'll say I'm there to do inventory or something."

Stoop was clearly intrigued. "Do you think it's still a crime scene, man? Yellow tape and a chalk outline and stuff?"

Bassett shrugged. "I'm focused on two things: removing the toolbox, and finding some more receipts that can lead us to our customers. They have no idea how much trouble they're in."

Tess slowed down and pulled alongside the curb across the street from **ttrp**. There was no crime scene tape. The block was quiet. Eerily so. There were no unmarked sedans lingering anywhere, nor were there any police cars.

"What about us?" Emerson bit on her lower lip as Bassett moved to get out of the RV. "I hate waiting."

"I know you do. Why don't you look up Linus Fields? He told me he was a ghost. Now I'm curious. If we can figure out who he was, maybe we can figure out who was out to get him. And who's framing me for his killing."

"And who The Butcher and the Agent *really* are?"

"Exactly." Bassett carefully shut the door behind him. It felt final and fearsome, almost as if he had been abandoned and was now on his own, even though friends waited just a few yards away.

For all intents and purposes, he had a feeling he would be alone while he saved the world.

Chapter Sixteen

Bassett felt like an intruder in his own bar. Sneaking through the back alley door. Tiptoeing like some criminal in a bad straight-to-rental movie. He didn't flip the light switch, but instead groped his way through the darkness. He stubbed his toe more times than he could count before he even got through the back room the accountants had rented and where Linus Fields had been murdered. Finally, with a rush of breath exhaled, both from relief and from a lack of oxygen (he had been holding it) he was inside the actual bar.

Lighting had never been great anyway, but now it was like a tomb. Shadowy shapes and bulging silhouettes resembled hulking harbingers of death. The ice machine in the kitchen kicked on, and the rapid-fire sound nearly caused Bassett to have a stroke. He walked right into the dangling pocket watches that were meant to convey whimsy and atmosphere, and after his heartbeat went back down to a normal level, he ripped one down and threw it on the floor. It made him feel a little better.

First, he went behind the counter to the cash register, but it had already been cleared out of its receipts. He'd have to dig a little further. Had he moved them, or had Margarita? He couldn't remember. He probably took them upstairs to file at some point. And by file, of course he meant stash in a milk crate at random. Lila's flighty way of life had been passed on to him in some areas. Like filing. It figured.

He closed the cash register. His eyes had adjusted somewhat to the darkness, and the hulking shapes no longer bothered his psyche. Now they just looked like his own tables and stools and chairs and decorations. He moved toward the door to his upstairs apartment.

His hands slid along the walls on each side as he climbed the narrow stairwell. His living quarters consisted of his bedroom, a bathroom, a small kitchenette, and a tiny office. The bedroom was where the toolbox had been, so he headed there first, confident in his footing even in the dark.

That was when he tripped over the naked man.

* * *

"This is taking too long. I'm getting really nervous." Emerson bit her fingernails down in anxiety. "I'm gonna call Poochikin's Pet Palace and see if they can take Winnie."

Stoop and Tess were playing cards on the pull-out table. "I'm sure he's fine. You can tell the bar is empty. Nothing to worry about." Stoop played a full house.

"How can we tell that? No shadows of ax murderers waltzing by the windows? No serial killers conveniently turning on all the lights? No fake special agents ringing the doorbell?"

"You're sarcastic when you're nervous."

"I'm sarcastic when I'm happy," she corrected. "I'm a psycho when I'm nervous."

"Awesome."

"Hey, guys?" Tess was looking out Rhonda's window, pulling aside the paisley curtains. "Um, what did you say the money was in?"

"A toolbox." Emerson frowned, then winced as she bit too viciously and ripped a cuticle. "Ouch!"

"Like how big of a toolbox? Abnormally large?"

Stoop quit shuffling the cards. "No, regularly large. Why do you ask?" He moved closer to Tess.

"Because our friend here seems to be really struggling under the weight of this, uh, floppy, human-shaped thing he's carrying." She moved to the door and opened it wide.

Bassett arrived, panting under the strain of his load, and gasped out a request for help, but not before he smacked the head portion of his cargo against the RV. "Sorry, buddy," he apologized, winded. "Stoop, help me out. Get him inside and then let's get out of here."

"Get who in here? What is happening?" Emerson appeared. "Who is this? Where's the toolbox? I mean, salutations to the guy here and all that, but what about the toolbox?"

"Simmer down, Scrooge McDuck," Stoop admonished with his tongue between his teeth. With Bassett shoving from the outside, and Stoop pulling from the inside, the body – wrapped in Bassett's quilt from his bed – was deposited on the nearest captain's chair. "Who is this, and is he dead?"

"Drive, Tess." Bassett flopped down on the other seat. "I didn't get his name yet. He was conscious for long enough to express regret for being naked in my apartment, but then he passed out again."

"Maybe it was when you banged his head against the vehicle," Stoop suggested.

"Haha. No, it was right after I tripped over him and pretty much fell on his face, shrieking like a peacock. But right before that, I grabbed the nearest object, which happened to be my umbrella, and smacked him a few times in self-defense. Or maybe after? Anyway, he was polite for a naked intruder." Bassett wiped his sweaty face with the sleeve of the turtleneck sweater. Then, rethinking, he pulled the whole thing off and sprawled with his head back on the seat, his arms reclining behind him.

"These seats are great, Tess. I really like the leather option."

Tess had already fired up Rhonda and was working on making a right turn on red, so she didn't reply. Emerson, however had plenty to say.

"What the hell, Tiger? Why is he naked? Why are we harboring a burglar? Why aren't you calling the cops? Okay, okay, the whole you're a wanted criminal thing, I know, but still! Why is he naked? Do you recognize him? How'd he get in there? Where's the toolbox?" Her eyes were huge and she was nearly jumping up and down in agitation as they pulled into a nearby parking lot. "And, why is he naked?"

"It's an unfortunate side effect of time traveling, my dear. I am so sorry. I do apologize." The naked man was speaking. He peeked out from his cocoon of quilts. He was an older gentleman, with a salt and pepper colored mustache that rivaled Sam Elliott's, and hair that would have been dark in his younger days. His eyes were a remarkable cognac-like brown and gold, but they were dwarfed in size by mammoth eyebrows that seemed to sprout from his forehead with reckless abandon. He spoke with a distinct British accent. "My, what a frightful throbbing in my head."

The group stared at him, then at one another. Only Tess seemed unperturbed as she rolled Rhonda through the parking lot, though she was excited. "I knew it! Where are you from and where are you going? I mean, when? I knew it about the clothes thing. I was just arguing this with Gus the other day. Like I'm not insecure enough, now I got to work out and eat right and join a gym and get a great body just to time travel?! Am I right?" She laughed, but no one joined her. Bassett stared at her as if she had three heads. "What?"

"Never mind." Emerson cautiously moved closer to Bassett. "So ... my name is Emerson DuPree. You met Bassett here, I believe. It's nice to meet you." She held out her hand but nearly snatched it back as the naked man's quilt began to fall.

He righted it, and blushed, before getting his arm out. Emerson was expecting to shake his hand, but instead the man bent his head and brushed his lips against her hand. Now, she blushed.

"Hey, watch it," Bassett instructed. "Keep your arms and legs inside the blanket at all times, buddy."

"Yes, of course. My name is Wells." The man pulled the blanket up around his ears. Now he looked like swaddled baby, with only his head sticking out. "Herbert to my friends. And that includes the lot of you, since you rescued me from wherever it is I found myself to be. Again, so sorry. Just unpleasant. The whole situation. And with a lady present!"

"You found yourself at the sight of a murder, Herb," Stoop answered. "In other words, of all the gin joints in all the towns in all the world, you had to walk into ours ..."

"Yes." Herbert twitched his nose as he spoke, as if he had an itch on his face he couldn't scratch. Which made sense, since he wasn't allowed to remove his hands from the blanket. "Again, I apologize. You see, my calibrations may have been off slightly. I meant to go to Amsterdam, 1750."

Emerson couldn't help snorting in laughter. "Your calibrations were way off! Wait." She quit laughing. "Did I just take it as face value when you said time travel?" She looked at Bassett with desperation in her face.

Bassett shrugged. "I know. I'm becoming a convert myself. At least we're sharing our delusions."

"It's super romantic."

"Come kiss me, you fool."

"Let's not get sidetracked, okay?" Tess said from the driver's seat, pulling back into traffic. "Bassett, did you get the receipts and the toolbox or not?"

"I was a little distracted by the naked guy," Bassett defended himself.

"That is no excuse. If I had a nickel every time I was distracted by a naked guy … I'm only kidding! Lighten up, you guys. If you don't have your sense of humor you don't have anything."

"I wish we had the toolbox," Emerson said, glumly.

"Is it a red, metal box?" Herbert interjected. "If so, I saw it lying under the bed as I lay on your floor, my good sir. Right before you fell on me."

"Yay!" Emerson clapped. "We're still rich! Sorta."

"But what about the customers?" Tess was still concerned. She kept driving, nowhere in particular in mind. They'd passed the same intersection twice now.

"We'll have to see if Babs and Joey and their team know anything about them." Stoop was confident. "Honestly, my peeps, half of the regulars pay with cash anyway. I know MJ and Bruce always do. Paper trails and conspiracy theories and government watchdogs, I guess. Special Agent Whatsherface is probably having just as hard a time as we are tracking them down."

"Whatsherface? Is that German?" Herbert asked, politely.

"Where are we even going?" Stoop went on. "We can't just circle the block forever."

"And Rhonda's getting low on gas," Tess agreed.

"Well, Herb here needs something to wear." Emerson was still not looking directly at their visitor for fear of the quilt slipping.

Bassett tossed him the turtleneck.

"Yes, well, that's a start." Emerson took a deep breath. "But pants are good, too."

"So, what, we swing by Macy's?" Stoop offered. Now he was being sarcastic. "We're a little beyond a shopping trip. We've got important save-the-world crap to do."

"Who is this Macy? Macy Whatsherface, is it?" Herbert's voice was muffled as he pulled on the sweater. His mustache was awry as his head popped through the neck hole. "If this is hers as well, I'm confident her trousers will not fit me. I'm afraid I've been enjoying a bit too much port these days, to say nothing of my fondness for sticky pudding." He pulled the sweater down over his belly, at least as far as he could. The sweater was stretched taut and showed off his paunch. Emerson averted her eyes again, but then she gathered her courage.

"Oh, come here," she said to the man. He stood before her, wobbly as a newborn fawn in the moving RV, looking as uncomfortable as a full-grown man in a bedspread should look, and she began to rearrange the thin quilt. In a few moments, Herbert was wearing a flamboyant floor-length skirt, tied in a double-knot (a very firm double-knot) on one side. There was a wide band of flabby, white skin showing between the black sweater and what formed the waistband of the skirt, but it would have to do. "Don't do any cartwheels or anything and I'll think you'll be okay," Emerson promised. Then she turned to Bassett and whispered a promise. "If you ever want to fool around with me again, you're getting all new bedding, Tiger."

Chapter Seventeen

Tess expertly maneuvered Rhonda into the gas station and pulled up for fuel. She filled the tank, Stoop hovering around her all the while like a lovesick bumblebee. Emerson was busy trying to make coffee. So far all she'd found was a canister of instant Folgers. She stared at it in dismay.

"I thought we were going to be friends," she hollered out the window to Tess.

"What?"

"It's not going to work out. It's not me, it's you."

"Um, okay?"

Emerson closed the window with a sigh.

"My good man," Herbert cleared his throat as he addressed Bassett, "I must ask you about your theatrical cosmetics. Do all men wear such a face in this day and age? Or perhaps you are Kabuki? I have, of course, traveled through many countries, so I am somewhat familiar with the art."

Bassett gazed blankly at the man. "Oh! This. Yes." He touched his face wryly. His fingers, when he pulled them back, were a ghostly shade of white. "It's a disguise. I guess we haven't told you the whole story."

"I do so love a good story." Herbert settled back in the captain's chair, crossing his ankles beneath the quilt. "Begin."

"This would be better with coffee," Emerson groused. She wound up her hair and anchored it with a spoon she'd found on the countertop.

"You see," Bassett began slowly. He wasn't sure what to say, or how to say it. Should he go along with yet another odd human who believed in time travel? And one who didn't just believe in the possibility, but who believed he already had? He took a deep breath and began again. "You see, I own the bar you, er, woke up in. It's called **time travelers' rally point,** and it's a … well, it's a rally point for time travelers." *Accidentally, but whatever.* "Lately, quite a few strange things have been happening – your arrival being only one of them, actually – and now it seems we're on the run from someone. An enemy. Or two. Hell, for all I know, an entire government." *Kudos, Bassy, you've graduated to conspiracy theories.* "We're worried for the safety of my patrons, so finding them and warning them is high on our priority list, as is, you know, getting my bar back. Oh, and someone sent me a whole lot of money."

"The toolbox, eh?"

"Eh."

Herbert grimaced, which made him look like a hairy raisin. His face smoothed out again as he smiled. "Sounds like you've got yourself an adventure, my good sir! Pray, do you mind if I stick it out with you? See where this quest ends up?"

"Feel free. Seeing as how you're kind of stuck here now. In the 21st century I mean." *Did he just say that out loud?* Bassett couldn't believe what was coming out of his own mouth. Obviously, this guy was a loony. Probably escaped from a mental hospital or something. Wandered away from the Blurry Recollections Retirement Home for Dementia Patients. He should probably have Emerson put an ad on Craigslist in case someone was looking for him.

"Dear me! Is that where we are? Well, I was expecting moveable homes by now, so I must say, I got some things right." Herbert glanced around at the RV. Tess and Stoop were back in the front seats and Rhonda was mobile again. "Does it fly, too?"

Emerson laughed. "Nope."

"Pity. I expected more out of your generation, no offense meant."

"Oh, none taken," Emerson replied, cheerfully. "We haven't gotten a whole lot smarter since – where did you say you were from? I mean, when? Guess I'll have to get used to phrasing the question that way from now on."

"1930, my dear girl."

"Oh!" She seemed surprised. "The English have such a nice way of talking that I always assume you're all from Victorian times. Lady Di, the Doctor and all his companions, Gwyneth Paltrow, Adele …"

"Gwyneth Paltrow isn't English, she's American," Tess piped up.

"Really? Why does she always have an accent then?"

"I think she just plays a lot of British characters."

Emerson frowned. "No, I don't think so. I think when she's playing an American, that's when she does her accent. From the English, her mother tongue."

"Okay, forget Gwyneth, and let's solve the pants question," Stoop interrupted. "And then go get Joey."

"Look, Rhonda is roomy, but we're going to have to stop picking up random people eventually," Tess pointed out. "Also, it's kind of my house, so, you all have to leave sometime."

"Even me?" Stoop asked casually.

"Are you batting your eyes at me?"

"Yes. Is it working?"

"No. Here. Walmart. Somebody go buy this man some pants." She made a hard left turn and went barreling into the parking lot. "On second thought, let's all go. I need to stretch my legs."

"But," Bassett gestured to his face, "I don't really want to."

"Well, then, wash up. You're in a, what did you call this, Herb? A moveable house. Use the sink. Be a problem solver." Tess jumped out of the RV.

"You're not my mom," Bassett muttered, but he did as he was told.

*   *   *

Walmart was crowded, and the group felt conspicuous. Even passing by the heavy-set lady in cat print leggings, they felt conspicuous. Chatting with an older man with a cart full of hunting rifles, they felt conspicuous. A teenager driving a motorized shopping cart nearly ran them down. He shouted, "For Narnia!" and rammed into the closet accessories aisle. They still felt conspicuous.

"Is it me, or is everyone looking at us?" Stoop whispered. They had picked out pants for Herbert – who was a maddeningly slow shopper – and were waiting in line. Of course, they did make something of a spectacle of themselves: Herbert was still wrapped in the quilt from the waist down, and he was snacking on a bag of chips and speaking loudly to everyone with his heavy accent.

"I think it's just that we have our guard up. We're suspicious of everyone now." But Bassett was uneasy, too. It wasn't just Herbert. He felt as though everyone was watching him.

"Or maybe it's because I'm so good looking?" Stoop offered.

"Yeah. That's probably not it. We're just imagining things."

"Good. Except that I'm imagining they're all zombies and like, the end of the world is happening, and we're the last to find out about it."

"Really, Stoo? I was just worried that Special Agent Katie was going to come around the corner, but your delusions are better."

"Special Agent Katie." Emerson joined them in line – she had gotten distracted in the book aisle – and scowled at the mention of her nemesis. She karate-kicked the gum stand. "I hate her. Sorry." The apology was to the gum stand. "How'd you get back here so fast, Tiger?"

"Hm?"

"I'm just saying, you must have really booked it to have beat me to the line. When we were jogging through the desert earlier you didn't seem nearly so fast." She helped herself to Herbert's bag of chips.

"What are you talking about? I've been in line for like, 10 minutes. This place needs more checkers."

Emerson frowned. "Uh, that's not right. I saw you pass by the books like 90 seconds ago."

"Yeah, no you didn't. You need coffee. You're starting to hallucinate." Bassett adjusted the spoon in her hair.

"Yes, I did!" Emerson batted his hand away from her head. Then she frowned. "But you weren't wearing those clothes."

Bassett looked down at his A Flock of Seagulls shirt. "I've been wearing this all day. Well, except for the hour I was wearing Tess's sweater."

"Nuh uh." She shook her head vehemently. "You were wearing a

Hawaiian shirt and board shorts. I thought you had just bought them here or something."

Bassett felt a distinct headache coming on. He rubbed his temples. Something about this weird conversation felt familiar. Oh yeah. He'd been spotted in the hardware store wearing a Hawaiian shirt, too. Once was peculiar. Twice was downright freaky.

Herbert was staring at the two arguing lovebirds. Chip crumbs were stuck in his mustache, hanging there like space particles. "My good sir, you aren't crossing paths with yourself, are you?"

"What do you mean?" Bassett moved up in line. Finally, they were getting somewhere. The woman in front of them had to be buying at least $400 worth of groceries. Why did he always pick the wrong lines? It was a knack he had. "Crossing paths with myself? I'm not the one hallucinating."

Herbert munched thoughtfully. "You're the expert, naturally, dear boy, so I know I don't need to remind you of paradoxes and being in the same parallel universe as yourself. Just be careful."

"Yeah. I will." Bassett said, resisting the urge to roll his eyes back in his head until they popped out the other side. In fact, the willpower it took to keep from rolling them had become a strain. That probably explained the headache, now that he thought about it.

Emerson was still staring at him, a faraway look in her own green eyes. She appeared deep in thought. She wasn't buying this, was she? Bassett sighed inwardly. He glanced down at his t- shirt again.

"And I raaaaaan," he sang, under his breath, "I ran so far away …"

Chapter Eighteen

Stoop paid for Herbert's new pants (and his chips), and they were once again back in the RV. Bassett had the fleeting thought that perhaps they should head back to the book aisle to search for his lookalike, but dismissed it. If there really was another version of Bassett Clark running around town shopping, he'd run into him eventually, he supposed. And then what? Time travel paradoxes? This was getting ludicrous.

Tess drove Rhonda to the house where Stoop had grown up. Living in the same neighborhood as the bar meant they drove by **ttrp.** Tess slowed down a bit as she drove past, and each passenger peeked through their respective windows as she did. There didn't seem to be any action. No unmarked sedans, no police vans. If the cops were still wanting to question Bassett for the murder of Linus Fields, they weren't doing much of a job tracking him down.

"Hey, maybe they'll arrest the Hawaiian shirt guy," he joked. "That'd be a spot of luck for me."

No one laughed. He supposed the situation wasn't funny anymore.

Betty and Joey's house was a cute split-level on a cul-de-sac. Stoop and Joey's father had passed away a few years ago, leaving Stoop to fill that void, at least for Joey. He didn't live there, but he spent plenty of time in Betty's house. Tess pulled up carefully along the sidewalk and let Rhonda idle.

"Well?" she asked. "Is this where I leave you guys? I need to get back at some point. Sawyer has a history test tomorrow that I know he hasn't prepped for, and I have school in the morning myself. It takes me an hour to flat-iron my perm."

"I don't know." Stoop paused as he was exiting the RV. "I'm worried for you. I feel like we should all stay together. Or at least you and I should stay together. Forever."

Tess pushed him the rest of the way out of the vehicle. "Get out of here, goof. I'll be fine. Text me if you come up with a plan, okay?"

Stoop agreed. The remaining four – Emerson, Bassett, Herbert, and Stoop – walked up to the house. Rhonda rumbled away as Stoop used his key in the front door. "A plan," he muttered, repeating Tess's words. "A plan would be righteous right about now."

He was attacked by a blurry streak of pigtails and denim. Joey scrambled up his long, skinny body like a spider monkey.

"Hi, squirt!" Stoop wrestled her back to the floor.

"Boy, am I ever glad to see you guys!" Joey was breathless. "Uncle B! You're not dead! That's great!" She embraced him too, though not as forcefully as she had her big brother.

"Why did you think I was dead?" Bassett inquired, closing the door behind him. "Did your Neighborhood Watch dig up some deets I should know about?"

"Deets?" Joey chuckled. She never giggled, only chuckled. She was an old soul. Giggling would have been beneath her. "Stop trying to be cool, Uncle B."

"I'm not cool, I'm phat."

"Sure ya are. Last I heard from the Watch – we've been totally staking out your place, FYI – you'd been kidnapped by some gorgeous but way evil lady ..."

"She was not that gorgeous," Emerson interrupted. "Quite frankly, I thought she was funny looking. Big teeth. Just my honest opinion."

"… and then Stoo was all, 'my best friend is dead! Wah wah wah!'"

"Aw, Stoop, you big softy." Bassett winked at his friend.

"What, he didn't shed any tears for me?" Emerson was offended.

"He was humming—" Stoop quickly covered up Joey's mouth, but the muffled sounds of Ding Dong, the Witch is Dead filtered through.

"Hilarious." Emerson glared at him. "Let's get down to business. Joey, we need to find some of our regular customers and we're having trouble. They could be in danger."

Joey quit humming, and put on her best serious and businesslike expression. "Roger that, E. Babs and I are one step ahead of you. Who's this guy?" She lowered her voice and motioned with her head toward Herbert.

He introduced himself, kissing Joey's hand as he had Emerson's. Joey surreptitiously wiped it on the back of her jeans. "So, he's one of us?" She was suspicious. "Because I haven't cleared him, Uncle B, and if you want my protection, you have to stop collecting new buddies like stamps. I can't safeguard you if you're always surrounding yourself with questionable people."

"Sorry, boss." Bassett put on what he hoped was a hangdog countenance. "Herb's okay. What did you and Babs find out?"

"Come in to the kitchen and I'll tell you what we know." Joey began walking briskly. "I always do my best planning and strategizing over chocolate milk."

"Me, too," Bassett agreed.

"Definitely." Emerson followed.

"Sounds delightful!" Herbert approved wholeheartedly.

Babs was already in the kitchen, dunking cookies into her own tall glass of chocolate milk. She jumped to her feet, wiped her milk mustache with the back of her hand, and saluted Bassett smartly. The teenage boy, Quinn, was there, too. He didn't jump up and salute but he slowed his chewing and regarded the group solemnly. Bassett thought him an odd duck.

"Good to see you." Babs smacked Bassett on his back with enough force to cause him to choke on his cookie, had he taken a bite yet. "Looks like we've had some action recently, huh? Not to worry, not to worry. We've got a plan. We were expecting this all along, frankly. Surprised it didn't happen before. Well, we're one step ahead of it all, don't you lose any sleep over that." She adjusted the strap of her overalls, held together with a safety pin.

Bassett smiled. He caught Emerson's eye; she was trying to control her laughter. "You saw this coming, did you?" He helped himself to some cookies. He seemed to be living on cookies lately. "I sure didn't. Maybe next time you can tip me off before I, you know, get kidnapped and threatened with violence."

"You're on a need to know basis, mister," Quinn replied. He held up his phone and snapped a photo of both Bassett and Herb.

That warranted a reply, but Bassett couldn't come up with one. For the hundredth time, he wondered dimly how he got in this predicament and what he should do to get out of it. The whole thing was just ridiculous. He should be able to go to the police like a normal victim, but he knew they'd never believe him. Not with Linus Fields' blood barely even dry on his bar floor. Which reminded him...

"Hey, E, what did you find out about Linus Fields?"

"Oh yeah. Nothing. He really was a ghost. Or that wasn't his real name." Emerson began rummaging through Betty's cupboards, looking for a coffee mug. There was a pot of this morning's brew on the counter. It wasn't freshly pressed Ethiopian Blend, nor was it fair trade or organic, but it was better than nothing. "I mean, I didn't spend a ton of time searching, but I didn't find anything when I Googled him."

Bassett savagely munched his cookie and swallowed. "I still don't even know if he was a good guy or a bad guy. Hell, this thing is so confusing I don't even know if I'm a bad guy or a good guy."

"You're the good guy, Uncle B," Joey assured him. "That much we know."

"And the Butcher was definitely a bad guy," Emerson added.

"Or possibly just misunderstood," Stoop offered. "Just kidding. Don't hit me."

"So, what would the good guys do in a situation like this?" Bassett continued. He wasn't sure who he was addressing, but his gaze wandered back to Babs. She might be sort of nutty, but she'd lived this long, which was a point in her favor. Also, she looked like she could just about take the Butcher.

Babs pursed her thin lips in thought. They nearly disappeared. "Well, they wouldn't hide out at their mom's house, that's for sure and certain. And they wouldn't go to the coppers and expect them to do their dirty work for them. I'd say they'd march straight back to the scene of the crime and not back down."

"Just reopen like nothing strange is happening?" Bassett wasn't sure. Actually, he *was* sure. Sure that it was a stupid idea.

"Well, you have to sort out who's working for whom, and who's the head basher. If you build it, they will come."

They all stared at her, not comprehending.

"Or in other words, if you reopen it, they will come."

"Just hang up the Open sign and hope nobody else gets killed?"

"This time we're all on guard," Emerson pointed out. "We'll all be watching. But just in case, I'm going to leave Winnie at the doggy daycare until we get this straightened out. It's going to cost me a fortune. I might need toolbox money."

"Yeah, but what about the police?" Bassett wasn't concerned about Winnie. He was concerned about becoming a jailbird. "I'm not putting the mime makeup back on."

"It was goth, not mime. More KISS, less French improv street performer."

"Whatever." Bassett was getting cranky. All he wanted was his bar back, his old bar, O'Malley's. Okay, maybe he wouldn't go that far, but still. He wanted things back the way they were before questionable Special Agents and Butchers and dead bodies. "I looked dumb."

"If I may?" Herbert spoke up. He had changed into his new pants. They looked a bit odd on him; almost like his body had not been made to wear modern cuts. And he still wore Tess's sweater. They probably should have sprung for a new shirt too, but Bassett was tired of stiffing his friends with the bills for things ever since his wallet had gone the way of his cell phone. Another reason to go back to **ttrp** and retrieve the toolbox.

"Go ahead." Babs nodded her head graciously.

"I just wanted to remind you that you do have infinite knowledge at your fingertips." They continued to stare blankly at Herbert. He pressed on, seemingly unperturbed. "I propose one of you go back to catch the killer."

"Go back?" Emerson polished off her coffee. There was a sparkle in her eyes and a healthy flush to her cheeks again.

"Naturally. It does seem the most logical way, does it not?"

"Um, yeah. Sure." Bassett scratched his chin. His beard needed a trim badly. It was at the itchy stage. And he hadn't had time to look into a mirror recently, but he was pretty sure that his seven gray pals had had babies in the past week. He was going to look like Santa Claus if he didn't watch himself.

Herbert puffed out his chest, which likely had a different result during the times he was not wearing a lady's size small turtleneck. "If I may, my dear boy, nominate myself? I am, after all, accustomed to the side-effects and perils of time travel. Also, no one knows me, so I'll be under the radar, so to speak. I can just make a stop on my way back. It's really no problem."

"Amsterdam, 1750?" Emerson hid her amusement admirably.

"Well, sadly not. I'd had my suspicions that was not going to be a real option in the first place. After all, I can't go back to a time before I've invented my time machine, can I?" He chuckled at himself. "But it's worth a try! No, home I shall go. But first, to your very own, a few days ago. Well, do we have a deal?" He looked rather pleased with himself. Bassett realized this was because he thought he was saving the day. He tried not to groan, but instead pasted a cheerful smile on his own face. He felt his right eye begin to tic.

Blurry Recollections Retirement Home for Dementia Patients, he thought. *I could drop him there, or I could let him try to manipulate time and space.*

Talk about an impossible choice.

Chapter Nineteen

They spent the early evening planning, plotting, and otherwise strategizing. The cookies made way for pizza delivery. Stoop's wallet was slowly emptying out. Bassett was going to have to give him a raise. Babs even drew an elaborate map of the bar. She had spidery, childish handwriting and illustrations. Walter and Nugget arrived, but apparently the two moms from the Neighborhood Watch group were busy; the teen daughters had a sports thing, and the baby had an ear infection. Bassett was trying to keep calm and not give away the fact that he thought this whole situation was ludicrous. Every time someone said something idiotic in a serious tone, he ate another bite of pizza before he could say something sarcastic. His stomach hurt. He'd eaten seven pieces.

Finally, their respective jobs rehearsed and quizzed by Babs several times over, the strange little group of vigilantes made their way to Bassett's bar. They walked, which Bassett also found a bit on the pathetic side, but Joey assured him it was very appropriate for the situation.

"Picture us in slow mo," she said, dreamily. "Our trench coats blowing in the wind, something exploding behind us. We're so cool, we don't even turn around to look." She demonstrated, strutting in slow motion, swinging her arms and putting on her best hero face. "KABOOM!"

As far as superheroes or vigilantes went, Bassett privately thought they were a sad bunch, but then again, what did he know? Maybe Herb could travel back in time, snag Linus' murderer (or stop it from happening altogether), and they could put this whole thing behind them. Wouldn't that be swell?

The streetlights were dim and flickering. It didn't help matters that they had to walk at the speed of a herd of turtles since Walter was approximately 100 years old and Nugget had to pee on a bush every five seconds.

"Tell me again about your time travel machine," Joey bounded back to Herbert. She was like an excited little dog herself. She bounced up and down on the toes of her Converse shoes.

Bassett caught Emerson's eyes and rolled his own. He hoped she wasn't buying this whole plan. He wasn't. Surely. At least, not completely. Barely at all really. She winked at him. That didn't clear up whether or not she was down with this plan.

Herbert described his contraption. "It's about this high," he measured to his hairline, "and made of your typical ingredients. Things that work at the speed of light, naturally."

"Naturally." Joey was all ears.

"And that's all I'm going to tell you, child." Herbert patted her on the head.

"But you can trust me!"

"Yes, yes, I trust you implicitly. But you see, I don't understand much of it myself, and what I do understand is very difficult to explain. And we cannot have this discovery falling into the wrong hands."

Joey made a face, but she was too polite and mature to argue with her elders. She skipped off to walk with her brother instead. They were nearly there. Bassett could see his beloved bar now. And thankfully, there was still no action on his street. No cars, no thugs, nothing.

He still wasn't sure what they were doing, despite Babs' complicated and thought-out planning and explanations.

"I didn't notice any time machine in my apartment when I tripped over Herb," he whispered to Emerson. "I mean, of course I didn't, because he's not a time traveler, but you know what I mean."

"If he's not, how'd he get in your apartment?" she whispered back. *Oh, great. She really was getting into this.*

"Who the heck knows? It's not like my security is stellar." He jutted with his whiskered chin to the gang, a few steps behind him. They were nearly at the bar now. "After all, someone got in to kill Linus. And how'd Linus get there in the first place? Now that I think about it, my bar is crawling with intruders lately. I'm going to have to invest in some security cameras or bars on the windows or something."

"Or quit keeping your spare key under the potted plants," she pointed out.

He bent down to move the terracotta pot of gardenias. "Good point." He pulled out the key. "Okay, let's get this party started."

He opened the door and gestured inside. The group entered **ttrp** with varying degrees of trepidation. Bassett was just thrilled that he didn't step on any naked people, hear Margarita Jones screeching at the top of her lungs, or have a wall explode as they walked in. Instead, all seemed quiet. There was the scent of onion rings still lingering in the air. He wondered if he had forgotten to take out the garbage. Well, no one could fault him that, he'd been a little busy. He also detected something vaguely minty. He could see the shiny shards of glass from the pocket watch he had broken when he was here last. They glinted on the floor in the dim lighting of the moon. The door to his upstairs apartment was ajar, the way he had left it. After all, it was nearly impossible to close it behind him when he was carrying an unconscious and extremely heavy Herbert. All was calm.

Well, except for the Butcher, sitting still in the farthest booth. But nobody could see him in the shadows, and nobody turned on a light. He sipped a freshly made mint julep and waited.

*   *   *

Each member of the team had a job. Bassett's was to get the toolbox, and to look for the file of receipts while he was upstairs. Like Stoop had said, most of the regulars paid with cash, but there had to be some sort of paper trail they could follow. Otherwise, it was back to Babs' idea: just reopen the bar and let everyone walk in like flies to a spider web.

Emerson was to go through the accountants' belongings in the back room, and she took Joey and Babs with her. Since none of them knew what a genuine, bona fide time machine looked like, Bassett wasn't sure what the point was. But he supposed if it looked like the accountants were ahead of the pack, so to speak, then it was likely them that Special Agent Katie wanted.

Herbert accompanied Bassett. Stoop was in charge of checking the voice mail messages and going through the mail. At first that seemed a waste of precious time, but then Bassett remembered what had begun this crazy adventure in the first place: a few text messages from the future and a UPS delivery.

Walter, Nugget, and Quinn were on look-out duty in the alley.

"I say, dear boy," said Herbert as they finished climbing the stairs and entered Bassett's apartment, "I do hope I didn't offend Joey with my little white lies."

"Hm?" Bassett reached under the bed and pulled out the toolbox. He flipped the latch. Still there. He wiped his brow in relief and snapped the box shut again. "What lie is that?"

"That I have a time machine," Herbert lowered his voice to a whisper. His mustache quivered with emotion. "I don't like telling falsehoods to small children."

"So, you don't have a time machine?" Bassett failed in his attempt to sound surprised. *Of course, he didn't have a time machine. He was probably just a naked transient who had crawled in through a window.* Bassett sat down on his own bed, sans quilt.

"No, I'm afraid I don't. Not exactly." Herbert got down on his hands and knees suddenly. "What I do have however … is … where in the bloody hell is it? Oh, here we go. I knew it must have rolled off when you wrapped me in your blanket. Very kind of you, by the way, I do so hope I conveyed my thanks." He sat back on his heels, looking satisfied. He had pulled something small from beneath Bassett's nightstand.

"Yeah, sure, you're welcome. What do you have there?" Bassett squinted at the object that Herbert held out to him. It looked like a smallish globe, made of different metals and something that glowed oddly. It seemed to pulsate in Herbert's palm, like a living thing.

"Well, my dear boy," he puffed out his cheeks and let out a giant burst of air, "you see, time machines are rather overrated, aren't they? They're completely superfluous once you understand how moving at the speed of light works. Also, they're rather dangerous. No one wants a rocket ship in your attic, especially your wife. I speak from experience. And I'm sure I don't have to tell you, being that you're an expert already, but there's only one way to eliminate the need for speed when time traveling."

"Of course …" Bassett trailed off, like he was used to doing when cornered in the bar by a regular who wanted to talk time travel with him. "It's obviously a … a … what would you call it exactly?"

"It's a wormhole," Herbert replied, proudly. "My very own wormhole."

* * *

Emerson uncovered the contraption that was in the back room. Whatever it was – a welded together mash-up of bicycle parts, crystals, a fax machine, and several smallish engines – it had been blanketed by a tarp in one corner of the room.

"Um, time machine?" she guessed. She looked at Babs, who threw up her hands.

"How the hell should I know?" she barked. "Does it look legit?"

"How the hell should I know?" Emerson muttered, under her breath. "Joey?"

"How the h-" she began.

"Watch your language, young lady," Emerson responded.

"I was just going to say, want me to try it out?" Joey cracked her knuckles.

"Definitely not. There's a scenario I don't want to explain to your mother."

They looked around at the rest of the rented back room. There were only a few folded chairs and some empty Chinese takeout containers. If the accountants had notes to go with their machine, or some sort of an owner's manual, they must have taken it with them.

"Well, if it is legit," Joey said, practically, "they'll be chomping at the bit to get back here. They're probably freaking out that the bar hasn't been opened for the past couple days."

"Good point."

"Well, I for one don't have time for lollygagging and gabbing like girls," Babs broke in. She placed her hands on her hips. "What's the next step?"

"I thought you were the one with the plan." Emerson was visibly annoyed with the woman. She was bossy. Emerson liked to be the bossy one; deep down inside she was still the 14-year-old captain of her gymnastics team and always would be.

"Let's go see if Stoop found out anything," Joey suggested. "Unless you wanna, like, send a fax to the past or something?" She chuckled her old soul chuckle.

It was sort of an intriguing idea, but they resisted the impulse to try.

* * *

"Of course it's a wormhole, I see that now." Bassett moved uneasily toward the stairwell, clutching the toolbox close and trying to remember to distribute his weight properly, for fear of blowing a hammy. He knew the guy was nuts before but now it was irrefutable. "Silly me."

The thing was still pulsating in Herbert's palm. Small little lightning strikes flickered and flashed out of the orb. Well, wormhole or no wormhole, it looked practically radioactive. Even though it was probably just some sort of light-up dog toy, Bassett didn't want to be anywhere near it.

"So," he continued, "what was the plan next? You're just going to uh, pop over to last Friday night and stop Linus Fields from getting himself bashed to death, right?"

"Right-o!" Herbert beamed. "At least, that's my plan. You know me and my calibrations. Haha!" He elbowed Bassett in a brotherly sort of way.

"Yeah. Those. Okay, well, should I just leave you to it then?" Bassett took another step towards the stairs.

"That's probably best. The less you know about my methods the less you will able to convey to the enemy should you be captured."

"Okay. Well, then. It was nice meeting you." Bassett said. It was mostly sincere.

Herbert raised the orb as if in a salute. "Safe travels, my dear boy," he said.

Bassett moved through the doorway with a barely concealed grin, toolbox in hand, and shut the door behind him with a click.

He really hoped the old man didn't blow anything up or jump out the second story window in his efforts to *disappear*.

Chapter Twenty

As they gathered in the kitchen, Stoop relayed his findings.

"Two messages from Lizard Buttons, and one from the accountant group. They're a little antsy about getting back into their room. Another message from your mother, she says her boyfriend was asking about you. So, that's probably not great, him being a cop and all."

"Don't remind me." Bassett cradled his head in his hands. He had poured himself a dark beer and Emerson a glass of wine. Joey had her normal cream soda. Stoop and Babs weren't interested in drinks, and Walter, Quinn, and Nugget were still outside, keeping watch.

"No mysterious UPS packages though." Stoop intentionally kept his voice light. "So, that's good, right?"

"Hey, speaking of those, is that it? Your fortune, Uncle B?" Joey swallowed a burp. "Can I see it? I've never seen so much money before."

"I think it's cursed. Better not."

She ignored him and came closer. "Hey, Butterscotch! I have that sticker at home."

Bassett had forgotten about the My Little Pony sticker that decorated the toolbox. "You do?"

"Well, I did. I lost it. I was kinda bummed 'cuz it's my favorite."

The group was silent as they regarded Joey. She blushed. "What? I mean, it *used* to be my favorite. Of course, I'm not into kid stuff anymore. What are you looking at?"

Bassett shook his head to clear it. "Nothing. Never mind." *I am starting to hate freaky coincidences, that's all.* "So, now what?"

"Where's Herb?" Emerson sipped her wine.

Bassett updated them all on Herbert's supposed wormhole and how he left him upstairs to work it.

"Man!" Joey was irritated and she banged her empty soda bottle on the countertop with a thud. "He could have told me! Letting me think he had a dumb time machine when all the time he had his very own wormhole! That's brilliant, by the way. If you can fold time, you don't really need a machine."

"He can't fold time." Bassett shook his head. "He's just a loon."

"Yeah, whatever." Joey was indignant and felt the need to stand up for Herbert. "I think millions of people would disagree with you, Uncle B."

"Millions of people?" He was amused.

"Yeah." She looked around at the group again. They were all staring at her with blank expressions. "Don't tell me you don't know who he is?" The blank expressions got even blanker.

"Sure, we do. It's Herb." Emerson was just as confused as Bassett was.

"Oh, for crying out loud, you guys, how did you ever make it through high school lit anyway? Herbert Wells? Still nothing?" Still blank. She shook her head as if disappointed in them. "Let me spell it out for you then: H.G. Wells is in your bedroom right now, Uncle B."
Except he wasn't.

Herb (or H.G.) Wells was gone. All that was left was the turtleneck sweater and his Walmart pants. The crew stared down at the pile on Bassett's bedroom floor. They were nicely folded.

"Was he barefoot all this time and I didn't notice?" Bassett mused at the lack of shoes.

"Not to mention the disturbing lack of underpants," Stoop added. "Weird."

"I can't believe you let him just leave like that!" Joey exploded. "Come on! Really? I mean, really?" She clapped her hands over her face and made a muffled screaming sound. "You had one job, Uncle B! One job!"

"Sorry, JoJo." Emerson put her arm around the child. "We're morons."

"Ya think?" Joey was still sullen but she relaxed a bit in Emerson's embrace. The thought came to Bassett that E would make an excellent mother someday. The realization gave him butterflies in his stomach. Those kids of Emerson's would be his, too. They had to be. That engagement ring became a solid piece of rock in his brain.

He didn't want to ruin the moment with his cynicism, but Bassett furtively took a peek under the bed. No Herb. He subtly yawned, stretched his arms out, and opened the closet door a crack. No Herb. The windows were still firmly locked. He hadn't gone out that way it seemed. "Holy crap," he murmured. It seemed Herb had been the real deal. How was that even possible?

"I didn't even get to say goodbye. Thanks a lot." Joey may have been snuggling in Emerson's arms, but she appeared a long way from forgiving Bassett. "Sometimes I wonder why you're even the head of this time traveling operation."

Bassett wasn't going to touch that insult. Meanwhile, if looks could kill, Joey's expression of wrath would have fried him by now. She had tears in her eyes and he knew they were the hot, angry kind.

"Come on," he said, eager to change the subject. "Let's get this money someplace safe and get out of here."

"We haven't gotten any closer to safeguarding our customers," Stoop pointed out.

"Sure we have. We have a phone number for the accountants, remember?"

"Okay," he acquiesced. "But what about the rest of them? I'm worried sick about MJ and Bruce. They're my homies."

"They'll be all right. We have Babs."

The aforementioned perked up at that. "Darn tootin' you do! Ain't nothing going to happen to them on my watch."

"Thanks, Babs."

"'Course my watch doesn't go 'round the clock. I gotta eat and sleep and fraternize with the opposite sex sometime. If you catch my meaning."

"Oh, Lord." Emerson stifled back a bad case of the giggles and buried her face in Joey's hair. She had told Bassett once that Joey smelled of bubble gum and that distinctive odor of blossoming pre-teen. She was trapped between needing nurturing and needing an antiperspirant. Emerson held her tight.

Bassett shooed everyone out of his bedroom. There were far too many people in his personal space, and the whole room felt off anyway. It was likely the lack of Ernest, may he rest in peace, and his bedspread. Whatever it was, the whole *feng shui* of the place was way off. He almost felt like he never wanted to come back. Buy a house in the suburbs with Emerson, that was his plan. Give up bartending and take up real estate or bean counting or underwater basket weaving.

He led the way downstairs once again, the toolbox swinging against his thigh. They entered the bar. It was even darker now. It had to be midnight if he didn't miss his guess. He snuck a peek at his watch. Yep. Betty was going to have his hide for keeping Joey out this long. He'd just blame Stoop. Betty never could stay mad at him for long. He had those hound-dog eyes that had gotten them out of a scrape or two as kids. There was the time with those Avery twins for example … what were their names? Jessica and Jennifer? Heather and Hannah? Melissa and Melanie? Bassett's reminiscing was cut short by a buzzing sensation in his pants. He jumped and fumbled in his pocket.

"Hello?" Bassett said, as he counted the heads going by, single file like a group of preschoolers. He shut the door to the upstairs quarters once the last person was through. "Mom?"

"Hello, Bassy. How are you?"

"Fine, Mom." He kept the impatience out of his tone. He motioned with his head for everyone leave the bar. "It's not a great time to talk though. Is there something I can do for you?"

"Oh, sorry, sweetie, I know how busy you are with," she paused. Bassett knew she was frowning and pursing her lips. "With whatever it is you do these days. Um, I was just wondering when I can expect Tess back? Sawyer is in my living room and since I was planning a little rendezvous with my silver fox tonight … well, I don't have to spell anything out for you, do I?"

"Ew. No, Mom. Gross. Isn't it a little late for a date though?" Bassett was the last to leave, and he hesitated before closing the door behind them all. "Hang on a second." Something glinted on the last table that he hadn't noticed before. "Just a minute," he told Emerson. "Be right there. No, Mom, not you, I was talking to E. Anyway, what did you say?"

"I was saying that Jonathan has unconventional hours, being a policeman. Midnight is his dinner break. I'm making spaghetti Bolognese and you know teenagers. Sawyer is going to eat it all when my back is turned. I can see it in his eyes. He looks just like you when you were 13."

"Oh, sure. Makes sense." Bassett walked back into the bar, toward the object. He approached it and picked it up. It was just a drinking glass. He sniffed it. mint julep. That explained the scent of mint lingering in the stale air. It didn't explain who had been drinking it though. He frowned. "He's looking for me, isn't he?"

"Who, dear?"

"Jonathan."

"Not that I know of ... didn't I tell you that he isn't trying to replace your father, Bassy?"

Bassett shook his head and put the glass back down on the table. Then he picked it up again. "No, not because of you two dating. Never mind. Why did you say you were calling again?"

"Tess. Can you release her from your little escapades now?"

"Wait, what? Tess went home a long time ago. Are you telling me she didn't pick up her kid?" Bassett tried to keep his voice neutral, but he knew the fear crept in anyway. He began to move toward the exit again but something else caught his eye. Something large and human-shaped in the darkness of the bar. It moved toward him with frightening speed. Bassett dropped his phone with a shout and flung the glass at the shape.

He missed. He'd never been one for sports. He was more of a chess club kid in high school. In 10th grade he went out for football and was pummeled to a sweaty pulp within an hour.

But the Butcher must have played a lot of ball in his days. He didn't miss.

His meaty fist made contact with Bassett's jaw and Bassett folded like a lawn chair. He hit the floor with a thud.

Chapter Twenty-One

"I said it's okay, Tiger. Stop struggling." The dulcet tones of Emerson DuPree's voice soothed Bassett, but only up to a point. He was confused, groggy, and his face hurt. Badly.

He made a sound like a dying windup toy and attempted opening his eyes. Approximating an over-the-top dramatic movie, he could see his own eyelids blinking rapidly and it made everything in front of him seem as though he was seeing it through the blades of an electric fan. There was Emerson, peering down at him in a worried fashion, her curly hair hanging down in his face and tickling him. Or it would have tickled him, had his face not been in so much pain. There was Stoop, behind her, wringing his big hands. He'd have to give him grief about that when Bassett found the energy to do so: Stoop looked like a stereotypical granny. There were Babs and Joey. The smallish figure of Walter was off to their right, and Bassett could only assume the sensation of his arm being licked was due to Nugget (he hoped). Quinn was standing close to Joey, his arm around her shoulders (Bassett was going to have watch that boy). And of course, there was the Butcher.

"The Butcher!" Bassett croaked and tried to sit up. He had to warn everyone. How were they not noticing this behemoth in their midst? They had to be seriously worried over Bassett's health not to see the monster before them. "Run!"

In hindsight, Bassett wished he had said something a little more courageous, a little more dauntless. Shouting for everyone to scatter like bunnies when they clearly outnumbered the bad guy, seven to one, could be misconstrued as embarrassing if you didn't understand the situation.

"It's okay, Tiger. Don't try to talk." Emerson leaned even closer and Bassett was hoping for a kiss (even in times of crisis – hell, especially in times of crisis – kisses were always welcome). But instead she was placing a zipper baggie of ice on his jaw. "He's not going to hurt you. Well, at least not any more than he already has."

"Sorry about that. Reflexes." The Butcher growled, and Bassett was chilled to the bone. *It was bad enough the man was huge and intimidating and had a name that brought to mind chunks of flesh being sawed apart and hacked into smallish pieces, but he had to have a gruff, guttural voice as well?*

"Reflexes?" Bassett tried to respond, but the ice was making his face numb. He sounded like a toddler trying to wake up from his nap.

"This is Kevin." Emerson said as she motioned to the Butcher. She smoothed Bassett's hair back from his clammy forehead.

"Kevin has a wicked right hook," Bassett muttered. *What was wrong with this group anyway? He'd been knocked senseless by a brute and now they had adopted him as one of their own?* "Why isn't someone killing him?"

"Settle down, Chuck Norris," Emerson replied, tenderly. "Turns out Kevin isn't so bad after all. I probably shouldn't have bashed him with that chair. Sorry about that." She addressed that last part to Kevin.

He nodded. "No problem, ma'am," he said. "I had it coming, or at least it would have seemed that way to you."

"Wait." Bassett pushed the ice away and tried to sit up. Talking really hurt, but he wasn't about to start a game of charades to satisfy his need for conversation. He tried to ignore the pain in his jaw. "You're a good guy now?"

Kevin shrugged in a self-deprecating way. "I've always been a good guy. I had a plan to get you two out of the storage unit when I was supposed to be torturing you, but your lady here beat me to it. When she hit me with that chair, I pretended to be knocked out so you could get away. It was better than my plan anyway, so I just rolled with it. I adapt. It's a strong suit of mine."

"Wait. I didn't actually knock you out?" Emerson couldn't keep the disappointment out of her voice.

"Sorry," Kevin answered, "but you're only knee-high to a grasshopper, ma'am. You did the best you could. I definitely had a scratch on my lower back if it makes you feel better," he added, helpfully. "Practically a welt. Here, look." He turned around and lifted his shirt.

To Bassett's disbelief and utter annoyance, Emerson complied. She peered closely. "Humph. Not even a bruise. And stop 'ma'am-ing' me." Only Emerson could boss around someone as terrifying as Kevin.

"What are you doing skulking around my bar?" Bassett wanted to know. He reached for the ice and placed it back on his jaw. He wondered dimly if any urgent care doctors were open around the clock. Then again, he was surrounded by liquor, so who needed pain killers? He motioned with his free hand toward the kitchen. "Stoo, I need a drink." His best friend immediately moved to provide one.

"I've been working with an organization that has been infiltrating time travelers," Kevin explained.

"Special Agent Skanky?" Bassett asked, since it looked like Emerson wasn't going to. She must have already gotten this whole story. Bassett wondered just how long he'd been out.

"No. That was my cover. My organization is on the right side."

Good. So, he didn't need to expect Katie Fitzgerald to come waltzing through his bar door. She was still a bad guy. Girl. Stoop arrived with his drink, a tumbler of whiskey. The good stuff.

"You have to understand, I've been almost as confused as you have been about who is on the up and up," Kevin confessed. He had dark circles under his hooded eyes.

Bassett tried to snort in disbelief, but it hurt. He settled for a pathetic sniffling. "I doubt that."

"Believe me." It was more of a command than a suggestion. "I needed to infiltrate everywhere that I could to start making any headway. It helps that I kind of look like a thug."

"You sure do. And did you?" Bassett really wished someone else would ask the questions. He drank the rest of the whiskey down quickly. "Make headway, I mean?"

Kevin reached up and stroked his chin. "Some," he responded.

Obviously, he wasn't going to be overly forthcoming. Awesome. Bassett handed the glass back to Stoop and sat up. His head swam a bit, and he wasn't sure if it was due to the injury or the whiskey. Emerson gave him her arm for support. "Why should we trust you?" Bassett moved his jaw carefully. It made a clicking sound which was rather alarming. He was pretty sure something in there was broken. Or at least, caved in. He was going to look like he was deformed. Good grief, he matched Ernest! The thought was both amusing and vaguely disquieting. Bassett shook the thoughts away with determination. He didn't need to be putting mysteries together that weren't even mysteries. So, the skull had a broken jaw, and now he had a broken jaw. On the same side. In the same place. Mere coincidence. Just like Joey's Butterscotch sticker showing up on the toolbox. Just like a lot of things. He was trying so hard to convince himself, he missed the next part of Kevin's story. "What was that?"

"I said I was here tonight waiting for someone to come back. I didn't know whether it would be the group with the rented back room, or you, or your friends, or Katie Fitzgerald, or one of your other regulars, but I knew someone would show. I didn't plan on ambushing anyone, but when you saw me and you threw that glass, well, like I said, reflexes."

"Bet you weren't expecting H.G. Wells either," Joey retorted, sourly. She was still cranky.

Kevin looked confused, which made Bassett cheer considerably. He was tired of being the only one around here confused all the time. "Sorry?"

"If your plan was to find the real-life, honest to goodness, time traveler amongst our group here, you missed him. He went back to the 1930s," Emerson explained.

"Or he scaled down the window using my sheets tied together," Bassett put in his own two cents. "And is wandering around outside, naked."

"I'm looking for someone rather *specific*," Kevin was still cagey. "And it's *not* H.G. Wells."

"And what about Katie?" Stoop interjected. "Does she know you're a double agent here? Or are you still buddy-buddy with the enemy? And just who does she work for anyway?"

Kevin sighed. "There are establishments out there you know nothing about, I'm afraid. Ekaterina is a consultant of sorts for one of the worst ones."

"And you're with one of the good ones?" Bassett was still skeptical. He also needed more whiskey, but this time he moved to get it himself. "We're just supposed to believe that?"

"Well, I could have done a lot worse than punch you," Kevin pointed out. "I could have killed you easily."

"Granted." Bassett reached the bar area and helped himself to the bottle left out on the counter. "But you don't have to rub it in."

"I'm actually trying to protect you guys. I mean, it's not my main objective, but I really am trying."

Protect us? Bassett took a sip. *My jaw calls shenanigans.* Protection from whom or what exactly?

"Did you call her Ekaterina?" Emerson asked. Kevin nodded. She pumped the air with her fist. "I knew someone that repugnant couldn't be named Katie. Ha! I was right, wasn't I, Tiger?"

But Bassett didn't reply. Something was nagging him, making his head throb worse than it had before. He tried to think back to right before the Butcher – Kevin – had flattened him. What had he been doing? Talking to his mother on the phone, that was it. Bassett's face went white and he put his glass down on the countertop. "Tess!"

The group looked at him from across the room. "What about her?" Stoop was automatically concerned.

"She never made it to pick up her son. My mom called right before Goliath here knocked me out." He couldn't keep the accusatory tone out of his voice. "I just remembered."

"Oh, hell," Emerson muttered, forgetting about Ekaterina. "That's not good."

"She's the goth one?" Kevin asked. He seemed to have a handle on all the regular customers. Bassett wasn't sure if that was a pro or a con.

"Yeah. Well, not really, but yeah," Emerson answered. "Don't run off half-cocked, Stoop. Let's figure this out." But Stoop was already leaving. "Okay, Lover Boy isn't waiting for a plan …" she trailed off.

Time Travelers' Rally Point

The remaining team, consisting of an injured, slightly drunk Bassett, two children, one elderly man and his dog, Babs, Emerson, and the suspicious Kevin, were left looking at one another in a state of indecision.

The bar's phone rang.

Chapter Twenty-Two

They all froze as though they heard the ticking of a bomb, not the relatively innocent sound of a ringing telephone. Bassett moved to answer it. His jaw throbbed the whole way there; it was like he could feel his heartbeat in his chin.

"Hello?"

There was the sound of heavy breathing on the other side of the line.

"Hello?" Bassett snapped the greeting the second time. He had no time for prank callers, or perverts. "Who is this?" A garbled and incoherent mumbling answered him. He was about to hang up the phone with a self-righteous slam when two words jumped out at him.

"Not Bassett."

Bassett frowned at his phone, as if the inanimate object was at fault. "This is Bassett. Hello? Who is this?"

The sound of a throat clearing. Then, another whisper, "It's me, Tess."

Relief washed over Bassett like a baptism. "Why are you whispering? Can you speak up? Where are you? Everyone was worried about you. Stoop tore out of here a minute ago like his pants were on fire ... Tess?"

"Bassett, pay attention to me, okay? I'm whispering because I don't want to attract any attention from the wrong people. Can you meet me? Something strange is going on." She was still hissing in his ear, and Bassett had to strain to make out the words. He massaged his sore jaw as he formed a reply.

"Sure, I guess so. Where are you?"

Tess gave him an address to a location on the outskirts of town. "I'll be there as soon as I can," he promised. He hung up and turned to find his new acquaintance hovering close. "Quit breathing down my neck." He scowled at Kevin, who was still not his favorite human on the planet.

"Sorry." Kevin moved a step backwards. Bassett felt guilty. A bit.

After explaining the nature of Tess's phone call, Bassett texted Stoop.

Your main squeeze is okay. Get back here. We're going to get her.

He hoped Stoop wasn't too hell bent on his own search that he couldn't hear his phone ping.

*   *   *

Maybe it was the lack of sleep, maybe it was the excitement of the night, maybe it was only that Tess was prone to fits of mania, but when the assembly arrived at the location, she was sound asleep in Rhonda. They had to bang on the windows to wake her after dismissing the taxicab driver. Now that he had the toolbox, Bassett finally got to pay for something and it felt good. A little committed, but good. *I spent some of the money. No going back now.*

Bassett could hear Tess fumbling with the lock inside the RV. Finally, she succeeded.

"Thanks for coming, guys. Sorry I dropped off. I'm not as young as I used to be." Tess yawned and stretched. A few strands of hair were stuck to her face and she plucked them off. "Gosh, I need a shower and a good night's sleep. I'm never going to make it to class tomorrow. Is it tomorrow now?"

"Yeah, we all need sleep. Why'd you call us out here?" Emerson yawned as well. The sight was contagious and soon everyone was yawning as they found places to sit. As vigilantes for time traveling justice went, they were a disappointing bunch.

"Okay, here goes." Tess rubbed her eyes. Without all the black eyeliner, she looked younger and more innocent. "It's going to sound really weird, though. I don't want you to think I'm crazy."

"We're all crazy here," Stoop assured her. The words were meant to be joking, but his tone was serious.

"Hang on," Bassett interrupted. "Before you start with your crazy story, I'm going to let my mom know you're okay. By the way, your kid is ruining her date."

"Oh my gosh, Sawyer! My little man! I'm so sorry!" Tess looked appalled.

"No worries. I'm proud of him, even if I've never met the little squirt." Bassett fired off a quick text to Lila.

"That's the problem with living in a drivable house. Sawyer and Sadie are going to need therapy. What kind of mom wanders off with their home?" She pulled at her own hair like a frustrated toddler. "Anyway. Moving right along. When I left you guys at Joey's house I was going home, right? Home sweet driveway. But I needed to drop off some books at the library, so I swung by there first. And who do I see, coming out of the post office across the street?" She waited for someone to guess, but no one obliged, so she went on. "You!" Tess pointed her finger at Bassett, who raised one eyebrow in response.

"I wasn't at—" he began.

"I know, right? I mean, I had just left you a few minutes before and I hit practically all the stoplights green, so I knew you couldn't have beat me there, especially on foot. Plus, you looked a little strange; like, I don't know, a little more … svelte, I guess you could say?"

Bassett found himself sucking in his gut. He knew he needed to exercise more; work on shrinking his beer belly. But still, having a woman subtly point it out to him was embarrassing.

"And you were wearing a Hawaiian shirt and I distinctly remembered your Flock of Seagulls shirt was what you had been wearing before, because honestly, I was never a fan. Of the band, I mean, not your shirt. I wasn't too into the whole New Wave craze, though I suppose now I'd get a kick out of it. Kinda sci-fi isn't it, in a way? Sorry, I'm digressing. Anyway, the way you combed your hair was different, too. But still, I'm not joking, it was *you!*" Tess punctuated the last word with a stomp of her foot, like a toddler trying to get her own way. Then she slumped her shoulders. "Okay, fine, start with the crazy accusations. I know, I sound like a loon."

"No, you don't." Emerson shrugged. "It just wasn't Bassett, that's all. Someone who looks similar. No biggie. We all have a doppelganger out there; it's practically science. How'd you end up here, though?"

Bassett tried to school his face to appear as nonchalant as his girlfriend, but he felt a bit sick to his stomach. What was with all the look-alike sightings? Was he going to run into this guy himself? What would they say to one another? *Hey, dude, give me back my face?*

"Yeah, just a similar looking guy," Stoop agreed. "I mean, it happens. I know I get mixed up with Denzel Washington all the freaking time. Super annoying."

Joey rolled her eyes. "You do not. Let Tess finish her story."

"Speaking of faces, though," Tess mused, "what happened to yours, Bassett?"

He opened his mouth and closed it again, treating them all to some interesting clicking noises. "I got punched by Kevin here." He motioned to the ogre in their midst. Up until now, Tess hadn't paid much attention to him, probably because she'd barely torn her eyes from Bassett, as if memorizing his face. Now she stared at the new guy.

"A bar fight? I guess that happens in your line of work, huh?"

"Not to the bartender, usually." Bassett stroked his jawline. It still hurt. He couldn't tell if it was bruised or swollen or both, but it must have been obvious to the naked eye if Tess knew to ask how it happened. "We'll fill you in later. Finish your story."

"So, I see you – or not you, but you know what I mean – and I decide I need to follow you. Not *you*, but the other you. Things have been getting so weird with the time travel and such, I just had to go with my gut. And my gut was screaming at me to follow this guy. So, I forgot all about my library books," she motioned over to the pile which was sitting by the driver's seat, "and off we went."

"Was I driving? Not me, but the other me? Or were you just tailing some poor pedestrian in your shady looking recreational vehicle?"

"Rhonda is not shady looking," Tess responded, primly. "She's a fully refabbed, upcycled, glamper. At first, he was on foot, so yeah, okay, I had to be super sneaky and drive really slow and try not to let him see me. But then, he gets on a bus. Okay, this next part is really boring. So, he takes the bus for a while, and of course there are all these stops the bus makes, and I'm trying to look casual every time someone gets off. It was difficult to look subtle because you know how Rhonda doesn't like to idle. She gets all cranky and loud. Anyway, after a while, the fake Bassett gets off the bus. And he starts walking again."

"Does this story have any action?" Babs cracked her knuckles.

Tess ignored her. "And he goes into this building."

"Which building?" Stoop peers out the window. There were several high-rise apartments to one side of the street, and a shopping plaza on the opposite. Anyone would have known the answer before she said it: the apartment building. The shopping plaza would have closed hours ago.

Tess moved closer to Stoop, who appeared delighted with the arrangement. She pushed his head aside and pointed up, out the window. "He's in that window, right there. Third floor, the corner one. Okay, the light's out now so you can't see, but I'm sure. I was watching the windows through binoculars when he went in. I felt like Jimmy Stewart in Rear Window."

"But without any violent murders?" Babs was obviously disappointed. She looked as though she was losing interest. Perhaps she had missed dinner, or some fraternizing with the opposite sex, in order to be here and was regretting it.

"No violent murders, at least not yet. But someone else was in the room with him." Tess kept her voice mysterious. Bassett thought she might have learned this trick from reading bedtime stories to her children.

"Agent Skank-a-licious?" Emerson piped up. "I'm gonna throat punch her!"

Bassett hurriedly put his arm around her shoulders. He wished he had a pot of fresh coffee and some bacon sandwiches. His girlfriend was getting out of control with this heretofore undiscovered penchant for violence.

"Nope, not a woman. A man."

"Who?" everyone demanded as one.

Tess grinned. "Casey, the accountant, that's who."

Chapter Twenty-Three

They debated walking up to the door, but couldn't figure out which door led to that window. There were too many "flies in the ointment," as Babs put it. The group felt a little defeated as Rhonda began the trek back to drop off her reluctant, but exhausted, passengers. First, the members of the Neighborhood Watch Team disembarked, one by one. Then Stoop arrived at his house, where he waved goodbye forlornly as the RV rolled away. Finally, Rhonda rumbled up to Lila Clark's house, so Tess could pick up her son, and Emerson and Bassett could spend the night. Bassett had no desire to wake up next to any naked time travelers or dead bodies, so sleeping in his own place still didn't feel like a viable option. They had left Kevin behind; he'd said he would walk from there, though Bassett got the feeling he wanted to stick around and watch the window. But why? He didn't know, and he was too sleepy to care.

"Your mama isn't getting any action tonight for sure now," Emerson teased Bassett, who choked back his gag reflex as they walked by the teepee. The flap door moved aside a smidge, and the same face as before peeked out, right before snapping it shut once more. They finished the jaunt up the walkway and entered the house.

Sawyer was curled up, fast asleep on Lila's couch, surrounded by miscellaneous remains of snack foods, drinking glasses, plates, wrappers, and silverware. The smell of spaghetti Bolognese lingered in the air. A faint snore erupted from Sawyer's nose.

"Mom, you didn't let him have any brownies, did you?" Bassett murmured disapprovingly, as Tess began waking her boy.

Lila glared at her own boy. "Of course not. He's just stuffed full of good food and he had a lot of exercise, that's all." As if on cue, Sawyer sat up and yawned. He was a good-looking boy, with the same mop of black hair that his mother had, and gangly legs and arms. "He mowed the whole back yard, and he weeded my petunias, too. Next week he's coming back to get rid of that wasp nest in my gutters, and he's going to prune the apple tree. You could say he's like the son I never had."

"Very funny. You know I'm allergic to wasps."

Sawyer wasn't the only guest in Lila's living room; Jonathan was there, too. Bassett swallowed a huge lump in his throat that suddenly arrived at the sight of the policeman, but he managed a small wave. Jonathan inclined his head.

"I'm going to have to face the music if I want to get **ttrp** back," he bent down and whispered to Emerson. She looked as nervous as he felt, but she nodded in agreement.

"He's going to believe us, Tiger; he has to. It's his job. I think."

Tess gave Bassett and Emerson each an affectionate hug and told Lila she wouldn't think of letting her pay Sawyer for the yard work (Sawyer's face showed some dismay, but the good boy and kept his mouth shut). The dark-haired pair left, with Tess promising to touch base in the morning.

Bassett was left standing in the room, feeling awkward and anxious. He cleared his throat, as did Jonathan. Emerson made a weak excuse about needing to use the little girl's room and beat a hasty retreat. "Traitor," Bassett muttered after her.

"What's that, Bassy?" Lila asked innocently enough.

"Nothing. Hey, Mom, if you have any of that spaghetti left, I'd love you forever for sharing it with me. I'm famished." It wasn't true – he could still feel the remains of all that pizza sitting like a brick in his gut – but his mom never could resist the temptation to feed her son. She bustled off, pleased, toward the kitchen.

"Soo...," Bassett began.

"Yes …" Jonathan replied.

"I expect you have some questions for me." Bassett's last word came out as a squeak and he hurriedly covered it with a cough. "Things being what they are and all."

"Well, I hardly know where to start, young man." The policeman seemed as ill at ease as Bassett was. Then again, arresting his girlfriend's son over spaghetti Bolognese was probably uncomfortable. As dates went, it was likely not high on his top ten. Poor guy. Bassett felt bad for him.

"It's just that …" Bassett began again.

At the same moment, Jonathan spoke. "What I was wanting was …"

The two men's sentences overlapped.

"You go first." Bassett flushed. He was glad his goatee had grown enough to cover the pink. At least he could keep his dignity.

"No, no, you finish."

"Have you made any progress in … well, you know what I'm talking about." *Have you arrested anyone else, by chance? 'Cuz that'd be awesome for me.*

"Well, that is," now it was Jonathan's turn to color, "well, there has been progress, yes. But I don't like to rush anything when it's this important. You understand?"

"Sure. I'm all about not rushing this, too."

"Good, good. I mean, it's imperative to get all the facts, do your research, see the big picture. Rushing things, well, rushing things is where mistakes get made."

"Totally."

"I'm glad you see my side."

"I'm trying, sir. I really am. Although you can see where it's a little hard for me. Being so closely involved and everything, I mean."

"Oh, of course!" The policeman's eyes lit up. "You are so important to both of us. I want you to know that."

"Uh, thanks." *Wait. 'We?' Was this Podunk town down to two cops now?* Sheesh, he knew there had been cutbacks, but good grief. Embarrassing really. Then again, it could be good for Bassett. Maybe they'd be spread so thinly that they'd forget about poor Linus Field and his unfortunate demise. And how Bassett had gone against orders and left town – even if it was under duress and by force by a whackadoo fake special agent.

Emerson and Lila were back. Emerson sat down on the sofa and began digging into Bassett's plate of spaghetti. She must not have had as much pizza as he'd had. Bassett spent a moment admiring the way she twirled the pasta and the way the fork flicked sauce onto her wonderful, Grecian nose. He wanted to lick it right off.

"Sorry, sir. What was that?" He pulled himself out of his daydreaming and back to the present.

"Bassett Clark," Jonathan began. His tone was extremely formal. Bassett's hopeful heart sunk, along with his good attitude.

Here came his rights being read, he knew it. He held his hands out in front of him, like a good criminal about to be cuffed.

"Bassett Clark," the policeman continued. But instead of taking out handcuffs, he walked over to where Lila sat on an overstuffed ottoman, and plopped down close to her. Jonathan took her hand in his. "I'm asking for your blessing to marry your mother.”

“Say what now?” Bassett dropped his arms and Emerson choked on her noodles.

Lila crowed with happiness and threw her arms around Jonathan. “Please say yes, Bassy, it means so much to us! I know I said he wouldn’t try to replace your father, but if you would consider allowing him to try? Please, Bassy?” Her eyes sparkled like diamonds.

“Sorry, what?” Bassett’s mind could not backtrack fast enough to understand what was going on right now. Emerson seemed to intuitively know the issue, and she put down her plate of pasta and hurried to his side.

She nuzzled his neck but it was a ruse to whisper in his ear. It didn’t work. One Emerson DuPree nuzzling Bassett’s neck was a surefire way to get his motor running, but not to ignite his brain cells. “Huh?” he whispered back, dimly.

“Your mom’s boyfriend wants to marry her and they want your blessing,” she said loudly.

Bassett sighed deeply and turned his attention back to the couple canoodling on the ottoman. “You want my blessing? You don’t want to …” *Arrest me*, Bassett thought briefly before adding, “… ask me something else?”

Jonathan halted his kissing of Lila’s knuckles one by one, to give Bassett a questioning glance. “Ask you what? Is there something I should ask you? Would you like to … vent your feelings? Lay some boundaries?” He straightened up and gave his future son-in-law his full attention. “Of course. Naturally. I’m willing to do whatever you need to feel comfortable in this union.”

"Gross," Emerson murmured, "he said 'union.' He's totally union-ing with Mama L."

"Shh." Bassett was still confused and his jaw began to throb again. He really needed a good night's sleep. Maybe he would be able to sort through this mess in the morning.

"Ask whatever you like, son. I'm an open book." Jonathan tossed his hair, stomped his foot, and threw open his arms as if to punctuate the claim with a little bit of interpretive dance.

"Maybe don't call him 'son' yet, Jonny," Lila said, under her breath. Jonathan scrambled to his feet.

"So sorry! Totally inappropriate." He was blushing. Bassett thought to himself he needed to grow a beard as well. At least he wasn't cursed with dimples. *Bet you weren't allowed to be a cop if you had dimples.*

"No problem, sir." He looked at Emerson. She shrugged. "You can have my blessing, I guess. I mean ..." he trailed off and looked at Lila. She seemed supremely happy. All of a sudden, his mood changed. "You never wanted to be married. You said it was an outdated institution, a sham, a way to keep women repressed! Honestly, Mom, what the hell?" He was suddenly more affected by this outcome than he would have thought he ever could have been. He'd always been the only man in Lila Clark's life. He felt ... replaced. It wasn't the best feeling, though it wasn't quite as bad as being sucker-punched by the Butcher.

"Bassett Zechariah Clark, don't you smart-mouth me," Lila replied to his little outburst. She used the same voice she used when Bassett was caught putting cherry bombs in the toilets in middle school, and she had to leave work to pick him up in the principal's office.

It was similar to being sucker-punched after all. To his utter humiliation, Bassett felt his eyes begin to leak. "Sorry, Mom," he said, contritely. He sniffed back a suddenly running nose. "Are you sure he's good enough for you? Are you good enough for her?" He turned his attention back to Jonathan, who stood ramrod straight and put on his best, respectable face. His face was still red, and Bassett took comfort in that.

"I'll do my best, or die trying," he promised. His voice cracked on the last word. It would have been endearing, if it hadn't been so irritating.

Bassett hoped it wouldn't come to Jonathan dying, even though he was reserving judgment of his mother's suitor.

"Well, I'm so happy for you both," Emerson broke in on the awkward conversation. "I love weddings," she coughed, elbowing Bassett, "as I keep telling my boyfriend here. Hint hint. Ahem. Well, we should probably hit the hay. We've had a long day. Not anything unusual or interesting," she hurried to cover her tracks as she obviously remembered she was speaking in front of a policeman, "just, you know, the normal, day-to-day, romance writer and bartender stuff. Nothing at all strange or illegal."

Bassett began pushing her toward the hallway before she spilled the proverbial beans. "We'll just help ourselves to some blankets and crash in the den, okay?"

"Goodnight, son!" the engaged couple called after them as one. A hushed reprimand from Lila, not meant for their ears, followed them down the hall. "Not yet, too soon, darling! Just call him Bassy for a bit until he comes around …"

Bassett wasn't sure he'd ever come around, but that was partially due to the fact that his new dad was in law enforcement. "So, he didn't even ask about Linus," he whispered, as he opened the linen closet and pulled out a stack of quilts.

"I know!" Emerson's emerald eyes were huge. "Is he just super distracted by your mom's hotness?"

"Ew. I don't know." Bassett shut the closet door, and they moved toward the den. His childhood bedroom had been converted into an art and yoga studio years ago and was so crammed with stuff that sleeping in there wouldn't be an option. Besides, his old bunk bed had been moved into the den. He used to have sleepovers with Stoop in that bunk bed, with their Star Wars sleeping bags, Bugles and cheese puffs for midnight snack attacks, and cans of Tab. They hated those pink cans but that was all Lila would buy. Pink cans or not, those were the good old days. Back when life was simple, no one was trying to kill or impersonate him, and he was the only man in his mother's life. His eyes weren't doing that annoying leaking thing anymore, but he still felt blue.

"Cheer up, Tiger," Emerson said, moving a cat off the bottom bunk. "Mama L. has found love, and you aren't locked up in the poky. Life is good." She moved another cat, and sneezed. "Is this one new?" She stared at the enormous tortoise shell as it slunk off in a huff.

"That's Mae West." Bassett crawled up the bunkbed ladder gingerly. He wasn't as fit and nimble as he used to be, as Tess had so recently reminded him. The bed swayed alarmingly. "Maybe you should take the top."

"No way, I get vertigo. Here," she tossed a pillow up to him. "Love you, Tiger. I'm glad you're not dead or incarcerated."

"Thanks. You too. See you in the morning." Bassett laid down, trying to get comfortable. There were only a few hours left till morning, but he knew he wouldn't be getting much sleep.

Chapter Twenty-Four

He was wrong. Bassett slept like a baby. The only thing that woke him was the pain in his jaw, the smell of coffee brewing, the sizzle of sausage in a pan, and the fact that there was a cat on his face.

He pushed off Mae West, who meowed in protest, and struggled to sit up. He smacked his head on the ceiling, then rubbed his jaw with one hand and his head with the other. He hung over the railing of the top bunk and peered down at the bottom. No Emerson. She had likely followed the aroma of steaming hot caffeine earlier and was in the kitchen with his mother. If Jonathan was sitting there in his pajamas – or worse, just his boxers, because he seemed like a boxers guy – Bassett was skipping breakfast and going straight to **ttrp.** He couldn't avoid reopening the bar any longer. He'd missed several night's income, and besides, his regulars would drift away and leave forever if he didn't show them some loyalty.

Since he hadn't been arrested for the murder of Fields, and since Kevin was now a good guy, there wasn't any reason to stay away. At least, not as many reasons as there used to be.

Emerson was alone in the kitchen, with a huge mug of Viennese Blend. The steam rose from the mug and curled the wisps of hair that had come undone from her bun while she slept. She looked as adorable as ever, and Bassett recalled her hint about weddings from the night before. He grinned at her. He wouldn't mind waking up to her in his kitchen every morning for the rest of his life.

But would she get bored? Restless? Fall out of love with him once she realized how much better she could do? His grin faded a bit, but grew again as she smiled at him.

"Guess what, Tiger?"

"Hm?" Bassett poured himself a cup of coffee and plated some sausages.

"I was talking with Jonathan this morning while you finished up your beauty sleep."

"And? Did he come to his senses about marrying my mom when he counted up the cats?"

"Nuh uh." She shook her head vehemently. "Guess again. Okay, never mind, don't guess. I want to tell you too badly. *He had never heard of Linus Fields.*"

"Yeah, I told you, the guy was a total ghost," Bassett agreed as he crammed a huge forkful of sausage in his mouth, then washed it down with hot coffee.

"No, you don't get it. I mean, he didn't even know what I was talking about! He was completely confused when I brought it up." She threw her hands up in the air.

"What do you mean? I don't get it."

"I mean," she spoke clearly and enunciated carefully, as if speaking to a toddler, "Linus Fields isn't dead. No one killed him. There was no murder in your bar, Tiger."

Bassett choked on a sausage. "Huh?"

"Don't you see? H.G. Wells did it!"

"He did what now?" Things were not getting any clearer. Bassett was completely baffled.

"Tiger, pay attention. Herb stopped the murder, just like he said he would. There's no other explanation." Emerson took his coffee cup out of his hands, put it down, and held both his hands in hers. She stared deeply into his eyes. "Time travel. He did it. It's possible."

* * *

On the way to **ttrp**, they had stopped by Poochikin's Pet Palace, where Winnie was ecstatic to see Emerson, peeing a little as she wiggled. She greeted Bassett by snapping and growling at his ankles. He had doled out more toolbox money to spring that piddling little ingrate from puppy prison, in addition to covering his team's expenses. Yet, it felt like the point of no return. Spending the money was getting him in deep; if he wasn't in over his head already, he would be soon.

As he turned the key to the bar's door, Bassett made a mental checklist. They were going to open tonight, but first things were first; clear out any naked people, glowing wormholes, dead bodies, or mint julep-sipping ogres. Emerson scratched Winnie behind the ears as she carried her around the bar. The action made Bassett miss Ernest. If time travel *was* possible, and they were about to discover the ability, he was going back to that storage unit to stop Emerson from smashing the poor skull to bits.

"Well, things look pretty normal to me," Emerson said, cheerfully. "Find anything out of the ordinary?"

Bassett shook his head. It had been days since he had turned on the lights, and he wasn't sure what to expect. There was still a lingering odor of mint and onion rings. Margarita Jones had not been back to clean since finding the body. He didn't blame her. Although ... if the murder hadn't happened *after all*, how did they have any memory of it? If he were to ask Margarita, would she stare at him blankly? Quit her job as subpar cleaning lady? But he and Emerson had memories of Linus. None of it made any sense. He'd barely passed high school algebra; this time travel science was likely to make his brain explode. A viewing of *Back to the Future III* was a definite in his weekend plans, along with some of Stoop's gourmet quesadillas, several beers, and some serious canoodling with Emerson DuPree. Bassett hoped it would help him get the time travel thing figured out.

Because, if he threw time travel out the window, the only other theory he could come up with was that Jonathan was so anxious to marry Lila that he was willing to cover up a murder to get his new stepson off the hook.

Appreciate the gesture, new dad, but that seems a tad bit immoral for a cop.

Maybe Stoop was right. As he would have put it: maybe the popo *were* corrupt.

"Tiger, are you listening?" Emerson called, snapping Bassett out of his thoughts regarding police corruption and the mysteries of time travel. He nodded mechanically in reply.

"As I was saying," Emerson continued, "taking Linus Fields off our plate, so to speak, is music to my ears. But don't forget: we still have a problem with our femme fatale, Ekaterina the Bimbo. And the fact that she's after our customers."

"Yeah. I haven't forgotten. At least we'll have strength in numbers. If they all come back, I mean." He was nervous about that. They were probably all regulars at Buffalo Wild Wings by now. Was there no justice in the world? Crime fighting was a lonely hobby. "I'm a lone wolf," he said, sadly.

"What?" Emerson wrinkled her brow and looked at him closely.

"Nothing," he said, wandering to the kitchen, where he peered into the cupboards and fridge. Just in case of supernatural activity. "Who ya gonna call?" he muttered. Nothing but Stoop's eclectic ingredients met his eye. A block of Gorgonzola cheese was perfuming everything else, in spite of the tight plastic wrap encasing it. There was a bowl of homemade hummus, several different salad dressings, vegetables, butter, milk. Nothing too weird (though he personally was not a fan of hummus). He went back to where Emerson and Winnie sat at the bar, and built himself a Guinness. He offered Emerson a glass of wine, but she raised a brow at the suggestion.

"It's barely lunchtime."

"It's been a rough week."

"Good point. Maybe a small Chardonnay. That seems like something a lady who lunches would sip on."

"Lady who lunches?" He opened a chilled bottle.

"It's a thing. Like, soccer moms who have brunch at the country club."

"Ah, now it's brunch, huh?" He winked at her. "Moving the acceptable drinking hour even earlier."

"That's why mimosas were invented, silly." She sipped her white wine.

"Do you want to be a soccer mom?" He was genuinely curious about the answer. Would they end up with a passel of kids like Quinn and Joey and Sawyer? He could sort of picture it, though the imagery was fuzzy.

"I want to be a karate mom, a painter mom, a basketball mom, a chess mom. Whatever my little Bassy Juniors want." Winnie chose the romantic moment to bark, as if in disagreement with this proposal.

"Bassy Juniors, plural, huh?" Bassett smiled behind his glass.

"Of course. At least six or seven."

"Holy buckets, girl." He choked on his beer.

"What are you complaining about? I'm the one who has to gestate them. Anyway, change of subject. What are we going to do about your doppelganger?"

Bassett shrugged. He was curious about the lookalike, sure, but he wasn't as obsessed with him as everyone else seemed to be. Honestly, if he stayed on his side of town, and Bassett stayed in the bar, then the problem solved itself, didn't it? He didn't truly believe the man who looked like him really was him. From the future. Or the past. Or wherever the hell time travelers came from.

"Should we do another stakeout? Or should we just track down Casey? Hey! We could take him out to that storage unit and do our own interrogation! Take Kevin along for intimidation purposes."

Bassett shook his head. "You and your latent maniacal tendencies. You scare me."

"Why, thank you."

"Besides, just because Casey the accountant is fraternizing with my doppelganger, doesn't mean either one of them mean any harm."

She frowned. "I don't know, Tiger. Seems like too much of a coincidence that they were just fraternizing. Something is definitely going on. We just have to figure out what."

"You figure it out then, Nancy Drew. I'm going back to being a curmudgeonly barkeep like the good Lord made me. Besides, we don't even know how to get ahold of Kevin the Butcher." He thought for a moment. "Even if we wanted to, which I'm not sure we do."

Emerson waved the notion away like a pesky fly. "I have the feeling he's the kind of guy who shows up when you need him. That's what operatives and spooks do."

"Yeah, they share that trait with the bad guys." Bassett's voice soured as he rubbed his jaw.

"Well, I trust him. At least, I'm pretty sure I do. Anyway, I don't think we have much of a choice. Pass me those sodas; I'll do your alley delivery. Gotta keep the Neighborhood Watch happy, don't you know?"

Chapter Twenty-Five

At first, the reopening of **ttrp** was an uneventful affair. Two days and nights went by with nary a disturbance. Bassett and Stoop were pleased and beginning to relax, if Stoop's lack of foot twitching and Bassett's lack of eye tics were any indication. Tess was back, in full goth gear, sipping the fuzzy navels Stoop now insisted on making himself. The drinks were prepared with extra care and usually came with a side of free finger food. The accountants had not returned; however, most of the other regulars had. Babs had taken to coming inside at least once per evening, and often three times, to "case the perps," as she called it. It seemed a mash-up of casing the joint and catching the perps, but Bassett didn't want to question Babs about her approach. He considered her harmless. She drank strawberry margaritas with extra tequila, minus the strawberry puree and ice. Once in a while, he spied her swallowing a pill from the little lacquered case she kept in the back pocket of her men's 501s. It was a dainty oval-shaped number, black with a red rose on top. Bassett was afraid to ask her about that, too.

It seemed the sudden lack of suspense and exciting happenings had Emerson morose. She sat in her usual booth, with Winnie curled up next to her, laptop opened on the table. She was behind in her writing deadlines now, and her muse was not musing. Her second glass of Malbec, awaiting her grasp, probably wasn't helping, either. Bassett slid in next to her.

"Well, you don't have to be an author, you know," he reminded her. "The bar is doing great, and don't forget our little nest egg in the toolbox."

"Please tell me you've actually put that in the bank by now?" She raised her head from where her chin had been cradled in her hands, elbows on table.

"I did. The teller nearly had a stroke. I was a little concerned she was going to call the cops on me. Normally, I'm making up stories about why my checks bounce. She didn't know what to say." He recalled the memory fondly. That had been a pretty good moment.

Emerson went back to staring glumly at the computer screen. "The whiteness is mocking me." She sighed dramatically. "The cursor is blinking and driving me crazy. I'm pretty sure it's using Morse code to tell me I'm a hack who can't write. You know what I need? I need a ghost writer for times like these."

Bassett raised his eyebrows so far they nearly disappeared into his hairline. "A ghost rider?"

She laughed. "No, genius, a ghost *writer*. Never mind. Maybe someday, when I'm rich and famous and supporting you in the fashion to which you'd like to become accustomed, I'll explain. In the meantime, I think I'm just going to kill off one of my main characters. That's a sure way to get my readers' attention, and get my mojo back. I saw it on Pinterest so it must be true." With that, she took a hearty swig from her glass.

"You can't kill a vampire; they're immortal." He ducked as she swatted him. "I'm kidding, I'm kidding!" He beat a hasty retreat. "You can stake them through the heart or drown them in holy water. Everyone knows that."

"There are no vampires!" she hollered. All the customers turned to look at her. She glared at them and raised her glass in a mock toast.

If looks could kill, Bassett would have been fried to a crisp by the time he made it back to the kitchen. Stoop was making something he called lettuce wraps, which seemed to Bassett to be a messy and overly difficult way of getting sustenance into one's mouth, but he hadn't been asked for an opinion so he kept quiet. It did smell good though, he would give him that. He snuck a bite when Stoop's back was turned. Sweet and spicy with a distinctive crunch.

"Are there peanuts in here?" he asked, around a mouthful.

"Peanut butter, my man. Organic and extra crunchy and ground by none other than Yours Truly."

Bassett grimaced. "In chicken?"

"You're so uncouth, dude. Peanut butter isn't just for PB and J sammies."

"It should be," he muttered, but he took another bite. If you took out the lettuce and the peanut butter, added a lot more chicken and maybe some beef, and put it all over some mashed potatoes or noodles, it'd be even tastier. And stick to your ribs better. That thought made Bassett suck in his gut self-consciously. He stuffed down his bite and his body shaming guilt by gnawing on a piece of lettuce.

"Hey, look who's here," Stoop motioned with his head. Bassett swung around to peer into the bar.

There was the mountainous Mr. Cavalry, adjusting his leather braces. The sad-eyed lady dabbed an embroidered handkerchief across her freckled nose. A couple in black turtlenecks and skinny trousers were having a polite but intense disagreement about whether existence precedes essence. And then Bassett noticed the accountants. Minus one.

"No Casey," he murmured.

"Interesting." Stoop drawled out the four-syllable word into at least six, and began scooping his chicken into a bowl next to the platter of large lettuce leaves. "And oh so suspicious."

"Should I ask after him?" Bassett inquired. He wasn't sure what the protocol was in this situation. "Ask where he's been? And if he's been hanging out with me, only the me that's not me?"

"Phrase it like that and it will make their heads swim," Stoop pointed out. "Play it cool, man."

"That advice has never worked for me." Bassett moved out from behind the counter that separated the kitchen area from the bar. "Remember 1993?"

There was confused silence from the kitchen for a moment, then Stoop burst out laughing his ginormous laugh. "Was that your year of grunge, man? That was the best. Flannel and greasy hair all the way. Smelled like teen spirit alright."

"Better than your year of hip hop circa 1990," he shot back, over his shoulder.

"I still have those pants. You can't touch this!"

"You couldn't pay me to touch them!" Just as he was about to reach the accountants, someone else even more interesting caught his peripheral vision. Kevin. He was just entering the bar. Bassett spun on his heel and headed toward the Butcher.

Emerson beat him to the man. At this point in her writer's block, she was leveraging every form of procrastination she could find, whether it be animal, vegetable, or ogre. Privately, Bassett thought Kevin fit all those descriptions. Winnie reached her small head out from under Emerson's arms, and whined at Kevin. He put his meaty hand out toward Winnie's usually snarling face and Bassett had a moment of pure happiness when he thought the dachshund might rip his throat out. Instead, the furry traitor licked him lovingly.

"Such a little beauty, isn't she?" Kevin crooned. He positively crooned. Okay, it sounded like he had a mouthful of marbles, but still, a croon. Bassett's right eye began its now familiar twitching. "Aren't you a pretty wee thing, sweet baby boo?"

"Isn't she though?" Emerson beamed. She put her dog into Kevin's arms, where Winnie nearly disappeared into the crook of his colossal elbow. That turncoat snuggled in with evident delight. Bassett's grinding teeth reminded him his jaw was still sore, and he hoped Winnie lost control of her bladder soon.

"You want a table or do you want to sit at the bar?" Bassett asked, trying to sound professional and not as astringent as the Angostura bitters he used to flavor the drink of the night: a Singapore sling.

"Come sit with me," Emerson suggested. "I need company, and Winnie loves you."

"Mint julep?" Bassett offered sullenly, as they moved away.

Kevin turned and smiled. It was a nice smile, Bassett had to admit. It transformed his ogre features into something that, while not quite handsome or attractive, were at the very least winsome and fascinating. His face was heavily lined with the grooves of his strangely shaped personal landscape, including pock marks and moles. When he smiled, his deeply-set eyes nearly retreated behind his sharp cheekbones. Likewise, his wide mouth traveled sideways until the edges of his lips were nearly touching his large ears and his massive nose flattened. "If you insist, I'd love one."

Bassett muttered under his breath, "I *don't* insist, but whatever, you dog-charming brute."

"Thanks, Mr. Clark. How's your jaw?" He appeared to ask out of genuine concern and curiosity; his victim's peevishness melted slightly.

"It's better, thanks." His eye seemed to have ceased its tic, as well. Perhaps Bassett's body was adjusting, and evolving into something less finicky and more adaptable. That was some sort of silver lining, he guessed. He moved to the bar area and began mixing Kevin his drink, along with a Singapore sling for himself. It made good business sense to know your product well. That knowledge led him to mix a second after he downed the first. He glanced over at the hulking man beast chatting with his girlfriend, and instead of the customary mint sprig, he garnished Kevin' mint julep with a long-handled pink parasol, the kind usually reserved for pina coladas and mai tais.

Bassett wiped his lips with his sleeve and delivered the femininely decorated libation to the booth, overhearing their conversation.

"You're *that* Emerson DuPree! Oh, I hadn't realized! You wrote *The Werewolf's Concubine?*" Kevin gasped, then jumped up and nearly spilled one snoozing wiener dog onto the floor. "I read it three times!"

Emerson radiated pure happiness. "You did not! You did? Tiger, I have a fan!"

"Oh, I am your biggest fan, Ms. DuPree." Kevin sat back down and accepted his mint julep. He pulled out the umbrella, gave it a quizzical glance, and then set it on the table. Then he adjusted Winnie with his substantial hands and stroked her gently. "You have such a way with words. And your character development was really something. When Margeaux LaFox threw off society's restraints and embraced her inner beast by saving the werewolf from the supernatural society of lesbian wiccans, well, it was just a thing of beauty and literary perfection. I don't mind saying, Miss, I cried at the end."

Emerson beamed. "I'm so glad you liked it. Did you see the parallels between the world Margeaux and Leo lived in and our own?"

"Oh, it was so clear," Kevin assured her. "Without being too in-your-face or preachy, I mean. You really have a way with words."

"You said that already," Bassett interrupted. "So, not to put too fine a point on it, but what is your point? I mean, why are you here? I mean, you're welcome to buy as many drinks as you like of course, but what I meant to say is—"

"Tiger, don't be rude." Emerson's beam dissolved into a frown that she aimed directly at her boyfriend. He tried not to wilt, but he really hated that expression, and more than that, he really hated being the reason for it.

"Sorry. Sorry. I just thought maybe he, er, you," he hastily tore his eyes from Emerson's glare and settled on the Butcher instead, "maybe *you* were here because you'd heard something about our mutual enemies." Honestly, Bassett wasn't crystal clear on the identities of said enemies but that was a moot point.

Kevin smiled again, doing that oddly mesmerizing thing with his face. "Thank you for keeping me on track, Mr. Clark. I could have talked plotlines and books for hours."

Emerson whimpered. She stared back at her blank white screen with a shadow of defeat in her eyes.

"Yes, I thought it was time to check in and compare notes on our mutual acquaintances," Kevin said, lowering his voice. "There are things you should know."

"Awesome." Bassett could see the past two days of simplicity fly out the window and take wing, never to be seen again. Soon, he would be a quivering mass of twitching eyes and anxiety. "On second thought, let's talk more about books. Don't you think Emerson needs a vampire protagonist?"

"Nice try, Tiger. Go on, Kevin. What do we need to know?"

Kevin looked over his shoulders and moved closer to Emerson in the booth, motioning to Bassett to get close enough to hear whispering voice.

Bassett had no choice but to squeeze in next to Winnie, the demon hound, and Kevin, the Butcher. He hoped neither tried to make a move on him. He sat, stiff as a board and ears perked, and wished for a third Singapore sling.

"It's like this," Kevin began. "You need to know there are people who aren't here to be your friends. Your operation is much larger than you initially anticipated, Mr. Clark. Things are being done here that are bigger than ourselves."

"I figured that out when H.G. Wells left his pants in my bedroom."

"Yes, well, he's not the only one who has discovered how to harness time."

"Is that what we're calling it?" Emerson suddenly began typing furiously. "That's good. I'm going to write that down."

"So, some of my other customers are time travelers?" Bassett helped himself to Emerson's glass of Malbec.

"Time harnessers, Tiger."

"Yeah. Those."

"Yes. I'm sure it comes to no surprise to you. After all, you have studied, and all who have studied have come to nearly the same conclusion: time travel is possible. And there are travelers among us." Kevin *seemed* sober, both alcohol-wise and in his manner of speaking, yet …

Bassett tried not to chuckle, but failed. It just sounded so hokey. "Among us? Like aliens or superheroes?"

He looked around, and for the first time, he felt something click. The sad-eyed lady who looked like she'd just stepped off the boat after fleeing the Potato Famine, Mr. Cavalry and his leather braces, the Beatniks discussing Sartre … it was all beginning to fit. But how could it be?

"Most of the time, nothing as interesting or unique as all that. Tourists, really." Kevin sipped his mint julep and, in approval, raised his mighty thumb. It was roughly the size of Emerson's wrist. She was still typing. The muse must have returned.

"Tourists?"

"From the future. It's a lucrative business about 100 years from now. That's when time traveling becomes more common. Of course, you'd have to be extremely wealthy or connected to be able to do it yourself, but some of the more expensive Ivy League and private universities are beginning to offer it as a living history course. And the celebrities. Naturally, the celebrities find it trendy, although to be frank, they get bored of it quickly. They find anything in the past backwards. So, the fashion of time travel comes and goes you see. I suppose you could say it always has and it always will. Ha ha, just a little time travel humor there."

Bassett smiled weakly. "Ha ha." He looked around his beloved bar. There were Tess and Adam and Gus, arguing over something in their college-rule notebooks. There was the old guy, the one with his little notepad and pen, that wandered around the bar. Babs had been here a few moments before, in her combat boots and wife beater tank, but he didn't see her now. There were Robbie and James, sans Casey. They had ordered their drinks from Stoop and were heading back into the rented back room. Bassett wasn't sure why he'd let them return, what with the damage they'd caused to the side of his bar. But he imagined they were anxious to get back to whatever it was they were building with the fax machine and bike parts and engines. There were MJ and Bruce, holding hands on top of the counter as they chatted with Stoop, watching in admiration as he wrapped hot chunks of spicy, peanut-y chicken in lettuce leaves. There was a group of four Bassett had never seen before; they seemed to be on a double date and had brought their own Parcheesi board. The only regulars they were missing tonight, besides Casey, were Lizard Buttons and the No Talent Hacks. Apparently, they had a gig at a bat mitzvah this weekend.

If Kevin was to be believed (and Bassett wasn't sure he was), at least one of these patrons was a time traveler from the future.

Or a time harnesser.

Whatever. Whatever you called them, they sounded like trouble.

Chapter Twenty-Six

Bassett said as much to Kevin.

"Trouble?" Kevin drained the last of his mint julep. "That's not the half of it, Mr. Clark. These individuals are worse than that. I beg your pardon if you thought I implied that these are mere tourists."

Bassett rubbed his right eyebrow. It was a handy trick he had learned recently that seemed to calm the nervous twitching. It brought the tic down to a manageable level of furious blinking, as opposed to lightning quick fluttering spasms. "Go on."

"Tourists you've had, sure. Who hasn't? They're all around us. We call them freaks and geeks and the eccentrics and the mentally unhealthy or the just plain odd, but they're really just trying to fit in with people and a way of life that is, in reality, quite far removed from them. Imagine you trying to blend in during, say, the Renaissance? Or the Stone Age? Well, no one has gone back that far, of course."

"But you can't travel back to before you were born, right?" Bassett had remembered this rule of thumb from his conversations with Herb.

"Well, actually, you can," Kevin said, twirling his mint julep cup in his ogre-like hands. "There are a lot of factors; however, we don't need to get into them right now. As I was saying, in another century or so, the technology becomes more easily accessible and ready to use for the common man. It's also quite popular in the medical world, as I'm sure you can imagine. Going back and meeting your ancestors is very helpful in acquiring your own medical history. Of course, if you cause a paradox it doesn't do you much good, so it's a very tricky process. You think it's difficult to become a doctor and graduate medical school *now*, do you?"

Bassett didn't reply. He hadn't thought much about it.

"Well," Kevin continued, "it's no peach later, let me tell you. A thesis and eight years of school isn't enough anymore. Your finals end up being during the Black Plague or you'll get dropped off during the polio epidemic and have to find your way back. Where was I?"

Emerson looked up from her laptop. "You were going to tell us who to watch out for, who isn't here merely for the old-timey atmosphere."

Kevin pointed at Emerson and made a gesture that could be described as a wink if his eyes weren't so oddly sized. More like an ocular shrug. "Yes. Thank you. I lose my train of thought at times. I get dreadful migraines in this era."

Bassett used the fact that his thumb and forefinger were rubbing out his tic to disguise the fact that he was also rolling his eyes. *In this era? Great. Another nutter.*

"Are you a doctor then?" Emerson seemed to find this fascinating. Her page was completely full of words Bassett could see but not quite decipher.

Was she writing a new novel? Starring an ugly beast of a man who was really a time traveling doctor under a spell, who could only be cured by the kiss of one romance author and her wiener dog?

"Oh my, no. No, I'm an agent with a specialized force who works with both the CIA and NASA."

"A special agent? Yeah, heard that one before. Tell me another." Bassett remembered Special Agent Skanky, and not fondly.

"I know. It's not easy to believe such claims, but please believe this, Mr. Clark: you're in danger here. This goes much deeper than you know, and I'm very worried you're about to be caught in the crosshairs."

Emerson rubbed her hands together in glee. "Yes! I knew this wasn't over. Kev, what do you know about a Bassy lookalike?" She wound her hair up and secured it with the umbrella skewer out of Kevin's drink. Obviously, she meant business.

Kevin shook his head. "Nothing, I'm afraid. Tell me."

She shut her laptop with a dramatic thump and leaned forward. She was practically on Kevin's lap, only Winnie was already taking up that real estate. Bassett leaned forward too, on the other side of Kevin. Now they were both nearly on each knee, like two mentally unstable adults mistaking the behemoth for Santa Claus. "Several people have had *sightings* of Bassett recently. Me being one of those people. It really is Bassett, only with slightly different hair and weird fashion."

"Weird fashion, huh?" Kevin responded. "Most experienced time travelers know better than to stick out like sore thumbs. They're all briefed on it before Customs allows them their passports. So, we can probably rule out Bassett's great-great-grandson or some such relative."

"Passports to another era?"

"Of course. You can imagine how dangerous it would be if we let just anyone travel willy-nilly around time. It's difficult enough securing borders without wormholes."

Bassett sighed. He was getting a headache. Of course, it might have been caused by drinking two Singapore slings and most of Emerson's Malbec, before a proper dinner.

"I can imagine." Emerson clearly agreed and was being taken in by Kevin's explanation of things. "I didn't mean that the fake Bassy was dressed like someone from the future, I just meant he dresses in stuff Bassy wouldn't like. Like Hawaiian shirts and board shorts. That's all."

"Hm. Well, my best guess is, it's you." Kevin nodded towards Bassett. "Though it's highly dangerous and I don't recommend it. Running into yourself never ends well."

"I don't time travel." Bassett's words were enunciated and ground out between his teeth with exaggerated patience. "Also, I don't wear Hawaiian shirts."

"Not right now, you don't. Who knows what you'll have figured out and embraced by, say, next Tuesday?"

"He has a point, Tiger."

This time Bassett didn't even try to be polite about hiding the eye roll. "Fine. Next Tuesday I learn to time travel, and discover a formerly hidden penchant for island wear. Looking forward to it. Now cut to the chase: who are we supposed to be looking out for?"

"I'm getting to it, Mr. Clark. Another mint julep first? I am parched."

* * *

For a long time after, Bassett would blame the Butcher's parched throat on what happened next. If he hadn't gone to fetch Kevin his mint julep like the well-trained barkeep he was, he might have gotten the full story. Might have learned the identity of his enemy. Might have known whom to avoid, tackle and take down.

Might have saved Babs' life.

* * *

By the time they all made it out the alley, it was too late. Quinn's shouts for help had alerted the whole bar before Bassett had even finished adding ice to Kevin's drink. It was a flashback moment to Margarita

Jones when she discovered the body of Linus Fields, only more chilling as it came from the throat of a young kid whose voice hadn't even changed yet. And this time, there was no Herb to go back in time and stop the murder from happening. *Where did that come from?* Bassett thought to himself angrily. *Herb was a nude transient who jumped out my window. That's all.* As for the police suddenly not recalling any murder at all, he was even more convinced it was a ploy by Jonathan to get his future son-in-law off the hook. Had to be.

Quinn was on the ground, with Babs. The crowd from **ttrp** pressed in until they formed a panicked, clamoring, semicircle of horror. Babs' head, with her gray crewcut, was cradled in Quinn's lap. Bassett thought this was very kind for a teenage boy. He wasn't sure what he would have done in Quinn's place at that age. Probably would have run in the opposite direction, shouting. Babs looked so peaceful. If it had been a violent death, there was no blood to show for it. Quinn wiped his eyes with a fierce motion and began to speak, locking eyes with Bassett.

"I found her like this. I just rounded the corner – I was gonna pick up our sodas, you know? And she was lying here. All … dead and stuff." He gently pushed her off his lap and stood up. "I was going to try CPR but there was no pulse." He huddled in his poncho, looking dejected and scared. "Should I do it anyway? Mouth to," he shuddered a bit, "mouth?"

Bassett looked down at his Neighborhood Watch leader. She was such a force to be reckoned with. How did she just stop living so abruptly? He had seen her only minutes before, a bit before Kevin had begun his story. Granted, it was a long, drawn-out story, peppered with plotline ideas for Emerson's book and waxing sentimental over Winnie and her diva-like qualities, but still. Approximately 20 minutes ago she had been alive and well and drinking tequila like a sailor with a day pass. What had happened?

"Was it a heart attack, do you think?" Emerson crouched down on the ground beside Bassett. She reached out and touched the dead woman's cheek tenderly.

"At her age ..." Bassett didn't know. She had seemed awfully healthy to him. She seemed healthy now, except for the line of spittle that had dribbled down and out her lips, and the fact that she was deceased. "It's certainly possible. I don't see any evidence of foul play."

"Foul play?" It was MJ. She looked terrified. "Why would you say that?" She clasped Bruce's arm so hard he winced.

"Nothing, nothing," Bassett rushed to assure her, and also all of his other patrons. "I'm sure it was a heart attack. Let's bring her, um, indoors. And uh, to the back room? Sorry, guys." The apology was meant for the accountants' ears.

"It's no problem." Robbie bent down and lifted Babs by her armpits. "You get her feet."

Emerson stood as tall as possible (she was still the shortest of the crowd, but her demeanor made up for the lack of height). She clapped her hands several times, like a preschool teacher getting the attention of a classroom of hyperactive toddlers. "If you've left anything in the bar, please fetch it. We will be closing early tonight. I'm sure you all understand. Once again, no need to panic. Thank you for your understanding."

The group of barflies obeyed without a qualm or argument. Small Emerson DuPree may have been, but fierceness and bossiness were two of her strongest traits. Winnie barked as if in agreement with her mistress. Stoop held the door open for everyone. He even let in Quinn. At this point in their adventure, a minor in the bar was the least of their worries. Tess had streaks on her cheeks from her tears, not to mention raccoon eyes from the mascara. Quinn looked on the verge of crying as well.

Bassett felt his own eyes begin to leak.

* * *

Once they placed Babs' body in the back room, and all but Stoop, Emerson, Tess, and Quinn had vacated the premises, Bassett called his mother's fiancé. It was an easy phone number for him to memorize, seeing as how it was three digits long and coincidentally connected him with the emergency dispatch.

Jonathan arrived with the usual suspects: an ambulance and the coroner. Bassett was jittery and nervous. How many bodies could be found in his bar before things started looking suspicious? If Jonathan had indeed covered up, or conveniently chosen to overlook, the first one, just how many could he get away with? Not that he wanted to, of course, but people seemed to keep walking into his bar and dying.

"It's really aggravating, to say the least," Bassett whispered to Stoop. They were sitting at the booth with the scuba diving helmet. Stoop's leg was shaking and jittery, and Bassett's right eye was twitching. Together, they looked like they'd been drinking shots of espresso with energy drink chasers. Emerson was making hot tea for herself and Quinn, who was sitting morosely at the bar. Tess was pacing, her brow furrowed beneath her white makeup. She seemed deep in thought about something.

"I mean, I don't mean to sound cruel or anything. I really did like Babs." Bassett knew he could talk about his feelings with his best friend and he wouldn't be judged.

"I get it, man." Stoop ran a hand through his hair, getting it stuck in his red afro. "Ow. This whole situation stinks. I wonder if she had any family. How do we find out?"

"Do you think they'll do an autopsy?"

"Like on the crime dramas?" Stoop swallowed. "I don't know, dude. I mean, you don't really think it was a heart attack?"

"I don't know what to think." And it was true. If his gut told him Babs was murdered, then he would have to ask why. And if he asked himself why, then he would conclude that all this craziness – the spooks, the kidnappers, the accountants, the Herbs in his bedroom, the mysterious Butcher and his claims – was due to time travelers and the people (or agencies) hired to stop them. That was a bunny trail he didn't feel like hopping down quite yet, though he was certainly dipping his whiskers in the water at this point. "I mean, of course it was a heart attack."

"Denial. You're spending a whole lot of time in Egypt, if you know what I mean."

"Agreed." It was Tess. She had finally stopped pacing, and had come to rest at their table. "You've got to quit denying all this is happening, Bassett. How long are you going to keep your head buried in the sand?"

"I like the sand," he protested weakly. "It's warm. And safe."

"Where the heck is Kevin?" Emerson hollered from the kitchen area. Then she clapped a hand over her mouth, clearly feeling guilty over yelling when there was a dead body and paramedics in the building somewhere. It seemed inappropriate. She gave a mug of steaming tea to Quinn, and came over to the table. He was texting on his phone; Bassett hoped he was seeking a ride, and not some salacious update posting on Facebook. Bassett read on the internet about today's teenagers; evidently, they were disrespectful hooligans who were constantly hazing, pillaging, skipping school, shoplifting, and bullying. Then they bragged about it on social media. Not like in his day, where they did mostly the same things but had to call their friends individually to brag about it, which took forever and got you in trouble with your mom who needed the line to call other moms about potlucks, perms, and Virginia Slims.

"Where the heck is Kevin?" she repeated, this time at a whisper. "He disappeared."

Tess answered. "He took off like a bat out of hell down the alley. Maybe he saw something, or someone."

"Awesome." Bassett rubbed his eyebrow. "This keeps getting better and better."

"Oh, good. I'm glad you think so, because here comes Agent Skanky."

Chapter Twenty-Seven

"Looking for Moose and Squirrel, are we?" Emerson glowered at the woman. She had jumped to her feet; the rest stayed seated, seemingly confused by the Russian's blasé entrance.

Ekaterina, aka Agent Katie Fitzgerald, looked the same as she had the last time they'd seen her; confident, sexy, and pretty much evil. Emerson stood next to her, arms crossed over her chest, shooting laser beams out of her green eyes at the much taller woman. There was a sense of bravado in the air, an I'm-not-afraid-of-you vibe, amongst the four. This could have been attributed to a sense of solidarity, but was likely due to there being several policemen in the bar.

"Simmer down, child," Ekaterina replied. "Go take a nap. No one likes a cranky toddler." She was letting her Russian accent come through now. Either Bassett hadn't noticed it before, due to being intimidated and then bound with zip ties, or she had been hiding it when she spoke in the storage unit.

Emerson responded with a well-placed kick to the shins, but the woman barely reacted. She simply looked annoyed, like a mildly exasperated mother with a disobedient child who was acting up in the supermarket.

Ekaterina smiled confidently. "Can I get a drink, please?"

The simple request, placed by a patron to a barkeep, made Bassett flinch, but Emerson leveled him with a stare. "Don't even think about it, Tiger," she clipped, absentmindedly rubbing her sore toe. Considering how tightly they were gritted, it was a feat that she could form words.

"I was going to poison it," Bassett offered righteously, sinking back down in his seat.

"Oh, let me guess," Ekaterina spoke, "our mutual friend, the Butcher, has been spreading lies about me. Such a surprise. And where is he now? Hmm? Gone, is he? How utterly predictable. You cannot trust him."

"Oh, tell me another," Emerson spat. "As if we needed Kevin to tell us stories about you anyway. You kidnapped us!"

She swatted the notion away as if it were a bad odor, and not an accusation worthy of a felony conviction. "Bygones and all that. You Americans are so easily offended. Crybabies. The rest of the world laughs at you."

"Hey!" Now Stoop took exception. "I'll have you know I am Cuban, Scottish, and African-American!"

"Oh, I see. But still American, yes?"

"Okay, she's good." Stoop was impressed.

Bassett wasn't listening. He had stood up and was moving toward the back room, where Babs' body lay, and where Jonathan, his soon-to-be step-father, was hopefully waiting with handcuffs. Maybe he'd have something with which to club the Russian agent over the head, if there was any justice in the world. He should have known better. Bassett arrived to find the back room already empty. Obviously, Jonathan had been kind enough to use the back door so as not to attract attention as they moved Babs' body to the ambulance. Bassett couldn't hold back the shout of frustration as he kicked the accountants' time machine, if that's even what it was. The fax machine came to life with a whirling sound and the lights began to flash. He had a momentary fantasy of turning the whole thing on and somehow escaping to another place and time.

Anywhere was better than here.

But he couldn't just leave the love of his life and his best friend out there with a crazy Russian spy. So, he went back the way he had come, cursing under his breath the whole while. There was the smell of death in the air. Whether it had come along with the coroner, had drifted off the body of his Neighborhood Watch lady, or had seeped into the carpet along with Linus Fields' lifeblood, Bassett didn't know. But it was there, burning his nostrils and making him feel faintly ill. He had never known the smell or feel of death before **ttrp.**

Suddenly, the inclination to bury his head in the sand, deny, and make excuses for all the insanity that had surrounded him for weeks now, was gone. With it, the faint sense of unease and insecurity; Bassett stood taller and took longer strides to get back to the table. He was done with this. If there were time travelers in his bar, especially the murdering kind, he would no longer turn a blind eye.

For the first time in his life, Bassett Clark made a solid decision.

"I'm in," he announced. The proclamation likely would have been more effective if his party had been where he had left them, but the only face to greet his newfound determination was the face of the scuba diving helmet. Bassett looked around, blinking in confusion. His head was swimming and the room was spinning. He regretted his pre-dinner imbibing. He blinked hard in slow motion, then took another look around the bar.

Ekaterina was helping herself behind the bar, shaking a cocktail expertly. Her perfectly cut and shaped hair shook along with the mixer. Stoop and Tess were nearby, on the other side of the counter as if nervous to get too close to the Russian femme fatale, and Emerson was ushering Quinn out the front door. Bassett had forgotten all about Quinn. How would he ever be a father? He had just left an innocent young man in the same room with a deranged kidnapper and possible murderer. He groaned aloud.

"Employees only," he snapped at Ekaterina. "Get out of my bar before I call the cops."

"The service here stinks," she replied evenly, pouring her drink into a martini glass. "And call the police if it makes you feel better. They will not help your cause. They will be more likely to arrest you for taking up their time."

"And just what is my cause? No, really. I'd like to know."

"Goodness, you are grumpy, aren't you?"

"I'm curmudgeonly. There's a difference."

"Ah." She nearly smiled. Not the creepy smile he had seen before, but the faintest hint of what could just possibly be her true and real smile. But before he could be sure, it had disappeared again into a straight line of ruby red lipstick. Or perhaps it was the blood of her enemies. "This is abysmal vodka. I am going to have some decent Russian bottles sent to you."

Bassett didn't know how to reply to that. He did buy cheap vodka. He had no defense.

"Look," Ekaterina brought her drink and came out from behind the bar. She put her martini glass down on the counter and sat on a stool. Tess and Stoop instinctively took a step back. "I'm not interested in playing games with you any longer. And before you start insulting me or accusing me," she held up a well-manicured hand, "no, I'm not going to gas you and take you out to some warehouse for questioning, though I would be within my rights."

"Excuse me? Did you just say within your rights?" Stoop drew it out as if baiting his little sister.

"When it comes to our government, my Cuban-American friend, we are all authorized to do whatever is necessary. All is fair in love, astronomy, politics, and, most especially, time travel. However, I do not think I need to use scare tactics. I have some questions, and I am sure you do, too. So, let us be," she paused, grimacing as she swallowed, "friends."

As if in agreement, Emerson's Grecian nose echoed Ekaterina's obvious distaste by flaring first, and then letting out an incredulous snort. "No. Way. Lady. And I call you that in the most vague and generous sense of the word."

"Shut up, munchkin. I am not talking to you."

Emerson made a sudden move toward Ekaterina, but Bassett intercepted her. "Talk," he demanded of the Russian. Emerson was taken aback by his tone and quit struggling in his arms.

"That is better." Ekaterina smiled. It was the creepy smile again. Bassett got the feeling she burned down orphanages in her spare time, or perhaps pushed old ladies out of crosswalks and into traffic for fun. "What do you want to know?"

"Who are you looking for? Is what Kevin said true about there being agencies and passports and all that? Who do you work for? Why are you bothering me? And also, why am I asking all this? I didn't even believe in any of this crap until about five minutes ago."

Tess opened her mouth as if to argue, but snapped it shut again. She was obviously annoyed at Bassett. Probably angry over the man supposedly in charge just now concluding something about time traveling she'd realized years ago. As for addressing that niggling personality trait, Bassett feared she might need to get in line: he had never been accused of being spontaneous or impulsive about anything. He took small lifetimes to decide on which brand of socks to purchase, and three more lifetimes to change his mind. He'd known immediately, within 30 seconds of meeting Emerson DuPree, that he would marry her or die trying, which was likely the most impulsive thing he'd ever experienced, and yet years had gone by and he still hadn't made it official.

Time Travelers' Rally Point

Spontaneous he was not.

Ekaterina sighed in an overly dramatic fashion. "I am bothering you because you had the empty-headed notion to start this bar. In a way, it was very helpful for us, I will concede that. Suddenly, there was a rally point, a meeting spot, where we could keep tabs on some of our most wanted fugitives and experts alike. In a way, you really did us a favor, all of us agencies. We wished we had thought of it. So simple. On the other hand, you were not being very discreet, were you? Opening the franchise in Florida, the other one in Budapest … Suddenly, keeping an eye and ear on you was becoming a full-time job. Hence, the need to have a spy in every bar."

"Wait. Hang on. What franchises?" Bassett asked what everyone else seemed to be thinking, their respective mouths hanging open.

"You franchised. You just do not know it yet. Well, perhaps you have not done it yet, but you are about to. What year is this? You are going to, let me put it that way. It is unimportant. Irrelevant. Time travel stuff."

"Time harnesser stuff," Emerson corrected, her voice sour. "Did we really franchise?"

"Please focus, midget, or I will get out my magic gas and put you down for a nap. Where was I?"

"Forget the franchise for now. I, for one, am interested in this agency you keep talking about," Bassett prodded.

"Ah. Yes. It is difficult for me to explain it. Let us just say I am an operative for a special offshoot of the Komitet Gosudarstvennoy Bezopasnosti, and leave it at that."

"Easy for you to say," Emerson muttered. She was still bundled firmly under Bassett's arms, but she had relaxed a bit. He no longer thought she would spring at Ekaterina's face and claw her eyes out. At least, he was mostly certain: he kept his grip tight anyway.

"The what now?" Stoop raised his red eyebrows in confusion. "Say that again?"

"The KGB," Tess answered for her. Her face was white, and it wasn't due to the goth cosmetics.

"The KGB?" Bassett couldn't help it. He laughed. Loudly and deeply. "Lady, I hate to break it to you, but this is the 21st century. Those days are gone. What do you think this is? The Cold War?"

Instead of laughing with him, Ekaterina simply stared at him. "Precisely. Now you understand."

"But. Wait. What?"

Tess held up her finger towards Bassett. "Time travel, Bassy," she reminded him.

"Huh?" His laugh stopped as abruptly as it had begun. His right eye began to twitch and he smacked his palm against it to stop it. It smarted and his eye began to water, but it stopped the tic.

Ekaterina turned her attention to Tess. "I am going to converse with you from now on. You seem to be the only one with any sense, and I am getting very, very bored. My agency has been … how do I say it? Adjusting the outcome of many periods in history for quite some time now. At times, we are successful. But, and I am being humble now, most of the experiments are a dismal failure. As I am sure you know, ripples in time are incredibly difficult to control. The outcome is nearly always impossible to predict. You think you have thought of every scenario, and then, suddenly another player is involved, or you accidentally put into motion an entirely different series of events that affects everything. It is tiresome work, and not as glamorous as you would expect." She sighed. "When I started, I was a young, vibrant college student, with stars in my eyes for my mother country, the Soviet Union. Now look at me; I am old before my time."

"I think you are very pretty," Tess replied.

Ekaterina smiled, and this time it was the genuine one. "Thank you."

"But I would imagine that being evil takes its toll. Wrinkles, ulcers, etc."

She laughed bitterly. "It certainly does. You, I like. I am going to do my best not to kill you. Now, where was I?"

Bassett took control of the conversation again. He wasn't sure if Tess was up to some sort of tricky plan or if she was simply too kind for her own good. He was pretty sure it was the latter. The mother hen in her. "So, you're trying to change the outcome of the Cold War? Or keep it going?"

"Ding ding! You have won a prize. And it is not my plan. It is what the agency has hired me for. I am just a pawn, you see. We do not give up easily. I go where and when they send me."

"In a time machine?" It was Stoop this time. He sounded like an eager 10-year-old, opening up a Red Ryder *Carbine* Action 200-shot Range Model *air rifle* with a compass in the stock and this thing which tells time.

She rolled her eyes. "Americans. Why must you always ask that?"

"Because at one point, we had a living, breathing, wormhole in our possession." Bassett literally bit his tongue two seconds after he offered this information. Suddenly, East/West relations were making him feel competitive. He wanted some sort of last word.

"Ah." Ekaterina downed the last of her dreadful vodka and shuddered. "Now we are getting somewhere, Mr. Clark. Do tell."

Bassett swallowed the lump in his throat. In for a penny, in for a pound, as his mother would have said. "We have H.G. Wells on our side." *Or we did at one point.*

"Yes, and I have Albert Einstein on ice," she replied. "As you would say, tell me another."

Chapter Twenty-Eight

As bizarre as it sounded, and with a palpable degree of awkwardness, Bassett, Emerson, Tess, Stoop, and their mutual enemy, Ekaterina, sat down to eat together that night at **ttrp.** Well, Ekaterina only picked at the plate of cold cuts and cheeses that Stoop put together. Fortunately, what was surely the most uncomfortable dinner party of their lives lasted less than an hour.

By the time the socializing – if that was what it was – was over, the last bit of salami on a toothpick had been consumed, and the bottom of the bottle of dreadful vodka was clearly visible, Bassett, for one, was just as confused as he had been before. He had more questions than answers as Ekaterina pulled on her coat and left as mysteriously as she had arrived.

"*Do svidaniya,*" she said softly, before the door shut. She, for one, seemed mollified and at peace with their meeting.

Bassett racked his brain, or what was left of it, to figure out what she had been after and at what point she had gotten it. She looked like the cat who ate the canary. Was it his slip of the tongue about Herb? Or had she merely been interested in roaming about his bar? Was it Tess's brain she had wanted to pick? Had she done something to Babs, or had the old woman died of natural causes? The last question swirling in his noggin reminded him to check his phone. He was unsurprised to find several logs of missed calls. One of them had to be about Babs. Before he could dial his voicemail however, Emerson began to speak in a wistful tone.

"I can't believe we just let her leave. What is wrong with us? I'm so sad I didn't throat punch her. We had Natasha Fatale in our grip, and we let her get away. Was it just me, or did it seem like she used some sort of mind control?"

"She's no good to us without Boris Badenov anyway." Stoop winked at her. For once, she allowed it, whereas before the whole adventure started she would have socked him.

"That's a good point," Tess mused. "Who does she work for? She *is* just a pawn; she admitted it and I believe her. Did the KGB really dabble in time travel? I suppose it wouldn't be all that shocking," she continued, answering her own question. "After all, the U.S. and the U.S.S.R. compete in everything – or at least they did during the Cold War. And if, in their opinion, the Cold War is still happening, well, there's your answer."

"Like a loop?" Stoop ate the last chunk of cheddar. "Just going back again and again to the same point in time, trying to change the outcome?"

Tess shrugged. "Not sure. Let's put our heads together. What do you all know about the late '70s, early '80s?"

"This is totally where you guys will be happy to have me," Emerson said with confidence. "This is my area of expertise."

"It is?" Bassett was baffled. He knew a lot about his girlfriend: her penchant for bad romance novels, her gymnastics training, her gift for snarky sarcasm, and the fact that she was absolutely the most beautiful goddess in the world, but he didn't recall anything about her vast knowledge of Cold War history. He said as much, choosing his words judiciously so as not to offend the woman he'd like to marry and beget children with one day soon.

Emerson grinned. "Tiger, did you forget? I have seen *White Nights* 124 times at last count."

Stoop appeared confused, but Bassett grinned back at her. Only the love of his life could think they could save the world with her unlimited knowledge of a 1985 Mikhail Baryshnikov and Gregory Hines movie.

But, if he were honest, it was more than the rest of them brought to the table.

* * *

Bassett scrolled through his text messages before listening to his voice mail. There was one from his mother, Lila:

Bassy, you will walk me down the aisle, won't you? And give me away? Kisses!

There was another from his sister, Peggy:

Why is mom getting married? What the heck? What happened to being against that institution? Do you think she's getting senile?

He sighed. He'd deal with the family drama later. He dialed in the code for his voice mail.

"Mr. Clark," said the recording, "we have a situation here at the **ttrp** in Miami. Please give the main office a call as soon as possible, sir. Or if you are able to get away, we can send the private jet to pick you up. It's fueled and the pilot is awaiting your instructions. This is a Code Red."

The message ended with a click. Bassett pulled the phone away from his ear and stared at it in total bewilderment. He looked around the bar. Between the lighting, his lack of good quality sleep, and the vodka-induced headache he was experiencing, the place seemed even more hazy than usual. Emerson gripped his arm to steady him as though intuitively realizing he was about to lose a fight with gravity.

"What's going on, Tiger?"

"Um. Well. Unless? No. It's like this … Okay. So …"

"Maybe try using your big boy words."

"Sorry. Okay. I have a message from somebody who says he's from the

Miami **time travelers' rally point."**

"Whoa!" Emerson let go of her boyfriend, so she could clap her hands with joy.

"No way!" Stoop shouted.

"I knew it!" (Tess exclaimed simultaneously).

"That's not all," Bassett continued. His legs wobbled as he sat down. "He said they have a *situation*."

"Cryptic. I love it."

"Yeah, I'm not sure I do. He also said the private jet is fueled and the pilot is awaiting instructions on whether to pick me up."

Emerson squealed like a preteen at a Justin Bieber concert. She clapped her hands over her mouth. "We have a private jet?"

"Evidently." He frowned. "Unless of course it's really Ekaterina and her KGB goons trying to capture us. We could be walking right into her trap."

"Seems overly elaborate, even for her. She's more the hire-a-thug-and-gas-us kind of girl."

"Yeah." He thought for a minute. "Wait, hang on. The toolbox. No, not the toolbox. The toolbox is now a bank account. Right. Hold on a minute." He brought his phone back out of his pocket and began scrolling through the apps. "I have the bank one here somewhere."

"Why?" Stoop began clearing away the plates from their impromptu dinner party. "What's the bank got to do with this?"

"Because if my balance has dwindled down considerably in the past few days, I'll know where the money went."

Emerson's eyes widened. "To the Florida and Budapest franchises?"

"Bingo."

* * *

Bassett's hunch was confirmed. Two huge transfers had been made, not long after he had opened the account. He didn't know much about money and buying real estate, especially in other states and countries, but the amounts seemed adequate for down payments on corporate real estate ventures. There were also several deposits made recently that he had no memory of making. Apparently, business was booming.

In just a few days? Time travel was confusing.

"Okay. We own a franchise. And I have a private jet. My head hurts."

"Talk about an overnight sensation," Stoop said. "Congratulations, my man."

"Thanks, I guess. What do I do about this jet and this *situation* thing the guy mentioned? Should I call him back?"

"I think you'd better. They could have a naked Herb running around or something."

"Good point." He rubbed his stiff neck. He felt like he needed a massage or a hot tub, both of which he could probably afford now. He felt a bit cheered at that thought. He could afford an engagement ring, too. A big one. One that would be so heavy on little Emerson that it would drag her hand down and cause her to turn in left circles. He chuckled aloud.

"What's so funny, Tiger? Are you losing it?" She was suspicious. "You have that crazy look in your eye again. Like when you went to bed with Ernest."

Bassett stopped chuckling and had a moment of silence for Ernest Hemingway, the best skull a guy could ever have. "Alright. I'm calling this man back. How does my voice sound?" He pulled up the number.

"Very boss-like. And sexy." She pecked him on the cheek as he connected the call.

"**time travelers' rally point 2.0,**" said a woman's voice on the line.

"2.0? Seriously? Good grief, I must have been drinking."

"I'm sorry? Can I help you?"

"Yes. This is Bassett Clark, um, your boss."

"Oh, Mr. Clark! Hello! How can I help you, sir? And may I say, it's just wonderful to hear your voice again!"

Again? But Bassett didn't question it. Hell, he was barely taken aback. "Yes, you too, um, I'm so sorry, with whom am I speaking?"

"Oh my gosh, Mr. Clark, I'm so sorry! It's Janet, sir. Do you want me to do it again? The phone intro? They've trained us to say our names and I'm so sorry. It's just been such a long day, what with the problem and all, and I do apologize. It'll never happen again, sir."

"Don't worry about it, Janet. I was actually hoping you could tell me about the problem."

"Oh yes, of course, sir. Of course I can. It's a Code Red, sir." And then she stopped talking. Bassett could hear her breathing on the other line. He waited for more explanation. Evidently, that was it.

"Janet? Could you elaborate?"

"Sir?"

"The Code Red? Um, I'm a bit fuzzy on that. Could you remind me of the descending uh, color codes?"

"The Emergency Codes? But sir, protocol says we aren't to discuss the codes over the telephone." Suddenly Janet sounded extremely stressed out. "Is this a test? Are you testing me, sir? Oh crap, they warned me about this. I never should have taken this job. And now I just said crap. Oh, crap. I said it again!"

"It's alright, Janet. Don't melt down because of me. I'm sorry I asked. I'll just look it up in the manual. We do have a manual, right?" Bassett hoped he hadn't used the same filing system he used prior to this: his messy box of receipts and bills.

"I don't know, sir." She seemed very defeated. "May I go, sir? I'm needed out front. Shall I send the jet for you then? You are coming, aren't you? Please say you're coming, sir. We are falling apart here, if you don't mind my saying so."

Whether it was the desperation in his poor secretary's voice, or his curiosity, or his inability to say no to women, Bassett assured Janet he was indeed coming.

"The jet will pick you up at the usual spot." Janet sounded relieved at his promise.

"Remind me where that is?" He did his best to sound casual, though if Janet wasn't suspicious and wary of her boss's demeanor by now, she wasn't the sharpest tool in the shed.

"Granger's Field. Can you be ready in two hours?"

"Sure. Why not?"

They both disconnected the call at the same time. Bassett looked at his three friends. "Get packed. We're going to Miami."

Chapter Twenty-Nine

Granger's Field was a baseball field back in Stoop and Bassett's day. Now it was unused and overgrown. The bleachers were rickety, and the play equipment that had once been shiny and new was dull and broken. A swing hung by one chain, the other side busted, and below the slide was a puddle of something that might be rain water but probably wasn't. There was a rust-colored merry-go-round, and it creaked slowly in a circle as the breeze pushed it around at a snail's pace. A nearby corn field also made strange noises in the night wind.

The only light was from the moon, which shone from the town across the highway, and the headlights of Stoop's Range Rover. Emerson was hopping from one foot to another, whether to keep warm or because she was excited was anyone's guess. Bassett paced nervously, his eyes on the sky. Stoop was snacking on peanuts from his pocket. Tess – who was not about to be left out of this adventure – was sitting on her suitcase, her chin in her hand. She had washed off her makeup. Bassett found the difference in her appearance startling once again. Stoop didn't really seem to notice either way; maybe love really was blind.

"I can't believe we're doing this, guys!" Emerson's voice was dreamy. "And in our own jet, too. I'd like to shove that in ol' Svetlana's face." She was running out of insults for Ekaterina and was resorting to rotating the only Russian names she knew. So far, she'd gone through Olga, Oksana, Anastasia, and La Femme Nikita.

"I, for one, am hoping we never see her again," Bassett answered, truthfully. "I can't help thinking she got what she wanted from us. I just wish I knew what *it* was."

Stoop shrugged. "It's the government's problem now. I wonder if we have a secret offshoot of the CIA dedicated to time travel things?"

"I assume so," Tess replied, pushing her black hair out of her eyes.

"Maybe that's where Kevin works."

"I can't help wondering where Kevin went," Emerson mused. She was still hopping and was working up a sweat in the night air. "Maybe he was following Babs' body." She tucked Winnie into her jacket, where the dog barked and stuck her nose out through the neck.

"For what? His own autopsy? Gross." Bassett hoped she was wrong. He really longed for confirmation that Babs had died from a heart attack, not from some sinister line of fire that he might have caused. How would he live with himself if that were the case? And it could have been one of the other Neighborhood Watch team members. Like Joey. His blood ran ice cold just thinking about it.

Suddenly, the wind picked up mightily. The merry-go-round began to creak at a faster pace, and the corn stalks rustled and blew sideways. It wasn't just the wind; it was a plane landing in Granger's Field.

The group watched, the women holding back blowing hair from their faces, and the men gathering the suitcases and bags. Bassett and Stoop locked eyes. They didn't have to say it, their body language and 35 years of friendship said it all: *Watch your back, and keep the girls safe.*

They didn't know if they were walking into an adventure or a trap. Unless they had missed an obvious alternative though, there was only one way to find out, and that was by boarding the jet.

So, they did.

* * *

Having never set foot in a private jet before, Bassett was unsure how impressed to be, but he tried to play it cool. This was supposed to be, after all, his very own private jet. And he had to admit, he liked the color scheme and the general feel of the thing. He'd never decorated one before (or had he?) but it seemed like the kind of décor he'd choose.

There were plush blue velvet seats that reminded him of Elvis in his blue suede shoes, and there was a vase of freshly cut daisies on the table. He knew daisies were Emerson's absolute favorite flower, so that was another indication of this being his/their plane. There were curtains on each window, and a round, oversized, and very luxurious-looking chair, topped with pillows and a cashmere throw. There were accents of bronze and elements of industrial styling that played with a steampunk theme. Bassett only knew that because Emerson had talked of doing a steampunk corner at **ttrp**. The lighting was bright, but not so much as to hurt their eyes coming in from the darkness of Granger's Field, and there was the smell of something delicious in the air. Something with garlic and tomatoes and maybe steak. Bassett's stomach growled loudly in anticipation.

There was a pilot of course. They could only see the back of his head from their seats, but he quite obviously wasn't Ekaterina, which had been a slight worry of Bassett's from the beginning of this journey. It was a woman, however, who had opened the door for them. Now she stood waiting patiently, her arms at her side. She had hair the color of wheat in one long braid over her shoulder, and she was dressed like a flight attendant, in a pencil skirt of blue and a blouse with a vest. White tights and blue heels completed her uniform. Bassett wondered if this was the nervous Janet he had spoken with on the phone.

"Hello, sir, and welcome." She crossed one heeled foot behind the other and dipped slightly in a curtsy. "I'm Alice. Please let me know if there's anything you need during your flight. I'll be serving dinner in approximately 30 minutes, at about the time we are over Boston. I know you and your guests enjoy a good view when you dine."

We do? "Yes, thank you, Alice."

He and Stoop had set the bags down near the door when they had entered, and now Alice gathered them one by one and set them in the overhead compartments, which were just as luxurious and expensive looking as the rest of the jet. They were covered in a buttery soft leather material in a shade of off-white, with tufts gathered the center. Cloudlike, all in all. Bassett wondered if that was what he had been going for when decorating. Funny how easily he was beginning to accept this. It was a very peaceful, almost spa-like feeling in the jet, except for Winnie's yapping. Emerson let her out of her coat, and she scampered off, sniffing madly. *If she marked her territory ...* Bassett glared at her furry butt and willed her to behave herself.

If he had any doubts at all whether this was somehow his very own private jet from the future, sent to pick him up and deliver him to a franchised bar of his very own making, they were erased when he saw the framed photographs to his left. They were arranged on an end table, one that could be folded up right into the wall, and there was another small vase of daisies beside those. Emerson and Tess had moved the other direction, toward the round lounging chair, but Stoop stopped and looked at the photos with him. Bassett's breath caught in his throat. There was one of the reopening of the original **ttrp,** after they'd done all that hard work at the thrift shops. Bassett remembered one of the customers taking it for him: he and Stoop were standing proudly, arms around one another, and Emerson was doing her best Vanna White impersonation, her hands thrown out as if to say, *Look at this place!*

The next photo was also one he remembered: it was his kindergarten graduation photo. His ears stuck out like Dumbo's and his dimples were hidden by his frown of concentration at the camera. His hair had been slicked back with water from the boy's restroom, and he was wearing corduroys and a paisley button-down shirt. It was his mother's favorite photo, and he was used to seeing it framed in a square of dried macaroni noodles and Elmer's glue, hanging by a magnet on her refrigerator, where it had been for 40 years.

The next photo was not something he remembered: it was of Emerson and himself, but he couldn't place the location. Some sort of fancy restaurant maybe? They were dressed to the nines too; Emerson was in a slinky gold dress that made Bassett's mouth water just looking at it, and he himself was in a tuxedo. A tux? He didn't even own a tux. He'd never been anywhere, done anything, which required such a getup. But that wasn't what made his heart skip a beat; it was what Emerson was doing in the photograph. She was holding out her hand to the camera, her left hand. Her left hand, with a ginormous diamond ring on it. He began to sweat. Profusely. Had he been wearing a tie, he would have loosened it. Instead, he pulled on the collar of his shirt, as if needing air. His right eye began to tic.

"Dude," whispered Stoop.

"I know," Bassett croaked back.

"I don't think you do, man." Stoop nudged his friend, whose eyes hadn't strayed from the engagement picture. "Look at this one."

There was a tiny voice in Bassett's head – perhaps his conscience, perhaps his inner common sense, perhaps the Holy Ghost – that bade him not to, but he looked anyway. The next photo was like the others; framed in silver and posed decoratively, but it was even more shocking than the others. This one showed all four of the people who were now in the jet: Stoop, Bassett, Emerson, and even Tess. And they were all dressed up once more, but in more of a beachy attire this time, no tuxes. The crashing waves of some tropical beach rolled in the background. Tess was out of her Goth gear, instead wearing a flowing dress and long earrings. She looked lovely, holding Stoop's hand. He was wearing trousers and a white dress shirt. Bassett had on a Hawaiian shirt and cargo pants. When he saw himself in the picture, he groaned aloud. But Emerson was the most shocking vision of all. She was wearing what appeared to be none other than a wedding dress. Bassett felt his heart skip at least two beats, possibly three. *How many could you skip before you needed CPR?* He hoped Alice was trained in such emergencies.

"Um, now look at this one," Stoop instructed, ignoring his friend's apparent heart attack. He glanced furtively over at the two ladies; they were both on the round chair, toasting one another with glasses of white wine.

"What now?" Bassett muttered. His heart had resumed beating, though it felt a bit sluggish. However, the next photograph kicked it into overdrive. It was now keeping time with his right eye. He felt as though his entire body was drumming like Lars Ulrich at a Metallica concert, but only if Lars had been drinking espressos laced with amphetamine and cocaine.

The last photograph was of a baby girl, if the pink blanket was any indication, with a mass of strawberry blonde curls, and two deep dimples. She was cradled in the arms of her beaming parents: one Mr. and Mrs. Bassett Clark.

He figured now was as good a time as any for that heart attack. He passed out.

*　*　*

Bassett was only unconscious for a minute or two, but the mind plays interesting tricks when it gets the chance. Apparently, his had decided it would be an excellent time to cause his life to flash before his eyes. And while it seemed impossible later when he came to and thought properly about it, he recalled all sorts of scenes and times and tidbits. Much more than could have been crammed into a mere two minutes of being passed out on the jet's floor. But then again, he would surmise, time travel was a strange thing. He was beginning to realize that now. Turns out, you do a bit of time traveling when a) passed out, or b) dying.

He saw himself as that kindergartener from the first picture, with dimples, and a cowlick that he had tried to paste down with water from the boy's restroom. He had known it was picture day at school and had dressed accordingly. His hair was blonder then; it hadn't darkened to the burnished brown of adulthood until his teenage years. He had lost both bottom teeth and one top one, and was careful about stowing his earnings from the Tooth Fairy (who was typically at least one night late, making the six-year-old increasingly suspicious, since his own mother wasn't exactly known for being punctual). He was saving up enough to buy a Rock 'Em Sock 'Em Robot game. But, by the time he had collected enough, he had changed his mind and went for a portable cassette recorder instead. He and Stoop used to interview one another with it. They also used it to spy on others, though the result was always disappointing. Grown-ups were incredibly boring. At some point, several years later, they had buried the recorder in the backyard in a sort of homemade time capsule. He assumed it was still there, along with a stack of baseball cards, a letter to the Rolling Stones, and half a Twinkie, all inside an Air Jordan shoebox.

While sprawled on the posh Oriental rug that covered the jet's floor, Bassett also had flashbacks of his days at summer sleepaway camp during middle school. He'd made enough lanyards to go into business for himself, but found out the hard way that there wasn't much money in it. He'd had a huge crush on one of the camp counselors. Alison ... he couldn't recall her last name. Not even his subconscious could locate that knowledge. Alison Somebody then. She had huge, fluffy, blonde hair and wore different colored mascaras for each day of the week: electric blue, shimmering violet, grass green. She chewed gum and had long, freckled legs. Unfortunately, the age gap of four years turned out to be insurmountable, no matter how large and hot a torch he carried for her.

He flashed back to the time when he first bought O'Malley's. Though not the type to be outwardly exuberant, he had uncharacteristically stepped out of his shell that day; buying his mother a fancy lunch at a seafood restaurant where the cloth napkins were folded as fans and placed inside their wine glasses. Lila had ordered a shrimp cocktail and crab cakes. After that, Bassett had made several telephone calls to share his good news, and he bought a round of drinks at Buffalo Wild Wings for a table of people he'd only just met when he'd dropped by for fried mozzarella sticks with Stoop. It had been a good day.

The next scene in the Movie of Bassett Clark's Life was the first time he'd ever laid eyes on Emerson DuPree. This scene was well-worn in the fabric of Bassett's memory; it was a scene he took out every so often, to touch, to smell, to remember. Was it any wonder it played slower in his brain than did the others?

It was an autumn day and the whole world seemed adrift in a crisp, cool still life of oranges and russets and yellows. He'd taken a walk – not because he was accustomed to do that sort of thing, but because the old Ford pickup he drove at the time was in the shop. He needed to buy some stamps at the post office – and that was when he saw her. She was a breath of summer on a cold day, a stamp in his passport, the perfectly written line in a song. She was everything, all at once, in her jeans and scarf and hair that glowed and whipped around her face in the wind. She had a Grecian nose that was pink from the breeze, and she was stomping on the sidewalk to keep her feet warm because she was wearing ridiculous sandals with peep-toes. Even with the heeled sandals, she was a little thing, but she was no child. She was waiting for the bus. Later, he learned she was going to her cousin's baby shower, hence the silly, dress-up shoes.

Naturally, Bassett had noticed and appreciated members of the opposite sex before. After all, there was Alison Whatshername, and there had been a couple of stolen kisses in high school with a girl named Emily after chess club, and he'd had one or two girlfriends since then. But this was different. Everything with Emerson was different. Life had been gray and methodical and predictable before her; now it was all going to change. It was like he'd never known what he wanted out of life until he met her. And then it was all so simple, so clear, he wondered how on earth he could have missed it before.

In his flashback, Bassett saw himself approach Emerson and mentally high-fived himself as he always did during this part of the memory. He could have kept walking right on by, but he didn't. He did the opposite of what was expected; he went right up to her and spoke.

"It's cold out and the buses are usually late. Do you want a ride?" he had said. He'd tried to make his voice sound a little deeper, a little sexier, a bit more husky and mysterious. It hadn't really worked: he sounded more like a perv. She admitted this to him much later, and had erupted into a laughing fit that made her cheeks red and her throat hurt, and made him laugh too.

Emerson had turned to him then and looked at him with her deep green eyes. She smiled a friendly enough smile; not enough for him to believe his love was requited, but enough to show her teeth and make his heart beat faster. "In what?" she'd asked.

"Huh?"

"You're not driving," she'd pointed out.

He'd been so embarrassed that he'd nearly turned tail and run. He could duck into the nearby alley, or find a wood somewhere close where he could live out his days in mortified seclusion. He'd be known as the man who lived in the wood. A feral man. He'd become an urban legend. It seemed doable and completely necessary after humiliating himself like this. He was poised on the balls of his feet, totally prepared to pivot and sprint towards the tree line. But, her eyes were so green and her hair looked so soft and her nose was so cute and pink. He was hypnotized. He didn't want to leave her side, even if it meant a lifetime of abject humiliation and scorn. It would be worth it to have her to look at.

They'd stared at one another for several seconds, Emerson's nose now a bright red and beginning to run, and Bassett's heart refusing to beat properly. He kind of wished he were dead, but only a little bit. Then she'd started giggling – not an annoying schoolgirl giggle, but a trickling creek kind of giggle that sounded like music – and Bassett started laughing too, and when it started to rain right then it seemed perfect somehow, like the best backdrop to a love story that began that day at a bus stop.

He'd never gotten the stamps. And she'd never gone to her cousin's baby shower. They'd fallen in love instead.

Chapter Thirty

When he came to, those eyes of green were looking down into his with concern. There were other heads lingering in his peripheral vision as well, but Bassett clung to Emerson's gaze to pull him out of his stupor. He had a headache, probably from falling over, and he was sprawled at an unnatural angle that made his left ankle throb. That was likely because Winnie was gnawing on it, though.

"What happened?" he croaked. Then it all came back, in a sudden rush. The photographs, his wedding to Emerson (when he hadn't even proposed yet?), and the birth of their daughter. Their daughter. A miniature Emerson DuPree-Clark. He felt faint again and his eyes began to roll back in his head.

"Oh, no you don't!" Emerson snapped her fingers in front of his face a few times, and then shook him by the shoulders. "Knock it off!"

"Okay," he agreed weakly. Winnie was biting down hard now and he kicked her off with no remorse.

"I uh," Stoop began, nodding his head ever so subtly in the direction of the little pull out table with the daisies and the framed pictures, "you know. Ahem. So, yeah."

They weren't complete sentences, they weren't even complete words, but Bassett got the drift. Stoop had removed the photographs while Bassett was busy fainting. Bassett frowned. He'd be willing to bet Sam Elliott had never fainted in his life. He wondered if he could blame it on food poisoning or a gas leak from the jet engines.

"Up you go." Emerson interrupted his train of thought and began pulling him to his feet. "That's better. How do you feel?"

"Good, fine, absolutely great. My blood sugar was probably just low or something. Actually, I think I tripped over Winnie, now that I think about it. Hit my head on the way down. Let's never talk about this again, alright?" He was anxious to put his temporary swoon behind them all. It was so embarrassing. Worse even than offering Emerson a ride in his invisible car that day all those years ago. He clapped his hands together briskly. "Let's eat!" he said, at Alice, almost as if he'd done that sort of thing before. She disappeared into the cabin, presumably to tell the pilot it was safe to take off.

The garlicky smell was pasta, a kind of ravioli that was a bright yellow-orange hue, with a creamy butter sauce. It was probably delicious, but Bassett couldn't taste anything. The women oohed and ahhed over it though, and moaned that they were going to gain several pounds each. Stoop was savoring his bites, rolling them around in his mouth, trying to divine the ingredients. He had come up with butternut squash, pumpkin, sage, brown sugar, white wine … It seemed a ridiculous list for something that was supposed to be dinner, so Bassett was not disappointed by his own lack of appetite. Who ate pumpkin in pasta? The world was getting stranger and stranger. He'd been raised on Rice-A-Roni and Hamburger Helper, which he'd learned to make himself at the age of nine because his mother was on a vegan kick and kept bringing home things like chocolate pudding made from carob and tofu. Luckily, she'd never been one to force her opinions on anyone else, even her own small son, so she'd provided enough grocery money for other culinary options. He'd eat his Tuna Helper straight out of the pot, the handle wrapped in a crocheted potholder, and take it to the television each evening, so as not to miss the Rockford Files. She'd cluck over his choices, and look at him with sad eyes, but she'd let it go. Meanwhile, she'd munch her sunflower seeds and dried apricots, and he'd eat his dinner with the same wooden spoon he'd use to stir it all together, and all in all, they'd made some good memories.

Now, Bassett shoved the last bite of ravioli in his mouth and forced himself to chew. It wouldn't do for Emerson to notice anything was amiss. He'd never really tried to lie to her but he knew instinctively he would stink at it. He swallowed the lumpy bit of pasta down and smiled at her weakly. "Next stop, **ttrp 2.0**," he said, coercing some brightness into his voice. "Can't wait to see it. I wonder if you decorated it, too?"

Emerson's eyes widened. "I hadn't thought of that! Won't it all seem familiar if we've been there before? This time harnessing stuff is super confusing. I feel like I'm getting less smart every day."

"I think it's one of those times where the more you know, the more you know you don't know. You know?" Tess offered. She speared the last ravioli on her plate with relish.

The plane dipped slightly and Winnie began to bark as if they'd been surrounded by ax murderers or set upon by rabid squirrels. Alice appeared, seemingly out of nowhere, and offered the yapping dog a rawhide bone. Once again, Bassett got the feeling that this had been done before. It was unsettling, but he was beginning to get used to the feeling.

*   *   *

The jet had landed, as smoothly as it had taken off, and they exited onto a tarmac in a location that was much warmer than the one they had left behind. Well, it was Florida after all, but still, the humid morning air was a bit of a shock to the group. Everyone but Bassett had slept on the plane. Every time he closed his exhausted eyes, he saw the photograph of his not-yet-born daughter float disconcertingly before him. He was anxious to see the franchise, and learn about the 'situation' that had caused such a commotion. They all had theories. Stoop and Bassett leaned toward the dramatic and pessimistic, while Emerson thought this was the perfect opportunity to show their leadership skills and problem-solving expertise. She was also hoping that Ekaterina would show, because she had learned a sleeper hold from YouTube she wanted to try. Bassett found the fact that you could learn such a thing off a tutorial a bit distressing. *What kind of a world was he bringing his theoretical daughter into anyway?*

Tess had theories about their trip too, but she was mainly there for fodder for her senior project/essay, and because Stoop wanted her there. He had a way of looking at her when she wasn't looking back that made Bassett's eyes water. He knew that look. *Be careful,* he wanted to shout at his friend, *or you'll end up in Hawaiian shirts on a tropical beach, marrying her, and having no memory of it!*

Bassett knew he had to shake off this lingering feeling of unease over the photographs and concentrate on the problems at hand. It wasn't as though he didn't want to marry Emerson – he'd known long ago he wanted that very thing – but he felt it a mean trick of Father Time or Mother Nature to ruin the surprise. That was probably why Stoop had instinctively hidden the photos. It was like secretly peeling back the Transformers wrapping paper from your Christmas gifts in November, only to be required to fake a delighted, surprised expression when you re-opened them in December. The tape would have that non-sticky, reused feeling to it, and the corners wouldn't properly conceal the packages. And you had to feign excitement for your mom, who was watching suspiciously from behind her cup of eggnog. All in all, no one wanted a Christmas like the one Bassett had had back in 1984.

And he didn't want a wedding like that either.

With that thought on his mind, he climbed into a navy sedan that was waiting for them at the end of the tarmac.

* * *

"When did we become the sort of people who have sedans and private jets and bodyguards?" Emerson whispered to Bassett on their way to the bar. "I mean, not that I'm complaining. A girl could get used to this."

They did, indeed, have a bodyguard. Stereotypes were always so unfair, lumping certain body types or ethnicities or genders into a little box. At least that's what Bassett had always thought before, probably due to his mother's inclusivity and ability to push one out of one's comfort zone. But he re-evaluated that belief now. His own bodyguard, Leif, was the most stereotypical bodyguard who had ever lived. He was enormous (even giving Kevin a run for his money in the height department), silent as a monk, and dressed in a black suit with a skinny black tie. Aviator sunglasses concealed his eyes, and he was roped in thick sinews of muscle that at some points – mainly on his neck – looked as though they were thicker than Bassett's thighs. He was an impressive gentleman, solid as a tower, and just as quiet. Bassett could only hope and assume his gray matter was not as rock-like as the rest of him. He wondered if he'd been the one who had hired Leif. *What an interesting interview process that must have been.* He wished he could remember it.

The driver of the navy sedan was named Philbert (pronounced like the nut, he had explained) and it was he who had referred to the bodyguard as Leif. All four of the newcomers wondered how difficult it was going to be to try to look as though they were not experiencing all of this for the first time.

"Do you like it?" Bassett whispered back, answering Emerson's earlier question.

"It's like Lifestyles of the Rich and Famous," she answered, with a giggle. "I keep expecting Robin Leach to pop out of the trunk."

Tess was anxiously gnawing on her bottom lip, and her legs were trembling. "I hope we don't regret this," she said. "I have kids, you know."

Apparently, so do I, thought Bassett. His stomach did a flip that would have made the gymnast in Emerson envious.

"I mean, why do we need a bodyguard? Besides the obvious, you know. The Russian spies and the magic gasses and the kidnappings and the mysterious fortune." Tess had quit gnawing long enough to speak, but now she went back to her lip with abandon. Bassett worried she'd have no skin left to put her black lipstick on soon.

"Well, we can rest easy about one thing," Bassett said, looking down at his phone which had pinged a few times since exiting the plane. He scrolled through a couple of text messages. "Babs passed away of natural causes. At least, as far as they can tell. Turns out she had a bad heart, and had gotten all her affairs in order over the last few months. Seems like she knew she didn't have long. So, that's good. Well, not good ..." he trailed off, awkwardly, "but, you know."

"So, she wasn't murdered?" Emerson looked cheered. Adventure she liked, even a bit of violence, but murder seemed overly dramatic, even for her.

"She could have been poisoned," Tess suggested. "Just because they can easily rule out gunshot wounds or stabbings, doesn't mean she wasn't murdered. Don't you people ever read Agatha Christie?"

"I'm a John Grisham guy myself," Stoop said, apologetically, "but I'll totally try Christie."

"I only read super bad romantic fiction. The worse, the better," Emerson said, happily.

"I'm more of a back of the cereal box kind of guy," Bassett confessed.

"Good grief, we're all going to die," Tess muttered. "Hey, we're stopping. Are we there?"

A nod from the otherwise still as a statue Leif confirmed her guess. They were there all right: **ttrp 2.0** in Miami, Florida.

The door to the sedan opened, as if it were pulled by invisible strings. Bassett wished it had been so simple. A haunting, an invisible being, heck, even that pack of ax murderers or rabid squirrels would have been preferable to what opened the door for them.

The first thing they saw was someone's chest, as they, naturally, were all sitting down in the car and the person opening the door was standing. They saw the unusual watch on the wrist of the man as he offered his palm to Emerson, who was nearest the door. It matched Bassett's wristwatch – the one from his unknown father – exactly. The next thing they noticed was the brightly colored Hawaiian shirt and board shorts. Hairy legs. Then the man bent down to eye level at the same moment that Emerson took his hand.

She screamed.

The man was Bassett Clark himself.

*   *   *

Initially, Bassett had a moment of panic, recalling when Herb – *It was Herb, wasn't it? Or was it one of the accountants?* – had gently reprimanded him for being in two parallel universes at the same time. *Or was it that you shouldn't run into yourself when time traveling?*

Well, of course that last one seemed true. Even a non-expert like Bassett knew that much. He had learned the basics from *Back to the Future*. Whichever rule it was, however, he was sure he was now breaking them all. He felt distinctly clammy all over and his right eyebrow began to twitch.

Emerson had scurried back into the relative safety of the sedan, dropping the other Bassett Clark's hand like it was a snake. Instinctively, she scooted into Leif's lap. Bassett – the real Bassett – would have had a problem with that if he hadn't been so busy sorting out his thoughts while staring into his very own eyes.

It is an odd thing to stare into one's own eyes. Bassett wouldn't necessarily recommend it to anyone. It gave him a sinking sort of feeling in his gut and a clamminess that quickly broke into a cold sweat. The eyes were very much his own: the same basic, boring brown color that he could tell had the potential to look more hazel if he wore the right shirt. They had a subtly squinting look about them too, that Bassett knew was from a slight near-sightedness and from reacting to the sun because he could never remember where he had left his sunglasses. His eyebrows were wooly and unruly. Did this Bassett have his own Emerson who threatened him with her tweezers when his brows got out of control as well? There were some wrinkles around the eyes and mouth, too, and whether they were placed in exactly the same spots follicle-y speaking, there were precisely seven silver hairs in his goatee.

And the dimples. Yes, there they were, as Bassett-from-the-future beamed at the group. Emerson's screaming seemed not to have affected him much, although his over-the-top grin faded slightly. He still held out his hand, with the wristwatch on it, as though holding out hope that someone would accept it.

"Welcome to **time travelers' rally point**," he said in a rather booming voice. This was at odds with Bassett's voice, which tended to be on the quieter side. Not Leif quiet, but normal quiet. The Bassett stranger continued to beam, his mouth stretching wide, and he began forming more words. "I'm so glad you're here! We have a situation, as I know Janet told you. Anyway, Dad is waiting inside and I'm sure you all want to stretch your legs. Wait." The beaming stopped, and a frown replaced it. "Hang on. I'm putting two and two together and getting four here. The screaming makes more sense now. I thought you saw a spider. That's not it though, is it? We haven't met yet, have we? Man, I hate it when the time continuum gets fried. Okay, let's start from the beginning." The hand, which up until now hadn't wavered in the slightest, now began a pumping motion, though no one in the car had moved to take it. Stoop's good manners won out, and he reached out and shook it gingerly. "I'm Robert, but everyone calls me Topper. Topper Herriot. Bassy, buddy, I'm your twin brother."

Chapter Thirty-One

There was chaos in the sedan, and Bassett had to get out. All that noise made him feel claustrophobic and smothered. Had he been a runner, he would have jumped out of the vehicle and fled down the streets of Miami, perhaps never to be heard from again. But as history had already shown, he was not a runner. So, he simply exited and stood by the carbon copy of himself, his twin brother, Topper.

"So good to see you, little bro," Topper said, grinning widely once again. He reached out and clapped Bassett on the back with gusto. "I call you that because I was born first. Four minutes older I am, but I don't look it, huh? It's the Florida humidity. Keeps my skin supple and moisturized. Ha! Just joshing you. You look great! Hey, what time period did you come from? Sorry about all the confusion. We're still getting the hang of this stuff, too."

Bassett felt his stomach relax and suddenly it was as though the weight of the world had been lifted off his shoulders – or if not lifted exactly, then at least moved a bit to the left. He even found himself smiling, though such an action had seemed impossible only moments before, and he unbent enough to begin the long story. He started with the renaming of O'Malley's and the arrival of the toolbox, moving on to the adventure in the storage shed with La Femme Nikita, and then he told Topper all about H.G. Wells and the murder he had evidently gone back in time to prevent.

At least he would have told his newly found brother the whole sordid story, had he been able to speak properly. He did get his mouth to open and shut a few times, but nothing came out but a squeaking sound. He finally gave up, and just stared at Topper, trying not to look as dumb as he felt.

Well, it certainly explained some things. The Hawaiian shirt people kept spotting him in, for one. But it didn't explain the big things. Like Bassett having a brother at all.

Finally, he found his voice. "I didn't know I had a brother."

"I know, right?" Topper sounded rueful. "Tell me about it. I didn't know either, until recently. Turns out when our mother and father had us, they decided to split up, and each took one son. I grew up with our father, Zechariah. You grew up with Lila. Sorry, obviously, you knew that part."

"No, it's okay." Bassett waved away the apology. "Be as detailed as you can here. Don't assume I know anything at all."

"Sure thing. Okay, so I grew up here, in Miami. I'm an IT guy, you know, computers and geeky tech stuff? So, I found you and Lila quite a while ago, through the web, but I didn't know whether to reach out. Plus, Dad was real nervous about it. Turns out he and Mom weren't exactly a love match. More like a one-night stand. Gross, I know. Anyway, when they each took one of us to raise, they pretty much agreed to never see one another again, because they thought that would be fair and best for their kids. Whack, right? I know. My thoughts exactly. Where was I?"

"IT guy. You found us."

"Right. Hey, you want to finish this at the bar? Your friends look interested in hearing it, too. Hey, E! Sorry about scaring you there. Forgot you hadn't met me yet, at least not that you recall." He smiled at Emerson, who was getting out of the sedan. She didn't smile back. Bassett knew that look. She got the same look on her face when someone was trying to sell her something. She didn't fully trust Topper yet, that was for sure.

Bassett did though. Having his own face right across from him instilled a trust that couldn't be denied. "Nah, we can finish the story here. I mean, unless it's really long?"

Topper laughed. "It's time travel, little brother! Of course it's long. And short! Ha! Where was I?"

"What happened after you decided not to contact me?" Bassett prompted.

"Well, after a few years I told my dad. Sorry, our dad. His reaction was … unexpected. I thought he'd be upset, or really let me have it, but he got super sentimental. Said he'd never forgotten you and wondered what you'd be like. That's when we got the idea for the money."

"The toolbox?" Tess was out of the car now too.

"Yeah. We wanted to help you out with your business and stuff, but Dad didn't think you'd accept his money if you knew who it came from. Since he was kind of an absentee father and all. I mean, not that he meant to be, but you know. So, we cooked up this plan to be anonymous and mysterious, and send you on an adventure, so to speak."

"Oh, it's been an adventure." Emerson scowled. "We've nearly been killed, like, 20 times." In times of stress and when in a bad mood, Emerson tended to exaggerate.

Topper's face fell. "I'm so sorry. We've been in the same boat over here, more or less. This time travel stuff isn't an exact science. When we opened our branch of **ttrp** people started pouring in. Like, real time travelers, you know? The bona fide, genuine ones?"

"The same thing happened to us."

"I mean, we were just as surprised as you guys. I know computers, and Dad knows business, but neither of us had dabbled in this kind of thing before, not really. I mean, Dad used to study it and mess around with experiments and theories in college, but it was just a hobby. Oh, and Dad's a millionaire, you know."

"Yeah, I figured. Toolbox full of money." Bassett shrugged as if it weren't important.

"Right. I only mention it because … well, never mind."

"So, I didn't franchise? You just opened your own **ttrp**?" Finally, some things were making sense. Sort of.

"Well, yeah. I mean, you've been on board more than you realize. Like I said before, the time continuum is fried. It's like we're walking in different but parallel universes or something. I can't figure it out. But we've got a whole team of scientists working on it, so don't worry!"

"Um, yeah, I'm still gonna worry."

"Yeah, I know you will." Topper looked at him fondly. "But let me be the older brother, okay? I'll take care of you guys. You're on my turf now! So, any more questions, or can I show you around the bar? And, well," he seemed to be searching for words, "do you think you might want to meet our father? Again?"

What was Bassett Clark supposed to say to that? What had he said the first time? How many times had this happened?

"Yeah, sure," he croaked. "That'd be nice."

*　*　*

It was a short enough walk from the shaded employee parking spot to the front door of **ttrp 2.0**, but even so, Emerson's hair was extra-large and fluffy due to the Florida humidity, and Bassett was drenched in so much sweat he felt as though he had recently been swimming. Stoop was paranoid about the Miami bugs he'd heard so much about in urban legends, and was wide-eyed and jumpy. Tess, too, seemed nervous; almost as if she was regretting the trip. Bassett felt personally responsible for everyone's safety and that made him sweat even harder.

The bar itself was much more grandiose, polished, and modern than the original. Bassett's bar was old and falling apart at the seams, but this one was in a shiny new building, with a landscaped front, discreetly tinted windows, and outdoor seating. Bassett felt a pang of jealousy, then dismissed it when he remembered he owned this place, too. He and Topper. And their dad. Whom they were going to meet right now, this very minute. Bassett felt the pumpkin ravioli threaten to come back up.

There was a lone man seated at one of the patio tables, who didn't look up from his newspaper as they walked by. He wasn't much to look at – he was a Linus Fields type if there ever was one, as far as descriptions went – but there was an earpiece in his ear that gave Bassett pause. Probably just some sort of Bluetooth device, but it looked positively futuristic. It was also at odds with the newspaper he was reading; a paper that was dated 1856. Bassett sighed. Evidently, this was the new normal, and it was bizarre.

The inside of **ttrp 2.0** was just as sophisticated as the outside; modern and swanky, with clean lines and an air of classy, cultured refinement. It even smelled nice. Not like spilled white Russians and death. The seating was a mixture of private booths and leather sofas with coffee tables. The lighting was soft and gave a sense of seclusion that appeared like it would be inviting both to couples on dates who wanted to make out, and time-traveling spies who needed to go over murder plans.

The bartender was a jovial-looking type, a man of about 30, with a shaved head and a paunchy stomach. He raised his hand to the group in a wave and called out to Bassett, "Hey, Mr. Clark! Good to see you!"

Bassett waved back, figuring here was yet another person he had met in the future/past. They were stacking up like a stamp collection, these people.

"Dad's in back. He does the books, you know." Topper led the way.

They went through a door marked *Employees Only*. Here, it was brighter.

Not only were there a larger variety of lighting options, but one wall was made entirely of windows. It was pretty, Bassett had to admit, but not really the best decision if you were thinking of it from a Russian-spies-are-after-me-and-want-to-pickle-my-onions kind of way. Unless all six of them were going to cram under the businessman's desk, there was nowhere to hide if Ekaterina or one of her minions arrived, guns blazing.

That was Bassett's first thought. His second was this: Zechariah Herriot looked an awful lot like the old man who liked to wander around the original **ttrp**, the man who observed things and wrote his thoughts down in a little notebook.

*   *   *

"Hello, son," the man said. He got up from behind his desk rubbed his eye, apparently trying to stop a tic. Then he clasped his hands in front of his body, as if he didn't know what else to do with them. On his desk were stacks of pocket size notebooks, dozens of them, maybe even hundreds. He was a smallish man, Zechariah, with a graying mustache and a disheveled suit. Every time Bassett had seen him in the bar, he'd looked the same; like he'd been sleeping in his clothes. Or time traveling. That was bound to put some wrinkles in your suit, not to mention on your face. It was all coming together.

"I know you," Bassett accused "Why didn't you tell me who you were?" Was he hurt, or angry? Bassett wasn't entirely sure which emotion he was feeling.

Zechariah wiped his forehead with the back of his hand. "I wanted to. But I wasn't sure how you'd take it, and I knew you were busy, what with the bar's business and all that was going on. I thought I'd just observe for a while. And then, well, it just seemed awkward. And I wasn't sure you'd believe me."

"So, you started this whole thing?" Stoop asked. "With the helmet and the money and the picture album?"

"Why?" Emerson added.

The man flushed a deep pink, and wrung his hands. "It seemed a fun idea at first. You see, I'd always been interested in the subject. Wrote my thesis on the theories of time travel and parallel universes at Oxford back in the day."

Tess's eyes widened at that. "Do you still have that thesis?"

"Not now, Tess," Bassett growled. "More important things than your GPA, okay?"

She sighed. "Fine. Go on."

"I do have it, my dear, and you're welcome to it. I am something of a hoarder when it comes to writing things down and keeping them." Zechariah gestured to the desk where the notebooks were, to prove his point. "As a student, I knew that time travel was certainly possible, but I couldn't determine if anyone had accomplished it yet. And then I met someone, a clockmaker by the name of Sven. I needed a job during the summer, in my junior year. Not only was he kind enough to hire me, but he made something for me. Two somethings, actually. Topper?"

Bassett's brother held out his hand. Awkwardly, Bassett moved his own in response, thinking Topper wanted to shake hands. Then, just as Bassett's fingers grasped onto his twin brother's digits, the moment froze in time.

Not literally, of course, though Bassett was beginning to believe that possibility might exist. The moment froze in time figuratively, as the faces on the watches on each wrist were plainly displayed. They matched perfectly.

"I always thought they were just an oddly decorated set. I was never sure why Sven gave them to me, but as he had a good eye and had been such a good boss to me, I kept them. I gave one to Lila when you boys were born."

The "boys" let go of one another.

"So, the watches aren't watches?" Emerson interjected.

"They are, too!" Bassett blustered. "Mine keeps perfect time."

"They're watches, but not only watches. I guess you could more accurately describe them as timepieces," Zechariah answered. "In the broadest sense of the word. And to be frank, they don't keep perfect time, because time itself, you see, isn't perfect. Like Steven Hawking says, quote, time runs faster in space than it does down on Earth. Inside each spacecraft is a very precise clock. But despite being so accurate, they all gain around a third of a billionth of a second every day. The system has to correct for the drift, otherwise that tiny difference would upset the whole system, causing every GPS device on Earth to go out by about six miles a day. You can just imagine the mayhem that that would cause.

The problem doesn't lie with the clocks. They run fast because time itself runs faster in space than it does down below. And the reason for this extraordinary effect is the mass of the Earth. Einstein realized that matter drags on time and slows it down like the slow part of a river. The heavier the object, the more it drags on time. Unquote."

"Cool. So, are they wormholes? Let me see, Tiger." Emerson stood on tiptoes for a closer peek, though she'd seen Bassett's watch a million times before. "I haven't noticed any lightning flashes coming out like you said Herb's wormhole had."

"Herb? Wormhole?" Zechariah echoed.

"Is that what this is?" Bassett demanded. Suddenly, he wanted to get it off his wrist, and toss it like he would a live grenade. "Geez, Dad, I've been wearing this for 30 years! I probably have radiation poisoning at the very least." He didn't even notice the slip of his tongue, calling the man "Dad."

"No, no, I'm sure you're fine. Sven wouldn't have put anyone in danger. Hmm, a wormhole. That *is* intriguing. Who is Herb, if you don't mind my asking?"

"H.G. Wells. Maybe. He said he was." Bassett sighed. "I don't know what to believe anymore."

"Um, sorry to butt in here, but why is mine … pulsing?" Topper wanted to know. "Is yours acting like it wants to jump off your body right about now, little brother?"

Now that he mentioned it, it was. Bassett's wrist was also getting hot. Suddenly, the watch felt too tight on his wrist. Bassett and Topper both began fumbling with the clasping mechanisms, in a hurry to remove the devices.

"Are we going to blow up now?" Tess asked, worried.

"No, no," Zechariah rushed to calm the group, "there is nothing to worry about, I'm sure. At least, I'm fairly sure. But I do know, we all know now, that they react in a peculiar way to being in the same room at the same time, especially *this* time. Every time Topper here went near you, something would happen, but things would *really* happen at exactly 5:55."

"Hey, that's totally legit," Stoop agreed, looking back. "The Bassett sightings usually happened on days when other weirdness started happening."

"So, that's part of the reason we knew we had to involve you, son. And it seemed like as good a time as any to meet you. Especially once we realized how discombobulated time in general was becoming. Things are not running in a linear sequence anymore."

"Gee, I never noticed." Bassett couldn't help the sullen comment. The watch was finally off, and he placed it on his father's desk and rubbed his hot wrist.

"So, how do we stop it? Stop our timelines from becoming all wavy gravy and loop-dee-loo?" Stoop demanded.

"That's why we called a Code Red. We need the timepieces together in one place, not to mention all the players."

"Which players?" Bassett narrowed his eyes.

"All the players." Zechariah sounded apologetic. "I believe they'll all come to us now."

Chapter Thirty-Two

"What good will it do? This showdown at **time travelers' rally point**?" Emerson was feeling skeptical, and when she was skeptical, she stood with her hands on her hips and demanded answers. Combined with her curly hair, which was out of control in the heat, she looked like a disheveled, angry porcupine.

"I agree with Emerson," Tess said. "You plan to get all the players – as you called them – here, and then what? Blow up the bar? That seems awfully extreme."

"You can blow up Agent Skanky." Emerson took her hand off her hip and struck a more casual pose. "I can live with that."

"No, no, violence is not the answer." Zechariah offered. "I am a pacifist, after all. Did you know you these two dear boys were conceived at Woodstock?"

"Dad!" they both shouted, as one. They looked at one another and grinned.

"Sorry," Topper said. "He always brings that up, and it's so-"

"Embarrassing," Bassett finished the sentence. "I know, believe me."

"Let's get back to the plans." Tess was still jumpy and agitated. "I need to call home and check on my kids soon. So, if you aren't planning on killing anyone, sir, what is the point of gathering us all in one spot?"

"Here's the problem I think we're facing." Zechariah steepled his fingers together and touched his lips with his two index fingers. He tapped them there once, twice, three times before resuming speaking. Bassett knew he was formulating his words carefully. He himself used to do that during tests in school, or when compiling his liquor orders. "The lines of time are indeed wavy gravy and loop-dee-loo, as you so eloquently put it, Stoop. I think dimensions are crossing over one another."

"Huh?" Bassett attempted to raise one eyebrow in confusion at the same time his eye tic decided to resume. The result made him look as though he'd just used an eye lubricant made of lemon juice.

"Think of it as telephone lines getting crossed. Or a receiver picking up other radio signals."

"So, our timeline is picking up another dimension's timeline? I don't get it."

"I'm with him," Topper agreed. "Dad and his team keep trying to explain it to me, but it's weird stuff. All we know is, the wristwatches are making it worse, so maybe if we figure out why and how, we can use them to our advantage. All this coming and going at the wrong times, on accident instead of on purpose, and then you add in Russian spies, and H.G. Wells, and well, it's tough to run a successful business properly. I mean, the health insurance premiums for our employees alone are just astronomical."

"Will we make it like it all never happened? Will everything go back to the way it was before?" Up until just this moment, Bassett thought he wanted that more than anything, but now he felt a pang of disappointment, which quickly morphed into fear.

Emerson too, looked as though she wanted to cry. "All of our hard work? The bar? The Neighborhood Watch Team? Herb?"

"No, no," Zechariah rushed to explain. "At least not in this parallel universe. My hope is we can prevent any more time loops from happening, not change what has already happened. That's kind of the first rule of time travel, you know. Don't try to change the past. It rarely works."

"Tell that to the Russians," Tess said, dryly. "They didn't seem to get the memo."

*   *   *

The bartender with the paunch brought drinks. He knew exactly what everyone liked, so Bassett guessed he had served them all before, whether they remembered. It was a frustrating feeling, like reverse *deja vu*. Was it because there were other Bassetts in other parallel universes? Every time they successfully changed the future or the past, did a new universe begin? He chugged his Guinness.

"So, you have a team?" prompted Emerson to Zechariah.

"One of the perks of being a millionaire," he replied, with a chuckle. "They're the leading experts in the field, scientists and genealogists, historians and mathematicians, genetics experts and philosophers. Even a few clockmakers, out of respect for Sven."

"And we thought our customers were odd." Emerson elbowed Bassett. "That sounds like quite a group."

"They're very eclectic. And they disagree constantly." Topper rolled his eyes. "We had to give them the banquet room, just for arguing and throwing chairs around in. But even that was distracting, so Dad bought the building next door for them."

"A whole building?"

"Time machines take up space."

Stoop crowed. "I knew we'd finally get to see a time machine!"

"Well, we have one, too," Bassett felt inclined to point out. "And ours comes with a fax machine. Very handy for uh, faxing the future."

"Wait. Is that why Ekaterina has been skulking around? Is she looking for your time machine and didn't know which **ttrp** was housing it?" Tess wondered aloud. She took a sip of her fuzzy navel. "By the way, Bassy, your dad's peach schnapps is better than yours."

"Everything's better here," Bassett replied. There was no rancor in his voice; it was simply true. Topper may dress like he was on a permanent tropical vacation, but he was obviously business savvy in ways Bassett wasn't.

He had a feeling they were going to make a pretty successful team, if they got out of this snafu alive.

* * *

Across the street from the bar was the building that Zechariah bought to house his eccentric team of time travel experts, and that was where the group headed. The building was arched in shape with rows of windows that seemed more to conceal than to let in light. Like dark stained-glass squares only meant for decoration. Yet, the moment its quirky shape called attention to itself, Bassett felt it was perfectly normal. After all, the best place to hide anything is in plain sight. Emerson, a fan of Edgar Allen Poe, often referred to that concept prevalent in *The Purloined Letter*. And as he realized this, having just left **ttrp 2.0**, Bassett began to wonder how many things—and more specifically, time travelers—had been hiding among them, in plain sight, all along.

As they walked, Topper explained that the group's theory was that perhaps the missing link in the time travel machine lay in the interaction of the two watches.

If using their power helped fuel the machine – which up until now had not been working properly – then they could …

Do what exactly? Bassett wanted to know. *Go back or forward? And why? And where? And what do we do about the Russians?*

They opened the building's doors fashioned of tinted black glass. Bassett knew instinctively it was one-way glass; the team of scientists could likely see out into the street, but anyone walking by couldn't peer inside. The sign on the door had read *VHS Repair. Keys Made While You Wait.*

"Obviously a cover," Emerson whispered as they filed inside. "Smart. No one uses VHS players anymore."

"I do," Bassett muttered, thinking of his beloved copy of *Back to the Future.* He wondered if there might be a market for *The Purloined VCR,* which Emerson could write after this experience concluded.

Inside was a large reception room, with a wrap-around mahogany desk that echoed the curvature at the top of the building. Behind the desk sat a small woman, with a tiny bun on top of her head. She beamed up at them through over-sized granny glasses.

"Mr. Clark! Yay! So glad to see you, sir!" The voice was recognizable.

Bassett smiled back. "Good to see you too, Janet." Suddenly, he knew where Zechariah and Topper had gotten the granny glasses for their little planting of the scuba helmet. And, Bassett frowned ... *Ernest.* Some things still hadn't been fully explained: the fact that Ernest's jaw was busted in the same place where he had been sucker punched; the Butterscotch My Little Pony sticker. *Of course, there were coincidences in life, sure, but still.*

"We'll be having an all-day meeting, Janet," Zechariah said. "Perhaps some sub sandwiches?"

"And coffee?" Emerson piped up, hopefully.

"Of course. Let me show you in." The receptionist came out from behind her desk and led the way to what Bassett could only assume was the boardroom. He wondered if they'd get to see the time machine. Or if Stoop would volunteer to take it for a spin. He could see his best friend and Tess making a habit of puttering through time, like other couples meandered through a Saturday's Farmer's Market. Emerson, too. She always had loved adventure. They'd probably have their own reality show soon; maybe even action figures. Bassett was the only one who liked his days safe and reliable and predictable. He couldn't help it.

Maybe he could be a stay-at-home husband, while his aspiring author wife brought home the bacon, figuratively speaking. His memory went back to the photo in the jet. He hadn't gotten a good look before he'd passed out, but it seemed like a cute baby they were going to have. How hard could it be?

Topper led the way as Janet held open the door to the boardroom, but it was really a hallway with a single elevator. The group piled into the elevator, which took them several floors up. They were in the top of the arch now, and then they seemed to shift forward, and back down. When the doors opened, Bassett was met with a sudden bright light that caused him to squint. It came partly from the fluorescent bulbs in the elevated ceiling, but mostly from the glowing, pulsing monstrosity in the center of the huge room.

Whatever it was looked more like a complicated ride at the state fair than anything. It was a cross between a Ferris wheel and … Bassett's imagination failed him. A futuristic Ferris wheel was all he could come up with. It wasn't as large as most, obviously – the ceilings weren't that high – and instead of having dozens of bucket seats, there was only one. Big enough to seat two. There was rope lighting that looped around the circular frame, of a similar color to Herb's wormhole lightning flashes.

Bassett and Topper had brought along their matching timepieces; Bassett's was in his pocket because he was no longer comfortable wearing it. Justifiably so, apparently, because as he approached the time machine, it began a disconcerting wiggling and moving about in his cargo pants. He hurriedly removed it and handed it over to the nearest scientist without even looking He could see the white lab coat and that was enough to satisfy him that the wearer was apt to be more familiar with the device than he was.

Had he not been in such awe of the time machine, and so concerned over the timepiece coming to life, he might have noticed that the scientist in the lab coat was MJ sooner.

"I knew you were the real deal!" Stoop exclaimed, embracing his favorite customer fondly.

She grinned back as she took Topper's watch as well. "Of course I am! Don't tell Bruce though. He thinks I'm at a quilting show in Kansas this weekend. The man is a dear, but he's a few sandwiches short of a picnic. After 50 years of quilt shows, you'd think he'd get suspicious that I can't sew a stitch." She winked.

"Mum's the word," Stoop promised. "What do you think of these?" He nodded toward the watches. "Are they the missing link to your machine here?"

MJ peered closely at them as they threatened to shimmy right off her palms. She curled her fingers firmly around them both and responded, "Seems promising. Ah yes. Sven was my brother. I don't know if Zechariah got around to telling you that?" She turned one of the watches over. "Zechariah and I both knew how close we were getting to unlocking the secrets of time travel during the Cold War."

"You knew one another back then?" Bassett asked his father.

"Yes, MJ worked in the front of the clockmaker's shop, while I worked in the back."

MJ continued, "One day, the same day that Zechariah here left to go to some music festival, we had a visit from the Russians. Sven hid his secrets in the watches and gave them to Zechariah. He was a long-haired hippie kid, so the Russians didn't look twice at him."

"I saved the world and didn't even know it," Zechariah said happily. "Those were the days."

MJ rolled her eyes. "Sort of. But now we're back where we started, in a manner of speaking. The Russians are sniffing around again, plus we have this problem with the time continuum being …"

"Fried?" Topper offered.

"Yes. But with these pieces right here," MJ grunted as she suddenly smashed one of the watches open with a small hammer lying nearby. Bassett and Topper yelped in protest. "Sorry, boys. Fate of the world and all that. I'll buy you new ones." Then she added, perhaps not intending for everyone to hear, with a weak smile, "Hopefully I haven't just given us all radiation poisoning."

The brothers, at the mention of radiation poisoning, both glared at their father, who looked away nonchalantly, his hands in his pockets.

"What do we do now? Who's going back? What's the plan?" Emerson put her hands on her hips.

"We find Sven, of course. He disappeared that same day, and since then, my searches have turned up nothing. Either he's locked up in the Kremlin or he's gone into hiding or he's dead. But I know my brother. He's out there. Problem is, we can't find him. So, we go back to that day and follow him. Bring him back here if we can. Stopping the Russians altogether would be icing on the cake." MJ sorted through the busted sections of the watch. She crowed triumphantly as she found what she was looking for: it seemed to be some sort of pebble, only of course, it wasn't.

"A magic bean?" Bassett snorted.

"Laugh it up, kid," she retorted. "This is serious stuff. I hope you're wearing rubber-soled shoes."

"Me?" Suddenly, Bassett got a dreadful feeling in his gut and his right eye began to twitch. He looked over at the glowing Ferris wheel in alarm. It shimmered.

"Naturally. This is your operation, after all. And besides, it can't be me or Zechariah. We could run into ourselves! I don't have to tell you how dangerous that is."

Emerson laced her arms through Bassett's and squeezed. "This is so awesome," she whispered, in a sing-song voice. "Room for two! You always said you'd run away with me, remember?" There was joy in her voice, like nothing he'd ever heard before except when she was daydreaming out loud about throat punching Ekaterina.

Well, if it was his time to go, he could think of worse ways than riding a wheel of death with Emerson DuPree by his side. *If we ever had time travel, we have time travel now.* He looked over at Topper as his brother nudged him with his elbow. Topper slipped something into Bassett's hand.

"You might not remember," Topper whispered, "but you wanted me to give you this at this point."

"I did?" His fingers curled around a small square box with rounded corners. He didn't remember telling Topper anything about this moment, but he knew instinctively what was inside.

Bassett Clark gestured toward the time machine. "Shall we?" he asked, with a little bow.

As they stepped in, MJ lowered the bar that served as a seat belt. Bassett swallowed his objections to the safety precautions that appeared a bit low-budget. Stoop and Tess stood as close to the machine as the scientists would permit them to stand, looking mildly terrified but mostly intrigued. Topper grinned from ear to ear and saluted as the machine began to whir.

"I love you, son!" shouted Zechariah.

The shimmer grew into a fearsome, throbbing light, as bright as lightning and twice as fast. Bassett covered Emerson's hand with his own, and as the room began to spin faster and faster, he slid the engagement ring Topper had given him onto her finger.

Whether the blinding light that followed was due to a machine malfunction, their arrival at their destination, the folding of time, or the look of bliss on Emerson's face, Bassett wasn't entirely sure. It really didn't matter either way. Bassett Clark was hanging on for dear life, and was going to enjoy the ride.

Epilogue

In the pirate booth, a group of five people sat, chuckling and making light conversation. A man and woman were in EMT uniforms, another man and woman were in matching hospital scrubs, and the remaining woman wore a white coat with a name embroidered on the chest and a stethoscope. They all drank water, and hadn't ordered any food. Bassett came by to see if he couldn't persuade them to open their wallets. Couldn't just have people taking up space without contributing to the bottom line.

The woman in the white coat informed Bassett that they were waiting for someone, who should arrive shortly. "But we do have these vouchers," she said, pulling a stack of paper out of her coat pocket.

Four free appetizers and six free drinks, Bassett read from the vouchers. *I didn't authorize this.* And yet, there was his signature at the bottom.

"Can you come back in a few minutes?" she chirped. Before Bassett could answer, she turned back to her colleagues.

Bassett mumbled to himself, "Great, someone comped these guys and forged my signature, and now I'm not even going to make any money off your table. You're taking up some prime real estate here, lady."

He didn't feel it, but as he headed back to the bar, Bassett unknowingly kicked a small black lacquer box that had been sitting on the carpet. Silently, it came to rest under the booth with the scuba helmet, where another group was sitting, enjoying their drinks and refreshments.

A sweaty man in a rumpled suit rushed in and approached the booth, a crumpled handkerchief in his hand.

"Sorry I'm running late," he offered to the water-swilling group. "Traffic was terrible."

One of the men scooted over and made room for the newcomer.

"Okay, okay," the man continued, catching his breath and checking his watch and the clock over the bar. "Gosh, I was afraid I'd miss it." His eyes came to rest on the bright yellow AED, and he seemed to relax his shoulders a bit. He took a sip of someone's water and nodded in appreciation. "Now, does everyone know what to do?"

The members of the group nodded and answered yes. "Don't worry," the female EMT said, patting the man's trembling hand. "We're ready."

"OK," the disheveled man said, wiping his brow and then reaching into his pocket. He pulled out a photo of a young woman. She had short hair, trimmed into a neat crewcut. She was leaning against a wall, wearing men's jeans and a white tank top that showed off her muscular arms. The photographer had captured her as she was just starting to laugh, a smile curving across her full lips. He ran his thumb over the glossy paper, looking lovingly at the figure in the photo. "My dear Barbara," he said wistfully. "I can't believe it's been 30 years since you enlisted. I'm so sorry that we lost touch." He gently pressed the photo to his lips and returned it to his wrinkled pocket, giving it a pat.

Just then, Babs walked into the bar. Evidently, it was time to case the perps. She reached into her back pocket and fished around. Then she patted down the front pockets of her 501s, apparently coming up empty. She looked distressed and checked her back pocket again. Then she looked back to where she'd entered the bar from the back alley, and slowly walked toward the door, looking carefully at the ground.

The man in the suit followed her briefly with his eyes, then sighed, "That's her." And then everyone at the table stood up. The female EMT grabbed the AED from the wall behind the bar and the group hurried toward the back door.

*   *   *

Penelope DuPree had her daddy's dimples and his round belly; fortunately, in her case the belly was due to baby fat, not beer. She had her mommy's green eyes, strawberry blonde hair, and ability to get into trouble at a moment's notice. And she and Winnie were thick as thieves and twice as mischievous.

If Bassett Clark thought that getting back in one piece after saving the world from time-traveling Russian spies had been difficult, it was nothing compared to being a stay-at-home dad.

"Penny, stop eating the dog food," he said absent-mindedly to his daughter, as he went through the mail in the back room of the original **ttrp.** Once the accountants had left – their time travel and fax machine combo a disaster and the tax season looming – Bassett had set it up as a playroom for Penelope. Having her in a bar was a little weird, but Jonathan, his mother's husband, always looked the other way. Penelope had both of her grandfathers twisted around her chubby little finger. They didn't even mind her kibble breath.

Back when Penny had only been a twinkle in her father's eye, her parents had gotten married. Not in a tropical locale as suggested on the jet, but at the top of a snowy mountain in Switzerland. Bassett had done two of the most impulsive and rule-breaking things of his life that year: he had proposed to his girlfriend and he had taken his knowledge of what was *supposed* to happen in the future and carved out his own destiny anyway. It had been somewhat comforting to chart his own path and walk it. Sometimes he wondered about the photographs he had seen in the jet that night. Had they disappeared since life had not, in fact, gone precisely in that direction? He didn't think Emerson's engagement ring was as ginormous as the photos had shown, and their wedding was a winter affair, to which Bassett had most assuredly not worn a Hawaiian shirt. Had the photos blurred and faded away like they did in *Back to the Future?* Bassett didn't know, would never know. He'd sold the jet to Kevin soon after he and Emerson had returned from a honeymoon in Budapest; Kevin needed it to chase Ekaterina across the skies. The details were a little hazy and Bassett hadn't probed for clarity. He preferred not to know every facet of what went on at all three **ttrp** locations. He and Emerson had honeymooned in Budapest, and they made monthly trips to **ttrp 2.0** to see Topper and Zechariah, but the original O'Malley's location still held Bassett's heart. Keeping up with the liquor orders and lining up weekend entertainment was Bassett's department. Lizard Buttons' No Talent Hacks had disbanded due to creative disputes last year. However, he handed over the time travel and most of what that entailed to Emerson, or Stoop and Tess.

So far, there were no action figures for the intrepid crew, but they were famous in their own right. After dating for many months, and working together after Tess's graduation, another wedding had taken place. This one right in the bar. Stoop had catered his own big day, and Tess walked down the aisle on Sawyer's arm. Now, their marriage thrived as they handled some of the more dangerous missions out of **ttrp**, or at least the most intricate and complicated ones. Tess was an excellent researcher and amateur historian, and her husband enjoyed the adrenaline rush each time he was strapped securely into Rhonda the Second, which was what they had christened the time machine in Florida. Often, however, Stoop could be found in the kitchen, planning exotic menus as the head chef for all three locations. Not to mention training his staff to deal with their customers' eccentricities. Barflies had always had odd tastes and demands, but barflies from other centuries really seemed to keep Stoop on his toes, gastronomically speaking.

Emerson had been put on bed rest during her pregnancy with Penelope. At first, this made her restless and anxious, but eventually she started work on a new novel, *The Time Harnesser's Revenge: My Story.* It was semi-autobiographical and revolved around her heroine tracking, and throat punching her enemy, a certain Agent Skanky. There were several sequels in the works.

The remainder of the Neighborhood Watch Team came around occasionally, but mostly they were busy with their respective lives. Joey was in high school now, Walter had gone into an assisted-living home, and the two mothers were busy with other pursuits. Quinn had sent Bassett a photo not long after an adventure. It was of Herb in Betty's kitchen, drinking his chocolate milk. It had taken Bassett a couple weeks to look up photographs of H.G. Wells on the internet for comparison's sake. If it wasn't Herb, it was a damn fine lookalike.

As for Margarita Jones, she had resigned after a romantic tryst with a nude British gentleman she had found in the bar one morning. She hadn't been seen since.

"Drop that!" Bassett said firmly to his daughter, who was merrily chasing Winnie under the table, brandishing a fistful of paper. She giggled and fell on her diapered butt. Bassett took away the soggy envelope she had been chewing on.

He opened it, his eyes scanning the content. He groaned. There was a safe deposit key taped to one side of a handwritten note. The letter read,

Backing and start-up monies for **space travelers' alien rendezvous (S.T.A.R.s)**. *Investment made in good faith that one Bassett Z. Clark will wisely instruct, counsel, and provide discretion in all matters of space travel, including but not limited to, points of location/eras/positioning, client confidentiality, rules and regulations, and high quality drinks and refreshments for said travelers. Sum: $2,000,000. Non-transferrable.*

Have fun and be safe out there.

About the Author

Justin Mitson is an engineer and manager for a semiconductor company in Boise, Idaho by day and a dedicated entrepreneur and freelance writer by night. Born in Butte, Montana, he spent most of his childhood roaming around the northwest, living in eighteen different locations before getting through high school. When not at his day or night job, Justin is also actively involved in the community, with his church, and as a small business owner. He utilizes his business ties and proceeds to give back to the local community, having raised funds for Boise area charities.